THE CHILD

BY
ANGEL VAN ATTA

1

Abraham died. He didn't do it of old age or natural causes. Unless you count a small child slicing you up with an old-fashioned barber's razor as natural. And then there's no way to tell if the razor cuts were really the true cause of his death by just looking. When the child was done, his body was mangled and gnawed to a point that even the most seasoned detectives on the scene the day it was found had to hide the urge to hurl behind gnarled fists.

One of the EMT's lost the struggle to keep his breakfast of cold coffee and peanut butter toast with pickle slices down. The taste of that breakfast was so bad coming back up he could never again enjoy that particular childhood throwback for the rest of his life. It was a struggle that would come back to haunt him years later when he walked into his mother's kitchen to see her feeding his niece the very same curious breakfast choice that had been handed down to the wee ones in the Miller family for generations. Even just the smell brought back the sight that Abraham's corpse would burn into that poor ambulance man's mind that gruesome Tuesday evening.

Abraham hadn't started that day knowing that it would end so badly in his favor. He had started it just like any other day. Alarm at five in the morning, in the shower by five-o-five. A quick bowl of Frosted Flakes, with tunes of Tony The Tiger exclaiming their greatness in his mind's inner television, followed by a quick brush and floss and then out the door by six. The long walk to work was his favorite part of the workday. He had two hours then to amble down the city blocks, watching with a small smile as the world awoke around him, coming to life in a secret way. A slow evolution from quiet to cacophony the closer he got to his office.

And then there had been the child. He was just a block away

from the safety of his boring job when he saw her. Boring was how Abraham liked it. He liked each day being similar to the last and the next. He liked not having to predict what would happen. He felt steady in the humdrum of a simple life, so when this new thing appeared, the frown that had pursed his lips hadn't done so just because he had felt sad for the crying child, but because it was unpredicted. It was new. It was not familiar.

The child was a girl. She had strawberry red hair, almost too bright to be real, that was pulled up into two high ponytails at the top of each side of her head. Her eyes were the brightest green eyes he had ever seen in the forty-seven years he had walked on this rock we call home. He had thought that perhaps they just seemed extra bright because of the tears that had welled in them. Her small cries were choked by sobs as she made eye contact with him. At that millisecond when their eyes had met, his whole body seemed to feel a shock and he jumped, though he felt silly for doing so.

"Are you okay?" he had asked her. His own voice trembling, too, as the shock started to set off alarms in his mind. The ones that warned you when something wasn't right. The ones that told you to run and never mind the social consequences. To get away and to do it right that second. But he hadn't ran because Abraham wasn't like most people. Abraham's life had been so simple, so mundane, so steady, that he hadn't ever needed to use his lizard brain before, so the feeling was unfamiliar to him.

At the sound of his weak man's voice, for surely Abraham had not been a strong man, the little girl had turned and ran into the alley that divided the quaint coffee shop he sometimes frequented, and the used bookstore that always seemed to be on the verge of closing. Probably would have, in fact, had the coffee shop not been right next door. The patrons of the coffee house loved the look they felt like it gave them to be reading the yellowed pages of yesterday's greats between pretending to work on their novels and hashtagging their selfies of themselves doing these things to countless internet strangers.

He had watched her go. The alarm bells caused confusion, but not fear. Her bright red pigtails bounced with each small child's step and the bright red skirt of her simple peasant's style dress fluttered a little in the slight breeze her gait created as she ran.

"Hey! Wait!" He called to her and began to follow her down the alleyway. "Little girl! Are you okay?" She stopped near a manhole where the cover had been slid back, and a dark gaping mouth of blackness seemed to ooze with dread in rivulets toward him. He could almost feel it pooling around his feet as he stopped a few yards away from her and that black gaping maw cut into the concrete at her feet.

"My puppy," she whimpered. Her voice soft and sad and scared all at once. "I threw his ball, and he ran, and I ran and then I saw the hole and he just fell in, and I can hear him but I'm too small!"

He looked at her then, sizing her up, and yes, she *was* too small! Five at the most, he guessed. Though he had no children of his own and his only brother lived on the other side of the country in a place called Florida where the sun never stopped shining and there were too many girls, apparently, for a man to settle down and procreate in a way that produced offspring.

She was way too small to be a threat to him, and he was a good guy. Certainly the type of guy who wouldn't turn his back on a sad child who needed his help. So, with one last look at the brightening world behind him, he set his fate and closed the last few feet to meet his doom.

"He's in there," she said as she raised a small fragile fist and extended a tiny child's finger toward the charcoal blackness of the uncovered city manhole.

"Aw, your puppy fell in?" he asked, his voice full of empathy for such a horrible thing to have happened. He remembered his own childhood dog. A Heinz Fifty-Seven if ever there had been. A shaggy doggo with light brown fur that stuck out in wiry tufts all over and always had a happy look on his face.

Chippers had died when Abraham was nine. He had been in a hurry to meet his friends at the creek behind the old baseball field and had forgotten to secure the latch on the white picket fence. His father had painstakingly installed that fence at the behest of his mother just that spring before. It wasn't a perfect fence, by any means, but his mother loved the feeling it gave her. A feeling of safety. A feeling of home.

3

Abraham himself had helped paint it white in the evenings after school as the year drew closer and closer to the ring of that last bell before summer, the bell that would unleash the children of the town into the neighborhoods and parks and creek beds. And, oh, how his family had laughed as they painted, joking about this thing or that and sometimes chasing each other around with thick white paint dripping from the ends of their brushes.

There had been love in that home, a great deal of it. And it had made Abraham the kind and good man that he was today. The kind of man who would stop and help a child in need. The kind of man who wouldn't think twice about doing a good deed like that. Even if it cost him everything. Even if it cost him his life.

Chippers had loved his child master as much as Abraham had loved him in return. When the scruffy pooch had noticed that his best friend had just skipped through the gate and that the gate bumped against the latch and then back open just an inch his little dog heart exploded with happiness. He ran down the steps of the quaint little porch and leaped after his most beloved friend. He slowed only to bump his wet little nose against the rough white wood to swing it open and then hurried on into the avenue to cross over to where Abraham had just stepped onto the curb. Chippers yipped with love in his little dog voice and the boy turned just in time to see the rusty front bumper of a 1964 Ford pickup collide with his first pet's shoulder. His trusting dog face still smiling that doggy grin of happiness, unaware that his heart was about to explode for the second time that morning. Only this time it wouldn't be figuratively, because this time it had the full weight of the rusty hulk of an automobile pushing its ribs right through it, accompanied by the sound of a slick crunch and pop as parts of the pooch's body reorganized themselves into unnatural places.

The truck had slammed on its brakes and the crumpled body of Chippers had flown through the air, a small fan of blood misting out around his muzzle as he flew. He landed with a wet flapping sound that would wake Abraham for years to come, haunting him in the smallest hours of the night. He had loved that dog with all of his little boy's heart and he would never again own a pet after losing him. He couldn't. It would be too hard to go through that

4

heartbreak more than once.

The little girl nodded, and more tears welled up in her eyes. "He's my most bestest friend, mister." Her voice so broken with sweet sadness that Abraham's heart began to break a little, too.

"Oh, no. Don't cry. I'm sure he's okay." But he wasn't sure, he only hoped and whispered to himself a silent wish that he wouldn't have to relive his childhood heartbreak through this small child. He bent his tall, thin body down and knelt before the hole. Squinting in through the darkness in hopes of seeing a puppy wagging his tail happily back up at him.

The child stood behind him now. He heard her shiny black shoes clicking against the dark pavement of the alleyway as she moved her small frame out of his line of sight. He thought nothing of it, though. She was just a kid who was in trouble, and he really did hope that he could save the day. It would be a nice start to this Friday morning and give him something to be proud about around the watercooler during the morning break. He would like that, he thought, because he was always listening to the stories and never really able to share. It was one of the bad things about being steady and stable and never venturing outside of your comfort zone. You never really had much to offer, conversationally speaking. Doers did and Abraham was not a doer.

He bent forward, a little into the darkness creeping up out at him. He grimaced at the dank smell of old water and grime unknown that lived below. At first, he hadn't seen anything. Just a thick blackness that felt almost as if it were a living thing down there. But then there had been a glint and he thought he could hear a small panting sound and suddenly there he was! A scruffy brown dog with bright loving eyes and a giant smile across his muzzle. And it looked like... but it couldn't be, could it? No, it was impossible after all these years, but still...

"What's your doggie's name?" he asked her. His voice was steady despite the uneasiness mixed with astonishment and maybe even joy he felt building inside of him at the sight of that familiar doggy face very much alive below him.

"It's Chippers," the child told him. Her voice still sounded sad, but also, maybe a little excited, too.

"Chippers?" he asked, the astonishment and joy now filling his heart. And with the sound of his voice saying that name the dog yipped his best Chippers yip and there had no longer been any doubt in Abraham's mind. He didn't know how or why, or even care, but that dog down there surely was his old best friend from years past and he called out to him, then. His heart and mind so happy. Happier than they had been in months or even years. "Chippers!!!"

He leaned even further down. His face extended an inch or two below the rim of the manhole. He desperately needed to get a better look at the miracle in front of him and just as he had reached the point where he could lean no farther forward it happened. In his excitement he had missed the small click and swish sound from behind and suddenly a bright lightning bolt of pain raced across his lower spine right above his tailbone. An area of skin that had been exposed when he leaned forward, revealing the bumps in his spinal cord to the world. A sight that had made the child's mouth water with anticipation and greed and want. And as she had brought the razor down with strength that was beyond her small child's body, his skin had opened up before her.

Like a hot knife through butter the razor parted the tissue and muscle and nerves, and like the Red Sea to Moses those two visible vertebrae split away from one another. Instantly his legs were rendered useless, and even before the bright red blood began to stain the tidiness of his whiteys, Abraham began to fall. The girl watched him go. A smile as sweet as peaches swollen on the tree spreading across her face. Her freckles lost amongst the dots of his blood that had settled there when her razor had kissed and spread his skin.

He fell forward and a part of him was happy that at least he would have his old friend. But when he landed with a slimy smack so similar to that sound that had haunted him for all of those years, there was no Chippers there to greet him. No wagging tail and rough wet tongue to lick away the tears of pain that were now coursing down his cheeks, and he knew. Chippers had never really been there at all.

Another part of him knew something else, too. The lizard part

6

of his brain had finally broken through, too late. It screamed now with all of its might. That thing was not a child, no matter how sweet it's smile. That thing was something evil and now he was going to die.

When he had fallen from the pavement of the garbage filled alley, he had done so head first and as his rendered useless bottom half had followed him through the opening, it had given him the momentum to do a kind of half flip so that when he landed, he landed on his back in the thick sludge that somewhat had broken his fall. And so, he saw her. The child that was somehow not. The sweet little girl of maybe five who couldn't be.

Her tiny figure appeared in the circle of bright light above him. She wasn't sad anymore, either. Oh, no. Now she seemed to be absolutely giddy with glee. A laugh as beautiful as a crystal bell's call tinkled in the too thick air and slowly, she invaded that circle of light. Her face seeming to grow and change as her frame eclipsed his new sun to this dark world below the city and the safety and the life of above.

Only a crescent of hope was left to him and in it he could see the bright blue of the summer sky. A sky that belonged to another where to him now. A sky that was no longer his.

The child sat and dangled her legs over the lip of the hole in the street. She giggled a chilling giggle that cut through his pain and caused the hair on the back of his neck to stand up.

"What are you?" he asked. His voice was shaking so badly with the effort it took not to scream in the agony that was consuming him.

That giggle came again, only the sound had changed from the melodious chime of a little girl's laughter to something much deeper. To something beastly and inhuman and ravenous. A guttural sound that, though he could no longer feel that part of his body and so had no way of knowing, caused his bowels to spew forth a liquid birthing of last night's dinner and his bladder to empty of the coffee he had drank before what was to be his final morning stroll through the wakening city streets. The liquids combined and mixed with the blood and though he hadn't been able to feel the relieving of himself, the smell was foul, and he had gagged then, barely winning the fight to keep his breakfast down.

The child dropped then from her perch above, landing with a squelch as her shiny black shoes stuck and then sunk into the thick ooze that covered the ground of this dank under place. He had looked up at her and saw that her features had somehow sharpened and changed. Her lips had stretched out across her face, thinning them from ear to ear and turning her into a nightmarish ghoul instead of the picture of innocence the child had been just moments before. A smile spread those lips then and he saw her teeth were too many for her child's head and all were pointy and looked as sharp as the razor that she had used to sever him with. Those were not the omnivorous teeth of a human, but, instead, the kind that were made for ripping flesh from bone and as she raised her razor above her head to slash, again and again, her eyes began to glow with a soft green light as if he were looking into the eyes of some creature of the night caught in the beam of a hunter's light. But there was no light down here, aside from that which softly shone from that uncovered hole above. And it certainly wasn't aimed into her face, but instead it haloed her from the ceiling of his tomb.

He screamed then as her razor did its work. He screamed and screamed. A sound of pain and fear and loss. He knew this was the end for him, and as the smell of his wasted adrenaline mixed with the smell of shit and piss and blood, he knew there was no hope. Blood splattered her face and the concrete wall behind him. Blood splattered her dress and her hair and her hands. And a frenzied laugh grew in the child's chest and rose and joined his screams. The sound of them mixed and danced and created something beautiful and terrifying.

The cuts she made were not too deep, oh no. Their job was not to kill him but instead to tenderize him with fear and pain. To take the joy he had just been feeling at the sight of his long-lost Chippers and marinate him in it through his blood that poured forth, covering him. Soaking into his pores and clothes and hair and pooling into the shallow spaces his eyes made above his cheeks. He could see her then, tinged red through the veil of his own life's blood. Manic and powerful and evil above him. That unnatural grin spreading and opening, too wide for the head it was attached to. A pointy, moist tongue slipping out through one corner, tasting the air

8

like a snake's tongue would.

"Please. Please just end it," he whispered huskily out of a swollen face. A slice in his right cheek showed the glistening white of bone and teeth that should be covered with flesh.

The child bent over the body. His body. Her blood-stained white legginged knees falling to the ground beside him and disappearing a little into the grime. She sniffed a deep and raspy sniff. A hungry sniff that started from his face and ended just below his now exposed belly button. A cut ran there from side to side, a thin layer of fat spread open, the color of yellow daisies in a summer-kissed field, and below that a deep red knot of muscle strained with the effort of living through all of his pain.

"Yes, I believe you're ready now." The child's voice that was no longer childlike spoke with glee and want and need. "I believe you're just!" He didn't know if those words were meant to comfort, but there had been only dread.

He put his hands up, trying to fend her off. His outstretched fingers quivering with the loss of blood and pain and fear. The pinky of his right hand was missing from the last knuckle up from one of the swipes of her blade and she grabbed that wrist and brought her long tongue to it. A fire even more deep than the one already burning there erupted as her tongue first made contact with the exposed tissue and gristle and bone. Her eyelids slowly closed in ecstasy as fresh screams erupted from his swollen lips and she brought his hand closer to her mouth at the same time she leaned her head forward toward the delicacy of his mutilated finger.

Her tongue disappeared back into that too wide mouth and with it so did his finger. Deeper and deeper, she suckled it in. Slowly it disappeared inside of her slick maw and his mind broke with the crunching sound he heard when finally, the last bit of pinky had been enveloped into that wet and dangerous place. The crunching sound of his pinky being severed from his fist and chewed. The pain was a new sound of hurt among his already singing body and he could finally take no more. He was screaming but he didn't even know it anymore. He didn't even care.

The child felt the snap of his brain and knew he was truly ready, for she was not here to merely eat of his flesh, but also of his essence. With a subtle snap and jerk of her tiny head it seemed to split in two as her jaw unhinged. Her stretched thin lips opened wider and wider, revealing shark like rows of jagged bloodstained teeth. There was a second of pause while her predator's eyes took him in for the last time and then she lunged. Those teeth ripping and tearing at all of his softest parts.

His cries finally lessened and only whimpers escaped him to join the squelching slurping sounds of her carnal feeding. The entire top of her body was now covered in his blood, but those too green eyes still shone out into the darkness and dampness of this place. The animals that called this corner of the sewer home had all fled when they felt her presence here. Returning only months later after her other self's stench finally drifted away. They could sense what she truly was under that child's guise, and they wanted nothing to do with it. Survival was their way of life, and they were trained through evolution to obey their lizard brains first. I guess you could say that's what makes them wild. I guess you could say that's what keeps them alive.

The child could feel that his time was almost up, so she abandoned her spot where she was gnawing into a ropey intestine, lavishing the taste of it like one would a Ballpark hotdog at the stadium. She crouched over him in a way that was entirely inhuman. Her arms and legs bent at odd angles and her blood-soaked pigtails slicked to the sides of her face and neck. She crept over his cut and mangled torso and up toward his face. A face that was frozen in a grimace of pain and fear. She was like a spider over its prey, gently bobbing up and down as her grimy black shoes found purchase on his ribs.

Her hands reached out and she splayed her fingers over either side of his head, digging her nails into the softer spots behind his ears. She bent as close as she could over his face, her bright green eyes a dazzling display in this dark world. She needed to see as his true him tried to leave his used and wasted husk. It was the part she loved the best. She searched his eyes and waited, listening to the slowing buh-bump of his heart as it drained the last bit of his life out into the pool of gore in which he now lay.

Buh. Bump. Her eyes glinted with the sound. In time with it.

Perfectly synced to his dying heart. Buh. A flashing glint and her eyes searched his and she saw it. His *his*ness there, swimming around, ready to run and be free.

Bump. She acted fast, before he could escape her. Her tongue shot out in lightning speed. It slid against his cheek and into the hollow of his eye, leaving a shiny trail of pink in the blood covered flesh of his face. Expertly it navigated into the space between the white squishy ball and the muscle that held it in place and folded itself underneath. Cradling his eyeball in her tongue she ripped it from his head, the cords and nerves dangling from below it and dripping a gooey redness that fell and disappeared in all that was already there. As quickly as she had invaded him his eye disappeared into her massive jaw, and she smiled at the feeling of the pop and saltiness of it as she swallowed.

Buuuuh. She repeated the process with the other side but this time she took it slowly as his chest rose and then fell for the last time. She relished the feel of the ball in her mouth, knowing how easily she could pop it between her teeth. Slowly and carefully, she allowed her tongue to roll it around, leaving a salty trail as it did so. Once it had been completely cleansed of its outside taste, she pushed it to the side with her tongue and clenched it between the top and bottom rows of teeth.

Gently she pressed. Slowly squishing his eye between those razor-sharp points and for a second it held. But then, when it finally could take no more no matter how gently she pressed, it gave way. With a pop and a gush it exploded delicious white goo. It was a favorite delicacy for her, and her childlike giggle returned.

With the return of her giggle, and the completion of her feast behind her, suddenly her jaw jerked and changed back to what it had been on the street above. Her lips slowly thickened, growing less and less wide across her face, and became hers again. A normal child's face now gleamed sticky from the light above. Only those eyes were the same. Too bright and glowing in the darkness.

She turned away from him, finally, and began walking through the sludge in the opposite direction of the street he had been strolling down not too long ago. Her dress and leggings were absolutely filthy, and her hair was slowly drying into clumps against her skin.

She would need a bath when she got home. She would make Mommy use the bubbles that smelled like strawberries. She loved strawberries. They were red and when you squished them in your fist they ran through your fingers like… well, like Abraham's insides had done when she pulled them to the outside. Yes. She really did love strawberries.

2

Sarah stood in the doorway of her daughter's room, her tallish silhouette outlining her slim figure from the yellow hallway light behind her, creating a shadow that lay across the softly carpeted floor and falling to an end at the foot of the twin sized bed. She watched as her daughter slept a peaceful sleep. Soft snores escaped her tiny nose every few inhales, creating a peaceful sound in the quiet space above where she lay. Sarah didn't smile as she would have once not too long ago because Sarah was terrified.

Emma *looked* like Emma. *Sounded* like Emma. Had the same freckles in the same *places* as Emma. Angels' kisses, she used to tell her as she lay with her in bed on stormy nights so the thunder that would shake the windows wouldn't scare the child. Then she would plant a bunch of smooches on Emma's cheeks and forehead and nose and how it would make Emma laugh.

A tear welled up and over Sarah's bottom right eyelid and her dull but beautiful green eyes shone with the threat of more tears to come. There was a wealth of sadness inside of Sarah's heart and she didn't know what to do about it anymore.

Was this Emma? Had she changed in such a cruel way so quickly? Or was there something else inside of her? Something ancient and evil? Something barbaric and monstrous? Or was Emma truly a psychopath finally emerging from her shell?

Either way, could she save her child? Remove the evil lurking inside of her? Separate this new thing from all of the good and innocence that was the Emma she knew and loved? The Emma she had carried inside of her? The Emma she had created and nurtured and taught to be kind? Oh, how she missed those days of happiness and laughter.

There was laughter still, oh yes. But it was the kind of sound that would make the hairs on the back of your neck stand up, because Sarah had been taught that it meant that something mean had happened. That pain had occurred or cruelty. A malevolent sound that no longer rang with purity and goodness, but instead had a darker and sinister meaning.

For a second Sarah wondered if she could do it. If she could end it all right here and now. Just walk across the room and wrap her hands around her child's throat and squeeze. If she had the strength inside of her and if she did, what then? There would be only one answer for her. To take her own life. To watch the light draining from her own child's eyes and then somehow make sure that the light would drain from her own eyes as well.

"I'm going crazy." She thought. Her lips moving with the words in her mind, but no sound coming out. She knew not to disturb Emma while she was sleeping. There would be consequences for that, and she was too tired to pay the toll tonight. Desperately so.

She quietly moved away from the door and headed down the hall to her own room, pausing only for a second to take in her messy strawberry blonde hair and softly freckled face. Her eyes were tired and sad and still shone with the threat of a heartbreak's worth of tears that seemed ever present now. Her hair was curly and long and dingy from needing a wash, the natural curls lost in knots here and there, which was unusual for Sarah's hair. Back in the before time she always took great care to keep it beautiful and healthy. She frowned at herself but was too exhausted to take a shower tonight; instead, she turned and walked through her own doorway and collapsed on the unmade bed.

She needed sleep and tomorrow would come too soon. There would be a full day of meeting Emma's demands. There would be a full day of keeping a child happy that found happiness in making others suffer. A full day of cleaning up after her, no matter how horrible that task may be. No matter how gruesome. A full day of redirecting as best she could the whims of a psychopath. A full day of doing the best she could and still almost always coming up short.

She didn't know how much more she could take, but she did know that she still loved Emma. If there was a chance that her Emma still existed in that imposter's body somewhere, she would gladly endure. With all of her heart and mind and soul she would endure. Until she knew for sure that her child was truly gone. Until that day, she would keep going. A mother's love is a magical thing. It was all she had to keep her sane and she clung to it like a life preserver.

She closed her eyes and let the memories of her Emma before the change drift with her into sleep. A small and peaceful smile spread across her face. This was her place. A safe spot where the evil couldn't reach her. Her dreams. Her memories. Her mother's love. And she slept wrapped in a cocoon of happiness, pushing the heartache away for a few short hours while the child slept.

A small snore escaped her, not unlike the ones the child made down the hall. Emma had her mother's nose. A cute button nose. And so they slept. Mother and daughter caught in a monster's web. Each one enveloped in their own dreams. The mother's those of times gone by. The daughter's a nightmare deep inside the corners of her own mind where the ancient thing held her prisoner. Both wanting nothing more than to be in the arms of the other. Both just doing their best to get by. Sarah awoke all at once instead of a little bit at a time. Her eyes snapped open with the feeling that something was there, staring at her. A small scream escaped her pursed lips at the sight of those bright green eyes. Eyes that were too bright to be Emma's even though they were the same shade of emerald. Emma tittered then, more than just a giggle, a mixture of mischief and something else. Something perversely satisfied at Sarah's fright.

"Good morning, Momma!" the child laughed. "Did I scare you? You're so silly!"

"Yes!" Sarah tried to sound happy, though she was anything but, and suddenly she had to pee. Her bladder pressed and throbbed against her abdomen as if counting down the time she had to make it to the bathroom before it would be too late. And wouldn't Emma laugh then? Wouldn't she find that hysterical? This new Emma with her twisted sense of humor? Oh, yes, she truly would! "I must have been having a bad dream just before you came in."

"I was watching you sleep for a while! You looked so peaceful laying there, Momma. I could have done anything at all to you and you wouldn't have been able to stop me." the little girl said matter-of-factly, climbing up on Sarah's plush floral covered duvet.

"Now you're the silly one!" Sarah laughed. A sound she hoped was buyable. She was getting pretty good at acting she thought as she put her arm around her child's body and pulled her close. She hugged her tightly and planting a loving kiss on the top of Emma's wavy ember hair. "You would never hurt me! I'm your mommy!" She stood then, trying to hide the fact that her daughter's statement had ran chills so icy cold down her spine that her bladder now felt like a block of ice inside of her instead of a boiling cauldron.

"Only as long as you're a good mommy." Emma's voice was now as cold as that ice running down her mother's back. A warning, not a joke. And Sarah knew it.

"Well, this good mommy has to potty." She turned her back to the child so that she could hide the look of terror she felt spreading across her face and walked across the room into the master bath, sliding the pocket door closed as she did so. Needing to have some sort of separation from that knowing gaze. Hoping not for the first time that the child couldn't read her mind even though it often felt like she could.

"And then breakfast?" Emma's soft voice through the door, sounding like she was standing just on the other side even though there hadn't been time for her to traverse the small room in just how long it took to slide the door shut.

Sarah gulped. She was constantly surprised at the child's new found abilities. Speed and stealth were just two of the things she could do. "Of course, my love! What would you like?" She pulled her pants down and sat, just in time, sighing at how good it felt to relieve her aching bladder.

"Uhhhhm…" A pause as the child considered her options. "Pancakes?" Sarah asked as she wiped and stood to flush, pulling her underwear and Hello Kitty pajama bottoms up. They were dark pink and had been Emma's favorite for her to wear before the change. She couldn't remember when she had put them on or how long it had been since she had changed. She felt grimy and dirty and longed for the shower. Maybe today she could sneak away for one.

"With strawberry syrup and whipped cream? I know how much you love strawberry syrup!"

"Uhm..., sure!" Emma's voice came through excited. "With sprinkles, too? And can you make the pancakes like rainbows?!" Sarah breathed a sigh of relief as she washed her hands, making the water extra warm and taking her time with the soap. Getting as much time in here alone as she could. Soaking in the water as much as possible, wishing she could be in the tub with the shower raining hotness down around her. Saturating her hair and cascading down her neck and back and arms and-

"Momma! With sprinkles and rainbowy?!" Her voice was now a little annoyed. She didn't like being ignored and the realization that this morning could quickly go sideways snapped Sarah back into the real world in a flash.

"Yes! Of course! And the whipped cream can be clouds!" Sarah answered happily. Or so she hoped it sounded happy.

"And crispy bacons? I *love* crispy bacons!" Emma jumped with the exhilaration of a child looking forward to something to come as Sarah slid the door back open.

"*And* sausages, too, if you want!" She bent and dipped up her child, swinging her around before resting her on her hip, as mothers do.

Emma giggled with delight and beamed happily into her mother's tired gaze. "I love you, mommy! You really are the bestest mommy I've ever had!"

Sarah bit her tongue before she could ask the child what that meant. She wasn't sure she wanted to know the answer. She just hoped it meant that this wasn't the real Emma and that she was in there, somewhere, just waiting to be rescued. And she hoped that she could figure out how to do that, before it was too late for them both.

After breakfast was usually the same. Emma watched cartoons geared toward the preschool-aged audience as Sarah cleaned up their mess. Sarah herself didn't usually eat very much, picking at whatever meal Emma had requested that morning and watching as the child shoveled mouthfuls of food into her greedy face. She ate as if she had been on the brink of starvation and didn't know when or

where her next meal might come.

In the beginning, Sarah had worried that the child would choke as she hardly chewed, instead just swallowing. She could almost see the giant forkfuls of food moving down Emma's throat in a bulge. She told herself that her eyes were playing tricks on her, but part of her wondered if that were true.

An even bigger mystery, though, was that the child was able to eat without getting messy. She hated to be messy, and Sarah now carried unscented wipes around with her in case of an accidental spill that would almost every time cause Emma to enter into hysterics until the spot or grime was wiped away.

There was only one exception to this rule, the times she returned after slipping away. Those times she seemed comfortable in the filth that covered her. Those times she seemed satisfied and lulled. She showed up in those moments completely covered in blood and dirt and sometimes shit and vomit or sludge unnamable. Always wanting a bath and then, after her mother had gently cleaned away every sign that something terrible had happened from her soft peach skin, the girl would sleep. For days, sometimes a week, she would sleep.

Those were Sarah's only moments of sanity. She would do whatever she could to ensure the child not wake in those days. She would unplug the fossilized landline cordless phone from the wall and double check that her cell was set to silent. She would park her car inside the garage and add a note to the door in case anyone came to

knock for a visit that Emma wasn't feeling well, so please don't disturb the sleeping child with a tap on the door or a ring of the bell.

Sarah would use the time to sleep herself. And eat. And shower. For hours she would shower. Letting the water turn cold before she would finally climb out of its comforting embrace. It was as if she were an embryo, safe inside her mother's womb. Even the soft glow through the pink shower curtain added to that feeling of being in utero. Her own heartbeat beating in her ears as if it came from some higher life form that carried her in this safe space.

She dreaded Emma disappearing and then showing back up like that, because she knew what it meant. She knew that the blood was too much to not mean anything less than some poor creatures' demise at the hands of her only child. But a small and selfish part of her prayed for those moments, too. They were her only solace in a world of chaos. They were all she had to look forward to in her new and twisted reality.

"Sarah, dear! Are you in there?" An old woman's high-pitched voice yanked her from the thoughts she had been losing herself in as she rinsed the last plate and loaded it into the dishwasher. "It's Mrs. McGregor, hun! Let me in, would you? I need to get off of these aching feet!"

Sarah froze, listening for the sound of the TV muting, praying that Dora would continue exploring and that she could get rid of the old hag without disturbing Emma's trance-like state as she stared at the fifty inch flat screen on the wall above the fireplace from her pink miniature recliner in the center of the living room floor. It was one of the only things the new Emma and the old one had in common, that trance-like state when morning cartoons were involved.

"That wasn't very nice," she sighed to herself, feeling guilty over the harsh feelings she had toward her elderly neighbor. "She's just lonely since her kids moved out of state and her husband is as lost in the television as Emma," she thought and dried her hands on her pink pajama bottoms.

"Dearie?" Mrs. McGregor called again. "Are you home?"

"Yes, I'm coming!" she called as quietly as she could and still be sure that she could be heard through the back kitchen door.

"Oh, Sarah! You are home!" The old woman's voice sounded rattled as she walked up the small stoop and pushed herself past Sarah and over to the table.

"Mrs. McGregor, good morning. I'm so sorry, though, right now is not a really good time. I have a migraine, you see, and-" Sarah started while holding the door open in hopes that her neighbor would get the hint.

"You're gonna wanna drink some hot tea and honey for that, it's what my dear passed momma would say." Mrs. McGregor ambled across the kitchen to the nearest chair and eased her old bones down into it.

She was a tall, thin woman, with graying hair that held just a hint of the rich blonde color that it used to be all pulled up into a messy bun at the top of her oval shaped head. Her mouth was set in a stern grimace, always, and her eyes were a dull stone color not unlike the color of her hair. She always wore plain colored house dresses with a small flower print, and today's was a dusty blue with tiny dots of yellow daisies. She wore no makeup on her pallid face, but her cheeks always shone with a natural blush, even in the darkest hours of the night.

"What can I help you with, Mrs. McGregor?" Sarah asked, resigning herself to the fact that she wouldn't be able to be rid of her company so easily today.

"It's my Peaches, Sarah! I haven't been able to find her anywhere and she's not the only one missing, either! The Garcia's say their little Stormy is gone, too and Joanna down the block told me just yesterday their new kitten hasn't been home in three days! Can you imagine? That poor little Tyler has been just in a fit about it!" Mrs. McGregor eyed the living room doorway shrewdly at the sound of the TV turning off in the next room. "You and Emma haven't seen any cats around here, have you?" Her voice suddenly cold and accusing when she said Emma's name.

"No, I'm so sorry, Mrs. McGregor, I am sure they will all be home soon, but you really have to leave, now. My head is bangin' up a storm. I just really would like to take a hot shower and get in a nap now that my morning chores are done." Sarah tried again, opening the door as wide as it would go and adding a small gesture with her other hand to drive home the fact that visiting hours were over.

"Hello, Mommy." Emma's voice from the doorway into the living room made both women jump as they had been engaged in a slight stare down. "Hello Mrs. McGregor," the child said, her tone equally as cold as the old woman's had been.

Mrs. McGregor stood. The air in the room had turned cold with the child's arrival and suddenly her bones weren't as unsteady as they had been when she had lowered herself at the table.

"Emma," she nodded to the girl's small frame, but was careful to avoid her gaze. "Have you seen my cat?" Mrs. McGregor tried to soften the accusation from her voice this time but failed, and somehow it came out harsher and more high pitched than she had intended.

"I don't like cats, Mrs. McGregor." The child's voice was steady and as cold and hard as frozen steel.

"Emma is allergic to cats, you see," Sarah lied and this time she wouldn't be dismissed. She could feel an electric current charging in the room and alarm bells were starting to ring. If this went on much longer she wasn't sure how it would end, but she knew it wouldn't be good for the poor old lady who loved her cat as much as Sarah herself loved Emma. "You really must go now, Mrs. McGregor. This headache is killing me." She crossed the room and placed a gentle hand on the older lady's elbow, guiding her softly to the back door and away from her young daughter's truly deadly gaze.

"Yes! I don't want to keep you!" Mrs. McGregor obliged as she started down the stairs. Her voice a little scared now. "Just please keep your eye out, won't you, Sarah. I'm going just sick with worry."

"Of course, I will," Sarah told her in a kind voice as she slowly swung the door shut. "Goodbye, now, and please give our love to Mr. McGregor!" she added just before the latch clicked home, not giving the old lady a chance to reply. She turned the deadbolt and peeked out the small square window that was built into the door and watched as the old lady disappeared around the side of the house back toward her own quaint dwelling.

"I don't like her, Mommy." Emma's voice startled Sarah and she looked over to see her standing in front of the sink and staring out the larger window there. "I don't like her very much at all."

"That's not very nice, now, Emma," Sarah told her, but gently, so as not to anger the child. She was skating on thin ice with Emma as it was, and she didn't want to push her luck.

"I know." Emma's voice, still cold but now also thoughtful, retorted as she continued to stare blankly at the spot where Mrs. McGregor had disappeared around the corner. A smile slowly spread across the child's face. It would have been a beautiful smile on the old Emma. Now it just caused Sarah's heart to flutter with anxiety and a dreadful anticipation. "I'm not very nice sometimes," the girl added. "I'm not very nice at all." With that she pushed away from the window, gave her mother a more normal child's grin and disappeared happily back into the living room.

Sarah watched her go and then leaned her tired body against the back door. Silent tears began to fall as she slid slowly down and into a sitting position on the floor. With her back against the cold, hard, wood and her knees brought up against her chest, she folded her arms up over her bent-forward face and cried silent tears. That last grin had reminded her so much of the child she loved. The Emma that was hopefully not lost to her, and she was suddenly so full of grief that she couldn't bear it anymore and her body needed to release it as best it could without disturbing the new Emma.

She knew it would sound crazy if she told anyone what she thought. They would lock her away and put Emma in a foster home and then what? She had to protect this child until she could figure it all out. She knew that Emma had to be in there, somewhere, but she wasn't sure what to do. If only Adam were still there, he would believe her. He would help her and they would figure it all out together. He had loved Emma as much as she did, and his loss was the absolute hardest thing she had ever been through. That was, until now.

And so, as the TV began to blare again from the other room, this time some other show with some other lesson to be learned, Sarah sat on the peeling linoleum floor, cradling herself in her own arms, and cried. She felt alone in this world now. She felt lost. She felt hopeless. Her heart was broken, and the tears ran in rivers out of her. Eventually, she slept.

About an hour passed before the child, as quiet as a mouse, crept into the kitchen doorway and watched the mother sleep. She smiled at the tired woman huddled there, against the door. She could feel the love for the mother that Emma felt, and it was good because that love would keep her safe. The mother would do whatever she could to keep the daughter safe and sound and happy.

The child could sense Sarah knew there was something different about her Emma. Some change that was unexplainable and dark. But she also knew that as long as she held her daughter hostage inside of this body with her, this was a mother who would do anything to keep her safe.

The child walked across the floor and lay a soft hand atop the mommy's greasy hair. This mommy was different, now, too. Tired and scared and unkempt compared to the mommy before the child had come into their lives. But that was okay. As long as she continued to be of service to the child then everything was okey dokey in the child's mind. She was a good mommy. She kept the child happy, so the child would keep her safe. For now.

She slid her hand further down Sarah's head and pulled out one of Sarah's hands folded below her sleeping face. "Come, Mommy, you're tired."

Sarah stood, as if in a trance, and allowed Emma to lead her to her bed. They walked slowly. The child first, with her hand behind her and up, lost in the bigger, elegantly shaped hand of her mother. Sarah took small steps and was barely even aware she was walking at all. It was like walking in a dream, and when the child turned her into her room and nudged her onto her bed, she fell atop the plush comforter and went even deeper into her sleeping mind.

The child watched her through Emma's eyes for a few minutes. She waited only to ensure that the sleep wish had worked, and that Sarah was, indeed, lost to it. When the child was satisfied Sarah was truly deep in her own dreams, she turned, a wicked smile playing across the freckled field of her innocent child's face.

Mrs. McGregor knew about the tasty little kitties. Mommy had suspected, too, so mommy had lied for her. Mommy kept her safe, but Mrs. McGregor didn't buy the lie and now Mrs. McGregor would have to play. That was okay with the child because the child loved to play. Playing was the best!

Emma's feet walked back through the house, stealthily and sure of every step. Her small child's hand turned the brass knob and let the child out onto the small back porch. She hummed a theme song to one of the many cartoons she watched in a sweet little tone and hopped down the steps with ease.

Skipping across the yard to disappear around the house the same place Mrs. McGregor had, the child began to giggle. She was so excited to be playing so soon after the doggy man that she almost couldn't contain herself. And, oh! How she hoped Mr. McGregor was home as well! Games were always more fun with more people!

The child squealed in delight at the thought of it and turned her skip into a gallop as if riding on the back of a giant white unicorn. A unicorn drenched in blood from razoring through crowds of delicious humans with its mighty horn. Humans ripe with fear-filled souls and bulging white eyes at the sight of her and her monstrous steed! She may have been an evil creature who had lurked in this world since time unknown, but she *was* still a child!

3

Mr. McGregor, Ralph to his friends, was known as a kind, gentle soul. People talked about what an outstanding man he was, always helping at the community dinners and never missing a chance to call the numbers at the local Baptist Church's weekly bingo nights.

The ladies liked to whisper to each other that Ralph's overall goodness stemmed from the universe trying to make it right that his wife should have so much bitterness inside of her own heart. Perhaps they would be different had they known the truth about Mr. McGregor and where Mrs. McGregor's bitterness truly stemmed from. Those ladies with their fancy haircuts and manicured nails might think differently of that kind old man had they known the kindness was just an act and the soul inside that man was not one filled with light, but instead, with a darkness that lurked there. Perhaps those ladies would be just a bit more kind to old lady McGregor had they known that though Ralph was a perfectly human man, he was capable of some very monster-like behavior.

Ralph McGregor had met Miss Nadine O'Delle at a church Christmas party held by his youth group. Nadine had just moved to town and her mother thought it would be a good way for the family to meet new people by attending the local Baptist church. Nadine had happily agreed and when she heard about the Christmas party she had been absolutely elated! Nadine had just turned seventeen that winter and wouldn't start school until after the holiday break. She was sincerely aching for friendship and thought it would be a good idea to get to know some of the local teens before she was the new kid in school.

Ralph had been going to every church youth function for almost a year now in hopes of meeting the right girl. Someone timid but still outgoing enough to make a good impression in those times where a fella's wife was needed to make one. Someone pretty, but not too pretty that she would catch the eye of every guy out there. *Some* eyes were okay, but not too many that it would be obvious to her that he was easily replaceable. She had to be smart, but not *too* smart and religious enough to believe that wives should obey their husbands.

He had had his eye on two different girls the night that Nadine O'Delle entered his life. Shelly Landon and Kelly Parks. The fact their names rhymed bothered him to no end. Shelly or Kelly? Kelly or Shelly? Which one will it be? He would lay awake at night, those words going through his head like a mantra. They both would make good choices as the wife he wanted to have. Both meek and not too ugly. A little less attractive than he really wanted, but all of the pretty girls around had good self-confidence, and that was a capitol NO in his book.

So far, Shelly had been winning the McGregor Wife Contest Extraordinaire, as he had dubbed it inside of his twisted mind. Her father had abandoned her and her mother when she was seven. It had been a relief for her mother who had tired of his angry fists and crueler tongue. But her mother soon found out how difficult it was to support a child on her own and ended up growing hard toward the girl. Shelly would try and reach out to her mother but would only get pushed further and further away. The only thing she wanted in the world was to be loved, and the fact that she had been abandoned first by her father physically and then emotionally so by her mother made her desperate for affection and certain that she had almost no self-worth at all.

This made her over value Ralph's affections and the more he would shower her with praise, the more she would crave it. Anything Ralph asked her to do, she did without question. She was younger than he, only sixteen to his eighteen, but he felt certain her mother would be glad to be rid of the responsibility that motherhood had bestowed upon her.

Shelly gave everything she had to give to Ralph. Her heart, her mind and her body had been his almost since they had met. She knew he had also been dating Kelly, and it made her so sad. So jealous. So much more convinced that she was worthless and that nobody would ever truly value her like she valued them. Her heart broke every night he was with Kelly and every time he would show up at her door, or call her on the phone, it would instantly mend itself. Stitching the pieces back together with a thick black string of hope and love and want and need for Ralph.

He had been good looking back then. He could have gotten any girl he wanted with his suave slicked-back, coal black hair and deep brown eyes the color of fresh brewed coffee on a cold winter's morning. His clean-shaven face, so perfect and blemish-free in a world full of pimples and half-grown mustaches. His deep dimples that accompanied his full lipped smile and the way one side of his grin would cockily perch higher than the other. All of this made him the most desirable boy at South Bend High, where they had gone to school all of those years ago. But it wasn't just *any* woman he wanted, and so far Shelly was ahead.

If only she had been a little bit prettier. A little less pudgy and maybe a few inches taller. He sighed and looked away from where Shelly had been sitting across the room. Where she was trying not to stare over at him and silently wishing he would come over and sit down. He actually *did* want to want her. To desire her as she did him. He knew she was everything he could want in a wife. But he just wasn't attracted to her. Not even a little. Sure, she could meet his needs when he asked it of her, and he had, plenty of times, but he always looked away or closed his eyes or ensured there be darkness where they did their deed. A man couldn't help how he felt in his heart.

Then there was Kelly. The far more attractive choice, if looks could be the only measurement. Sure, she wasn't as pretty as most of the girls, but he found her attractive in a more subtle way. The turn of her lips when she had something funny to say. The way her lighter brown eyes had of sparkling when she was happy. And that caboose was one a fella could lose himself in, yes indeedy!

But she had been raised in a loving home. A happy one. Her parents were very poor, and she had been clothed with hand me downs for the entirety of her life. She had seven older brothers and sisters and four younger. She was not the baby and also not the oldest. Lost somewhere in the middle of the pack. Overlooked, as she was not the squeaky wheel in the many wheels of her household.

She did her chores without incident. Her homework was always on time. She even kept her appearance tidy and neat. She knew love and kindness, but not so much in the kind that is special for the individual. More so as a shared thing between many hands and hearts. It wasn't until Ralph she learned the value of a love between two people. He was the one who had given her a taste of what it would be like to know that someone loves you more than anyone else in the world. That you weren't just one of many. That you were *more*. That you were *special*.

Ralph knew Kelly wouldn't make the perfect wife, though. She wasn't used to harsh tongues or painful fists. Her father had treated her mother as an equal, and so she would expect to be treated as equal. And then there was the fact that with such a large family and loving home it would be harder to keep her from leaving him. There would always be someone to give her security away from him once he started breaking her in, and that would be no good. It would take a long time to sever those relationships. The risk of her leaving him before he could would be too great.

He sighed again as he tore his glance away from her. *Her* he wanted. In a deeper way than just as his bride. More than just a possession to care for his home and his health. But a possession also to be possessed. He could see the lust in other young men's eyes as they looked at her and it made him want her even more. No, she wasn't the prettiest girl, but there *was* something about her and he knew he wasn't the only one who noticed.

But he couldn't let himself go down that path. He knew he couldn't and that's why he had stalled for so long. Going back and forth in his mind. Kelly or Shelly? Shelly or Kelly? Because he knew one would be the perfect wife, but he *wanted* the other one to fit. Even though she didn't. It wouldn't work out in the end. He knew that. And he also knew that his looks would fade and though he could be charming when it fit his needs, he wanted to get this part over with so that he could begin the next part. He knew that youth would eventually leave him and make replacing a wife so much harder.

The training part. Oh, how he looked forward to the training part. The breaking in would be so enjoyable. So fulfilling. So…

And then he saw her. She stepped through the doorway of the high school gymnasium where the church had arranged to hold the party. A beautiful blonde with shiny grey eyes the color of freshly poured steel, just cooled. Her lips were a bright Christmas red and there was a tiny blush playing high on her cheeks, as if each one had been kissed by an angel. Her hair had been teased and pinned up and she had carefully placed a bright white poinsettia bloom into the base of the bun resting high on her head. Her dress was a soft red and held to her perfect curves.

But the part that made him the most excited was the part he could feel pouring off of her in waves. There was something broken about her, too. She was lonely and scared and something else. Something darker. Something that would make her fit perfectly to him. Their pieces would fold into the other's, and it would be a beautiful thing. If, that is, you were into the darker kind of beauty. The kind that's tainted with pain and twisted turmoil.

Ralph stood and placed his very best smile upon his face. She was a little prettier than he would normally look for and he knew there would be competition in this group. A new girl to the small pond full of fish would be like blood in shark infested waters. But he was drawn to her, nonetheless.

Forgotten from his mind, and his heart, were both Kelly and Shelly. He didn't notice (and had he, he wouldn't have cared) that their gazes both tracked him as he walked across the room. They could both sense the want emanating from him as he took in this new and prettier girl. They could see her interest, too, as he reached her and held out his hand while tipping down a little, bowing to greet her. She giggled a giggle neither of them could hear, but heard anyway, with their hearts instead of their ears.

With the red that rushed to the new girl's cheeks, causing the blush that she had applied there to disappear into a pool of actual color and the embarrassed but happy way she couldn't quite meet his eyes, they knew. It was over between them and he. He was lost to them forever.

29

4

Kelly would be okay. She would go home that night and cry into her pillow. Her younger sister would awake to Kelly's soft sobs and would climb down from the top bunk and hug her tight. Telling her she loved her and that everything would be alright. Her mother would walk by and hear the whispering and pop her head in to see why they were awake so late. She would sit next to her daughter on her bed and hold her and let her cry it out. The right boy would come along, her mother would whisper, and Kelly would know that she is loved in a more personal way by her family. Kelly was lucky.

Shelly, on the other hand, not so much. She would later walk past the blooming new relationship of the boy she thought she was going to marry and the newcomer. She would meet Ralph's eyes only once, and, seeing the dismissive way they glared at her, and then changed to a softer look of want when they switched back to the pretty girl in his arms, she would go home to her own mother. Looking for acceptance and reassurance she would rush through her front door, tears streaming down her plain cheeks, and collapse on her couch, wailing in a sorrow and loss so deep it took her back to when her father had left them. Left her.

"Mama!" she called out and the tired looking silhouette of her mother appeared in the doorway leading to the kitchen. "Mama, he doesn't love me, anymore. He's met someone new. Someone better." The poor girl searched that silhouette where the face should be. Her eyes bright with the pain that bloomed so deep and so loud in her heart.

"Hhhhmph," the mother snorted as she walked all the way into the room and stopped, standing above the heartbroken daughter next to their worn and ragged couch. "I was wondering when that boy would come to his senses! He's so handsome and you're just so…" Shelly's mother searched in her overworked mind for the right words to describe what she was thinking. "Plain. Plain and boring is what you are." She sighed, a scornful look burning down onto her daughter's fragile state. "What am I going to do now, Shelly? I was counting on him taking you away. I'm so tired all the time. I can't manage this for much longer."

Shelly's heart shattered again, into a million pieces far finer than any man could make it do at this point in her life. Her mother's love was something she always assumed was there, even though she could hardly ever feel it at all. "Don't you love me, Mama?" She asked her mother, fearful of what answer might come.

"Well, yes, of course, I love you! But any creature on God's earth loves its child. It's the reason more mothers don't eat their babies in the wild. It's the reason humanity has grown as it has. My love for you has nothing to do with my *like* for you. I've fed you and clothed you and kept a roof over your head for all of these years by myself. I've lost loves because of your very existence more than once and have had to work extra shifts to make sure that you had new shoes when your old ones got too small. A mother does that because of love. If I didn't love you I wouldn't trade away my days and weeks and months and years to whatever job I can get my hands on just to make sure you don't have to live in a car under a bridge somewhere. I sacrifice getting things I would like so you can have what you need. But I can love you and not like you, too."

Shelly looked at her mother then, shattered pieces of her heart in a pile within her chest starting to burn with the pain of this evening and also of this new realization. Her words stolen from her tongue and her eyes too shocked to allow tears to spill. Even her breath was caught in the speech her mother was slowly letting flow from long, pursed lips.

"It's hard for me to like what took from me my first love. He was convinced he couldn't have kids, you see. Some accident had happened to him as a child and the word of a long-ago doctor still rang in his ears that it was an impossibility. And so, when you came along, he couldn't believe you were his, though you have his nose and his narrow chin. He grew more and more angry whenever you would cry for him or want him to teach you things."

Shelly's mom paused then to sit down on the chair next to the couch, as if her feet could no longer hold her weight after such a long day of scrubbing rich people's toilets and sinks.

"You were always wanting to learn, from the moment you appeared in this world. It's like you needed it," the mother continued. "You would demand to know things, sucking it from us like a little emotional vampire. The *needing* was so overwhelming sometimes. It was hard to think. You always cried and wanted and needed. Taking as much as you could from us until we had nothing left to give."

Shelly kept watching her mother silently. Trying to ignore the coldness that was seeping into her. From her toes on up into her heart and mind, she could feel the iciness creeping through her body. Through veins and muscle and bone, it crept. She was so afraid of what would happen when it filled her completely, but she didn't interrupt her mother. Good girls didn't do that.

"His family could see that you were his. It's obvious to look at you that you are. But he continued to deny. And the older you got the angrier he did. He started to drink, and he's always been a mean drunk. With the drinking came the hitting. And the screaming. And all because he thought I had went out on him. Ha! The thought of it. I had been as pure as fresh winter's snow on our wedding night and was true to him up until the day he left." She licked her lips, color growing deep within her cheeks as she began to grow angry from the memories this conversation was forcing into her now. Memories she fought hard to ignore.

"You would shower him with the love you had for him, and he hated it. So, he would drink to escape it. His family was very stern that he stayed with us. That you were his responsibility, and so deeper and deeper into the bottle he went. He never took it out on you. He told me you were just an innocent bystander. A mistake made out of matrimony, but not your fault. It was the whore he married whose fault it was, he would say. And I would beg with him, and plead, trying to get sense back into his head. But I wonder…" Her voice grew soft and thoughtful then.

"I wonder if he really did know that you were his. But that he just couldn't deal with all of it. The responsibility. The failure to answer all the questions that spouted forth from your mouth in never-ending streams. You were just so much work. Finally, he left. I was relieved by then. I was sad to lose the man I loved more than anyone else in the world, but that man had left me a long time ago. When you arrived, in fact."

Shelly looked up then and her mother's eyes met hers. They locked them into place with such a fierceness that Shelly was instantly terrified. She wanted to run from the room instead of hearing what was to come next. She would gladly just seep into the couch and under it, through the cracks in the hardwood floor. Down and down and down she wished she could go. Buried deep in the earth and safe from whatever was coming next. She didn't think she could stand it.

Her mother's gaze was ice as she held Shelly's to hers. Her voice, when she finally did speak, was deep and final. It rang in Shelly's ears like a death drum. "How could I ever be expected to like you. You ruined two lives the day you were brought into this world, screaming out in protest against everything and everyone around you."

The daughter stood, then. The ice had finished filling her all the way up. It gobbled her into some frozen maw that dripped and oozed with venom and acid, ready to dissolve her into the nothingness that was overtaking her mind.

Her mother was always tired, yes, for as long as she could remember it was true. But now Shelly thought that the tired creeping over Shelly herself had to be worse than anything her mom had ever felt. She was just SO tired. Every single part of her, her limbs, her lips, her *hair*, was tired. Every cell of her being felt as if it could lay down and sleep for an eternity or more.

Tired of not feeling love, even though her mom said it existed. Tired of not being wanted. Tired of not knowing what it was like to be chosen or valued or needed. She was tired of never being picked as partner in science class. She was tired of not having a best friend but getting to hear the giggles from the other girls with theirs as she passed them in the hallway after P.E. She was tired of not having anyone there to pick up the pieces of her heart and help her fit them back together.

Shelly didn't cry or say anything back. She just turned around and walked silently up to her room. As she went up the stairs, her shoes made hollow clicking sounds that mirrored the sound of her wounded soul, dying inside of her. When she got to her room, she slowly closed the door behind her. She walked across the thinning, blue-carpeted floor and sat down on the right side of her bed.

There was a glass of water on the nightstand there, still over half full from last night, in case she got thirsty while she slept. She stared at it. The way the lamp above it seemed to float atop its smooth surface. She wasn't even thinking anymore. Just staring at the water. Caught inside a world of numbness, she just sat. Eventually she heard her mother use the restroom and then go to bed. But she didn't really give it much thought. It was just background static. For hours she just stared at the clear glass sitting there.

Eventually she moved, though her thoughts were still lost to her. She slid the drawer of the bedside table open without deciding to do so. She acted from a part of her mind that was quiet. The part that takes over when you're overloaded with emotion. She pawed through the items there, all the way to the back. She pushed aside the white plastic handle of the brush she used. Slid away the pink, and then the red nail polish that she hadn't used in years gone by, tiny flakes of dried polish that had leaked from the stem falling to the wooden bottom of the drawer as she swept them aside. She moved away the small jewelry box her favorite aunt had given her when she had turned twelve, though there was no jewelry to keep inside.

Finally, her hand struck what she was looking for and her fingers closed around it. A clear orangish pill container with a white screw on safety lid. She had broken a leg over the summer and had been given a prescription of heavy pain relievers to help her through the worst of the painful days. Shelly had been a champ, though, and had only taken two or three and then only when she couldn't bear the pain. She hated drugs and prided herself on not needing them. She would never drink, either she often told herself. She would not be like her father had been.

She pulled the bottle out and placed it on the table next to the water and stared for a while more. Her lips quivering as if she were whispering a prayer, or perhaps shivering in the night of this cold winter's day. When she finally reached for the bottle, her hand was steady and did not shake. She pressed and twisted the cap with cold, dry fingers. It popped off in her hand with ease and she looked in. Nearly full. She smiled, but it was a sad smile. A serene smile.

"I love me, even if I'm the only one who does," she whispered to the empty room, only her childhood stuffed animals there to hear. "But I can't live like this anymore."

Shelly tipped the bottle on its side, carefully shaking out a row of large white tablets. When it was empty, she dropped it into the small trash can on the floor between her bed and the table and replaced it in her hand with the glass of water.

Shelly took the pills, one by one. Almost running out of water before she had finished. Then she sat the glass back down, a smile of relief on her face in the knowing that it would soon be over. She lay back against her pillow and reached up with a slow hand to turn off the lamp.

The darkness held her in a loving embrace, or so she fantasized as the slow ebb of the high took her in its hands. It held her close and rocked her steadily back and forth and as she drifted off into the blackness that awaited her, her heart finally quiet. Its sadness was gone and replaced only with darkness. She was finally at peace.

Shelly breathed her last breath and slipped away from this world into the darkness beyond while, just three blocks away, the man she thought would be her husband and who would finally show her what love was held the hand of the new girl as they sat on the porch swing of her family's new home.

Maybe Shelly was lucky. She wouldn't have to endure, or watch her children endure, Ralph's abuse. Nadine, on the other hand, would; a lifetime of it.

5

Ralph had found the perfect new young wife in Nadine. She had fallen head over heels with this handsome young man. Her family, growing up, had been broken, as was Shelly's. Her father had passed away in the war and so her mother had brought her up on her own. She had three older sisters, whose jobs it had been to take care of Nadine, and this left them all annoyed with her, and somewhat unkind. Unkind more in their impatience with her than anything else. Well, except for Cindy, who was just four years older than Nadine.

Cindy had remembered what it had been like to be the youngest. The one everyone else had loved the most. The spoiled one. The prized one. Then, along had come Nadine, and just after, her father had been pronounced dead by a knock on the door and the hushed words of a man in a uniform. Cindy's life had changed all at once. It was like the wind had gotten knocked out of her with her father's death, and every time she was passed by for the crying baby or had to stop playing to bring a bottle or a diaper, her breath would get sucked away again. Cindy knew exactly who to blame, too.

Cindy may have been jealous, but she wasn't dumb, no, not one little bit. She would wait to hurt the baby when nobody was around. She would sneak in quietly after school and tip toe into her room, which was also now the nursery. She would wait and listen for the sounds of anyone moving around in the house. Her mother would almost always be in the kitchen preparing dinner, and her sisters would be in their own room, talking about boys, or still walking home the long way from school. They were both in middle school and they liked to chat with their friends or stop and get some penny candy at the small market on L street.

When Cindy was sure that she wouldn't get caught, she would press Nadine's little toes together, slowly pressing harder and harder until finally the babe would awake with a start and a scream. Then she would quickly head out her door and duck into the bathroom before her mom could get to the hall. Sometimes she would pinch behind her knees or pinch her nose instead, just to liven things up a bit.

As Nadine grew, she learned to fear the child that was Cindy and try to keep her distance. But Cindy always found a way to get to her when nobody was around and the older she grew the worse and worse the abuse became. Nadine had often thought about going to her older sisters or her mother for help, but the last time she had done that the consequences were too painful.

Nadine had gone to Dina, her oldest sister, and said she needed help, her voice shaky and completely terrified.

"Help with what?" Dina had asked, while setting down the book she had been reading.

"It's Cindy," Nadine had whispered in one long outgoing breath.

"What do I need help with?" Cindy's voice had asked from behind. A voice that had been thick with threat and rang like warning bells in Nadine's mind.

"Uhm." Nadine had jumped, her Keds actually leaving the floor, even if just the tiniest bit. "I thought you needed toilet paper," the small child lied, blushing at the untrue words that came out of her mouth. Nadine hated lying.

"Nope. Wasn't me," Cindy had said in a sing song voice, and then turned to walk gaily back to their room.

Nadine had spent the rest of the evening helping her mother with dinner. Peeling potatoes and setting the giant white plates in their places around the table. She didn't want to be caught away from her mother's side and cried that night when her older sisters tucked her in. Nadine lay awake for hours dreading the thought of what would happen when she closed her eyes. Finally, sleep came and ushered her tired mind into soft dreams full of bunnies and butterflies.

Because the next morning had been a Saturday, Nadine slept in extra-long. She had been exhausted from the stress of the lesson Cindy would teach, when would it be, and where. So, her mind stayed happily lost in her own special land of sleepy time bliss. Finally, mother had woken her for breakfast, and she had yawned and stretched on her bottom bunk before curling her small hands into fists and rubbing out the sand that the Sleepy Man had left there.

Then she sat up. And then she screamed.

Laying in the lap of her soft yellow pajama bottoms was the twisted and mangled body of her pet guinea pig, Charlie. She had loved Charlie. With all of her heart. He was her best friend in the whole world. And she screamed again as she noticed how one of his dark little eyes was bulged out and staring up at her. She could sense the pain he had been in blazing out at her from that shiny, dead eye. Nadine screamed again. Again and again, she screamed. She hugged the stiff corpse against her face and a small dot of red, sticky, rodent blood smeared across her pale ivory cheek. Her mother and older sisters had all ran in, then. Cindy entering the room last, so that only Nadine could see the smug smile playing across her ugly, twisted lips.

"It's Charlie!" she cried, over and over again, her voice full of tight agony at the loss of her most beloved little friend. "It's Charlie! It's Charlie! It's Charlie!"

"Oh, honey." Her mother had swooped down and gently removed the pet from the sad clutches of her youngest child's hands. "I'm so, so sorry." Her mother's voice was gentle, and she was trying to hide the small amount of relief she couldn't help but feel at the loss of this furry oversized rat. She was not a mean woman, and while she felt her daughter's loss a great deal, she was also disgusted with that pet her brother had thought to present young Nadine with on her sixth birthday last year. She had insisted he take it back, but then relented at the child's glee. It wasn't often she was able to make her children this happy since she had to work a lot of long hours and money was tight, on top of the overwhelmingly horrible loss of their father. But she had had *one* condition. The giant mouse had to live outside.

Her brother, Harry, had happily obliged, and he took Nadine

on a special trip to the hardware store. He favored his youngest niece because she looked the most like his own lost child had looked, who had drowned ten years ago when she, too, had been six. He spoiled all of his nieces, but he could admit that he overdid it when it came to little Nadine. She even had the same name as his daughter. His sister had given her it in Harry's daughter's honor, as she had loved her niece as much as her own children and missed her greatly. Their families had been close in those days. Back before Harry's daughter had died and then his wife had left him. She couldn't take the loss and needed a new start. And with the death of his sister's husband, Harry tried his hardest to be there for the girls when he could, and help his sister make ends meet when she couldn't.

Harry and Nadine had purchased two-by-fours and plywood and chicken wire fencing. Then they had gone home and set to work building an outdoor pen. It ended up being pretty sturdy, even if it did *look* a little messy, and was big enough that Nadine could sit inside and crawl around with her Charlie for hours on end. She could almost even stand up!

Her mother had only regretted the decision once. Well, once until now. That had been on a rainy night not too long after Charlie had come to call their backyard home. There was thunder and wind and Nadine was worried that Charlie's fur would get wet. Mother had tried to explain that the house uncle Harry had built was very cozy and that the pine shavings they had put inside the little wooden box of a house inside the bigger cage would keep his little hairless bare feet all toasty and warm.

But Nadine had lay awake in bed, worried thoughts of flash floods going through her mind. She had seen a flash flood on TV once and it terrified her thinking that her fuzzy little guy would be lost to her. Just like her daddy had been. So, she had listened to the slow breathing from above for a while, the sound that meant that Cindy was fast asleep. When she was sure that she was safe from the all-seeing eyes of her next-oldest sister, she slipped her feet out from under the covers, and slowly stood, not wanting to make any creaks in her mattress as she did so.

Tiptoeing through the sleeping house, and silently letting

herself out the back door, she was relieved to see that the rain was just a small patterning and that no floods had invaded her backyard in a flash, as she had feared. She thought about going back inside and forgetting her whole idea of a rescue mission, but then she reasoned that it was still pretty cold outside, and heck, she had come this far!

Nadine crept back into bed a few minutes later and covered herself and Charlie up in the warm blanket. To Charlie's credit, he actually slept curled up in the empty space by her neck and under her jaw on her pillow and didn't awake again until morning, when Cindy was pointing and screaming at them both.

"Ewwww!!!! Mother!!!! There's a rat in Nadine's bed!" she had yelled into the waking house.

A few seconds later their mother had burst in, her hair curlers all askew from tossing and turning all night. She never slept well on stormy nights. Those were the nights she had missed her John the most.

"Nadine! Child! What in the world?" she had asked, but then she had broken into laughter at the sight of her daughter's sleepy eyes matching those smaller ones of the furry face beside her. They both looked up at her as if she was intruding on their sleep and the very idea that she could annoy a guinea pig was somehow hysterical to her. So, she laughed and when the other two sisters had come rushing in to see what the commotion was about, they had laughed, too. Then, so did Nadine. And when the mother looked again, finally getting her hysteria under control, she saw that Charlie ALSO seemed to find the whole situation hilarious, because there was (and she never forgot the look of it for the rest of her long years) a small guinea pig smile on those little lips amid the fur. She looked at that smile and broke down again, and at her renewed gales of laughter, the three other girls followed suit. It was a sound that would shine a bright light of joy and hope in anyone's heart. Well, in the hearts of the happy people of the world. Not in Cindy's, though. Her heart was shining, but the light was red and blaring. Nobody noticed the absence of her laughter. They were all too caught up in the magic in the room. They were taken away by it.

The mother sighed now and looked down on Nadine with pity in her eyes. "Jessica, get a shoebox, would you please? From the cabinet under the stairs."

"This is why mother told you not to sleep with it," Cindy's voice spoke up, emotionless so as not to give away the joy she felt at the sight of Nadine's grief.

"Cindy, that's not very nice to say right now," mother scolded, but softly.

"Sorry, mother," Cindy said, again with no emotion to hide the anger that replaced the bitter kind of happiness that was there. Of course, she would get scolded at a time when Nadine should be, she thought, and tried to hold her aching heart together inside of her chest.

"I didn't sleep with him! I woke up and he was just there!" Nadine protested through the tears that were streaming down her cheeks.

"Oh, honey, he couldn't have come in by himself. Maybe you were really tired when you got him," her mother said kindly.

"He's in a better place now." Cindy retorted. Her voice as cool as the back part of the freezer when it gets all full of frost.

Nadine met her eyes, and she knew what had happened the instant she felt the spark when her gaze met Cindy's. She knew then who had taken Charlie out of his cage. She knew then who had grabbed his body in both of her hands and who had twisted with a smear of hate across her face. She knew who had then placed him in Nadine's bed, atop the sleeping child's chest. And she knew why. Because she had almost talked. And talking got what you loved hurt. More than that, it got them killed.

So it went, over the years. Silent, inescapable abuse at the hands of her sister Cindy. Even now when it was just her, Cindy and mother at home, it was the same. Getting help was too risky. She always had a pet around. Cindy would make sure of it when nobody else happened to. Nadine would try not to love the new family kitten or puppy, but always would, in the end. She was an animal lover. Animals were always kind and loved unconditionally. And they never, ever, lied.

6

Ralph had been right when he had thought Nadine broken upon first sight. She knew fear and pain at the hands of another. She knew what it was like to love someone who hurt you, even though you hated them, too. But, perhaps most importantly, to Ralph, she knew how to keep the secret of it all and also about the consequences of not.

For Nadine, Ralph had been everything she had hoped to find in a young suitor. Tall, handsome, dark. But he had also been kind at first. Funny and wise about things. She could tell that he loved her, too, and she knew that her days left in her home with Cindy would be numbered. Too bad she didn't know that soon after marrying Ralph, there would be a lifetime of living how she had been with her jealous sister. Most of the time her new husband would be worse than Cindy had ever even hinted at.

Ralph had courted Nadine for three long weeks before popping the question. Nadine was sure it was going to happen when he pulled his car into the themed motel that was just off the highway three miles out of town. It was a mysterious place that the teenagers always whispered about, the girls giggling together about what it must be like inside and the boys all making up stories of when they had brought a girl there. The girl was always from out of town, a friend of a cousin or sister who was staying over and the stories were always unbelievable in how outrageous they were.

When he pulled in and parked, she knew that something magical would happen there tonight because this was a place that had caught all of their curiosities at school (even in the two short weeks she had attended she had become obsessed in the wonder). This was a place where imagination was born in their minds. Surely, he had big plans for this wonderful curiosity.

And Ralph did have big plans that night. Ginormous, in fact. He had gone around to her side of the shiny red car. He opened her door and as she leaned forward to get out, he caught her chin in one strong, but gentle grip. "Wait. I need you to do something for me."

Nadine rose her eyes to his, happy to oblige with anything he wanted that night because it was going to be the most memorable night of her entire life. "Of course."

"I need you to trust me," he said. His voice husky with emotion and also, something else, something more carnal.

"I trust you with my life, Ralph. You are my everything." Her voice was simple in its truthfulness and pleasant sounding to his ears.

"That's why I chose you," he told her, and a warmth grew around her heart. This is what love is really supposed to be like, she had thought. Her innocence and expectations only allowed her to see the good in him. Young love often takes its victims quickly and without any worry of how it will end.

Ralph leaned forward and gently slid a red handkerchief around her eyes, tying a hard, tight knot at the back of her head. She winced when a few golden strands of her shiny, thick hair, got stuck in the tying, and he had smiled at the sound. Unseen by her covered eyes, he had taken a sick and dirty need for that sound. He locked it away and played it again over the years, too many times to accurately give an account of. That small, sharp intake of breath. A tiny gasp like the tinkling of pure silver against sparkling crystal. It was the most beautiful sound he had ever heard in his life.

She let him take away her vision and trustfully took his hand to be led wherever he had the mind to lead. His hand was strong and sure and steady. He carefully navigated her up and out of the passenger seat, softly guiding her with his voice as well as the pull of his wrist. He closed the door of his shiny crimson beast, and led her, without incident, into their room.

She could sense the change from hard cement below her thin-soled sneakers to lush carpet. Thicker than any she had ever stepped foot on before. It felt soft through her shoes, and she wanted to kick them off and dig in her toes, being taken away into this mystery world completely and fully in doing so. Nadine knew only one thing in her foolish young heart of hearts at that moment. It was that she was hopelessly and irrevocably in love with Ralph. Tall, handsome, Ralph. Who she thought she knew in the certainty and blindness that is young love.

Ralph let go of her hand after walking her further into the room. Suddenly she was an island in the darkness that the blindfold had created and even when she opened her eyes, she was lost in a thick red fog through the neatly folded layers of the cotton bandana.

"Ralph?" she asked after a few seconds of being lost in the hazy red world without hearing any sound from him or feeling his steady grasp that had been lost to her hand. A little bit of uncertainty created an outline to her words.

"Okay! You can take it off now." His voice was full of confidence and her heart leaped up her chest and caught there. For a primal, panicky second, she thought she might choke on it. But then the moment passed, and it settled back down where it belonged, though at a much faster pace than it had been thump-thumping before.

Slowly, ever so slowly, she reached her shaking hands up and gently pushed the red fabric away from her eyes. The room was gently lit and as her view became unobstructed it was as if she were being transported away across the ocean and dumped onto a deserted island's sleepy oasis somewhere in the more tropical part of the world.

The ceiling was painted bright blue, with floating lazy clouds drifting forever in place across the wooden sky. The walls were artfully done so it was as if she stood in a clearing of palm trees, complete with adorable brown monkeys and brightly colored parrots living in their bushy green palms. A bar made of pale-yellow bamboo made up a quarter of the back wall and on it there sat a bottle of champagne in a shiny silver colored bucket full of ice. Two cups made of furry brown coconuts sat on either side of the celebratory bucket.

Next to the bar there was a door disguised as a small bamboo hut. It was slightly ajar and inside she could see sand colored tile leading up to a giant waterfall type bathtub made of giant grey stones. She sensed that if they turned on the faucet a waterfall would trickle down and fill the tub.

It was the bed, though, that was the centerpiece of the room. A giant pink and ivory colored oyster shell lay open against the wall to her left, gently lit from hidden lights within. The mattress looked soft and was covered in silky tongue colored pink sheets and round pearl white colored pillows. The comforter was thick and luxurious looking satin and round, also of the same shade as the sheets. This was a magical room alright, but the most exciting thing to her was Ralph himself.

Ralph was knelt before her. His dark grey dress pants sunk into the thick sandy-looking carpet at one knee, the other stood out before him, keeping him steady as he knelt. In his hands, which were raised out toward her, was a small black velvet box, opened to reveal a shiny gold ring. The diamond that sat at the center of the ring was not so big, but also not so small that she couldn't see it sparkling in the romantically lit room. Her heart this time exploded up and out of her chest, not stopping to get stuck in her throat. This time her heart raced out of her and shot into a million, billion fireworks above her. Fireworks that only she could feel and almost see as they banged and exploded with the sound of the love she held for him.

"I have been looking long and hard for the perfect wife. I've courted two women before you, but the day I saw you walk into that room, both of them were instantly erased from my mind. I knew the moment I saw you that I had to have you to be my bride. I wanted you then so fiercely that I could hardly wait to kneel before you and ask you to be my ever after. The woman who will care for me above all others and be the good Christian wife who makes my home and gives me children to pass my name onto." His voice was solemn. Serious. She knew that what he was saying held great weight to him. That what he was asking was important in his mind. That however she answered him tonight would be her real vows and that they would be entering into a contract here far before they did in front of God and family.

"Do not answer me lightly, Nadine. I need you to know and understand what I am asking. To be my wife, you will need to be strong. You will need to fulfill my desires and keep my home. You will need to smile to the world even when you feel like screaming. You will need to carry whatever load I need you to carry. I am not looking for just a friend to share my life with. I need a woman who will do as I ask and keep my secrets. When we marry you will be mine and my ears are the only ones who you will share your secrets with. I will be your husband and I will be the most important person in your life. I will have to be for this to work." She gulped at his words then, starting to understand, she thought, of what he was really saying, but still not completely grasping it at all.

"You will love, honor and obey me in our marriage as you will swear to do in front of God himself, in his own house. You will not falter or fail in this because, as my wife, that will be unacceptable. You must promise me now, before we go any further. I am telling you all of this before you decide because you have to know what I expect ahead of time. After we're married, my word, as your husband, will be law, as God has intended, and I will keep you in a home and provide for you and I will be your everything." He paused to consider if there was anything else he should add, and then went on.

"Will you take me as your husband? If you say yes, it's forever and cannot be undone by man's law, because God's law is the only law that matters." He finished, his eyes ablaze with the heaviness of his words and the lust he held for her. Something that he had been trying to control since he had first walked up to her that day not so long ago in that high school gym.

She met his fierce gaze with eyes full of emotion herself. "I have but one condition to your proposal." She knelt before him so that their eyes were level with each other and she could search his more fully as he answered. "Do you love me?"

It was a simple question, and he laughed. He had been worried that there would be some strings attached that he could not agree to without lying. But did he *love* her? That was an easy one to answer with all of the honesty in the fabric of all that there is and was and will be.

"Nadine, I have never loved another like I love you here, now. I have never wanted or needed a woman before with such ferocity as I need you. You are exactly what I have been searching for and I cannot imagine a day where my love for you will ever cease to be. I am asking for you to see me as your world, as I now see you at this moment," Ralph stated, licking his lips after the final word had left him.

"Then yes! Yes, I will marry you! I will be yours and you will be mine forever. I will be a dutiful wife as God intends for me to be and I will keep your home and bear your children happily forever and do it all with a smile on my face." She said these things but didn't understand the extent to which he meant them in the asking. She said them with a happy heart and mind set free. She loved him, and he loved her, and he would take her away from the silent hell she lived in and he would make all of her dreams of having a husband and being a mother and a wife come true. Or so she thought then, on that winters' night headed toward spring. She truly did believe it.

He had it all planned out. A summer wedding, just after graduation. They would go away for a few weeks afterward to a cabin his father owned in the woods a few hours north and spend the time exploring each other more fully. She had blushed at that, excited and nervous at the thought of what those words really meant.

Then they would come back and live in a quaint two bedroom his uncle rented out and he would go to work in the family business. They would start their family there, and once he had moved up in the ranks a little and they could afford to buy a home of their own, they would. Something bigger with a nice back yard in which to watch the children play.

She fell in love with him all over again hearing his plan for their future. It was a beautiful thing, a fairytale come true. And she couldn't wait for any of it to happen and with that impatience came the need to please him and keep him happy so she wouldn't lose him. She gave herself to him fully that night. In word and body and mind. She was his. He was no one's but his own.

They were wed in the church with the few friends she had made of her new classmates that year, her uncle, mother and sisters and their new families sitting on her side. His side was full of classmates, friends of the family, and family. He had a high charisma, so he could hide his darker side with ease and grace. He attracted people to him like a moth to a flame, and so his side of the church was full of a sea of smiling faces on the day they had wed.

Nadine had made her promise eagerly, for now on top of her vows to him, she had a secret. Soon she wouldn't be able to keep it hidden any longer. Her skirts and dresses had all been getting tight on her as of late and it had been a while since she had had a visit from that long-hated bitch called Auntie Flo. She had been too afraid to go to the doctor. It was a small town, and small towns are full of wagging tongues. So, she had spent almost four months in a state of disbelief and worry and hope that her period would suddenly start again. Late, but finally welcome, for once.

But her period hadn't come and so she waited, in a quiet desperation, for the day they could be wed. After that, it wouldn't matter if there was a bun in her oven. At that point it would be a blessing instead of a bastard who was shunned and gathered leery stares and whispers behind raised hands as it was passed by in the streets. She didn't think that he would welcome a bastard child, either. His beliefs were very strong and unwavering.

She had been agreeable to everything he had asked for. He took her to a different motel after that first magical night where he had taken from her the only true thing she had to give, her virginity. A motel that was cheaper, and dirty and always seemed to smell of long spilled beer no matter which room you had. The first few times she had been cautious and still timid and afraid. These trysts were getting less and less about her, and more about his needs each time they entered through the swollen, musty doors of this trashy place.

That first time, in the soft, silky mattress of the beautiful oyster bed, he had touched her gently, lovingly, softly. He had made her feel ecstasy unlike anything she had ever known in her young life, and she had wondered at how any human could make another human feel so good in such an unexpected way.

"Do you like this?" he had asked her in the middle of that first wonderful night.

"Yes," she had gasped at him, trying to catch her breath but finding it ever so hard to do so.

"Good," he whispered, his lips lightly brushing over the tender skin of her smooth left inner thigh. "Every time we do this after tonight, it will be your turn to make me feel this way." She had answered in a moan, and he had smiled. He almost had her trained and he had just begun the training. She really had been the perfect choice, and his heart soared.

The next few months, at that new motel, he had taught her how to please him. Where to put her hands and mouth and what to say and also what to take. He had given her not love and gentleness, but hardness and sometimes even pain. She had tried to get him to slow down, to be softer, but he had looked at her so fiercely that the heat coming from his eyes actually seemed to burn her skin. She could feel her cheeks ablaze with that hateful gaze. The disgust he looked on her when she tried to speak up cowed her in fear. Fear that he would not want her anymore.

Fear of being left by the first man who she had ever known love from. And, in a secret part of her, fear that he would never do those things he had done to her on that first night again. She needed that and lusted for it. Because of those things she kept going with him on those nights to this place. She bore the pain and the shame and did everything he wanted her to do and sometimes she was rewarded and that needing part of her rejoiced. She was addicted to it by the time she had started to worry about the possibility of her impending motherhood. She was addicted to that rare moment where he pleased her, even though she knew by then that he didn't please her for her enjoyment. No, he only did it when it was something that he had wanted to do. Not for her carnal pleasure, but for his own strange satisfaction.

And so, they stood in front of friends and family. In front of the preacher and the Lord, they stood. The rings were exchanged, and their vows were spoken and then the preacher man let them seal it with a kiss. Everyone cheered and threw the rice and then it was time for the party!

It was a somewhat lavish affair for a town so small. His family happily paid for everything as their business was going well. His mom even came along to pick out dresses with her and her mom and they all got along surprisingly well. His family knew he would

49

need the perfect wife, and they could tell that he had chosen well. God give her strength, they would say to their inside selves every time they saw her. They knew he was a monster, but still they were proud. He was their creation.

The reception was enjoyable to all. Even Cindy was happy at the beautiful wedding and big to do afterward. She laughed along at all the jokes that new family members told, and she smiled the happiest smiles in the wedding photos that she could. And they were *real* smiles. Because Cindy knew something that Nadine and their mother or sisters did not. Cindy could *sense* it and it made Cindy's wicked little heart warm and tickly.

Because Cindy herself was not a kind person, and because of the evil that lurked within, she could sense there was darkness inside of her dear sister's new husband. She knew that, though Nadine had happily rejoiced in the fact she was about to be rescued from Cindy's torturous grasp, she really wasn't being rescued much at all. Cindy's eyes were full of sparkle and a true joy, even if it came from a place of horribleness and charred edges. She knew that her sister had been duped and that she would never escape the clutches of someone like Cindy. Of someone like Ralph. Cindy was truly happy for the first time that day since before her dad had died. Yes. Cindy absolutely beamed!

Everyone danced and drank and ate. Money was pinned to Nadine's dress by her new aunts and uncles and cousins and there had been more than one stolen squeeze of a breast or butt or waist in the pinning. She had endured with the grace of a million years of women being forced to endure such things and she had gushed with praise and thanks at all of the money being given. One great uncle from the old country even dropped a silver coin in the modest bust of her white, flowing dress, and winked at her when she gasped in shock. A mischievous smile on his face as he sauntered away after.

Mostly, though, it had been a beautiful night on top of a beautiful wedding and Nadine would keep it in her mind. Looking back on it when she thought about the few happy times in her marriage over the years. She had been the happiest that night than at any other time in her life, happier, even, than the first night they had shared together at that themed motel off the highway.

Ralph finally swept Nadine away, back into the long white limo and on their way to the cabin. They would be there without a car for a few days, and then his brother and mother would drive his up, along with dropping off some groceries to hold them over the rest of their stay. Ralph would use that time before his car arrived to give her more lessons. Training a young new wife was a very important thing. You only really had one chance to get it right, otherwise you would spend the rest of your life in nagging hell. Marriage was a contract under God, and one he did not take lightly or see as an escapable arrangement.

They had arrived finally, at the end of a long dirt road. The cabin was beautiful to her. Absolutely stunning, in fact. It was two stories and made of actual logs that had been cut by hand. It was nestled within a canopy of elm trees, shading the whole area and adding an even more peaceful touch to the scene.

The cabin itself wasn't painted but stained a rich reddish brown which enhanced the natural look of the wood. The door and window seals were painted a dark rustic green that matched the thick grass below the stained wooden deck. A tire swing slowly swung in a lazy circle from one of the branches of a towering elm. The rope was thick and the soft yellow color of freshly baled hay.

She sighed with happiness as Ralph grabbed her up into his strong and steady arms and walked her over the threshold. He sat her down on the shining hardwood floor inside the door and beamed into her eyes as he did this.

"You're mine now." Ralph's voice was matter of fact.

"And you are mine," Nadine replied, a softer, love-filled tone.

The smack was sudden and loud, as if a gun had been shot off in the small room. Her face instantly blazed with pain as her left cheek started to swell and burn and her left eye poured a salty stream as if to cleanse itself of what had just happened. She stood there before him, a small, dainty hand held up to cover the bright red patch spreading across her shocked face. She looked at him, tears threatening to fall from her right eye as if it needed to match the left. Her gaze was screaming disbelief and hurt. Hurt beyond just the physical sensation, but deeper, as well. Her soul screamed with it.

"I am not yours, for The Holy Book itself does say that the wife belongs to the husband, and not vice versa. Eve was formed from Adam's rib, and so you are now formed from mine. You are mine. I own you. It is God's own words that dictate it so." His look to Nadine was one of compassion and love, even though he had just stolen her trust, and so she was confused.

Does he love me? She wondered. How could he look at me so and not have love in his heart for me?

"You will do as I say, and I will love you for it. If you deny me my rights as your husband, I will punish you as is my duty. If you disobey my words or teachings, I will punish you as is my holy position in our time on this earth. You have given yourself to me, fully, and have promised to obey under God's own roof, and so you shall, or I will correct you in your path. Our home will be a righteous one as it will be my job to make it so and keep it so. That starts now. This very second. You can have happiness as long as you choose to be the good, godly wife. You can have security as long as you obey as you have promised to obey. Will you choose so? Or will our life together be full of lessons? For there is no separation. You are mine forever." His voice was drenched with so much sincerity that she had no choice but to finally consider his words to her these past few months.

The slap had shown her the truth. Finally, her eyes had been opened so wide that she couldn't deny it any longer. This man would not give her the safety she so desired. Unless she played by the rules. Unless she granted every whim and obeyed every word. She felt that he really did love her, and she couldn't help her love for him, even now. And so, Nadine resigned herself to it and nodded her agreement to the pact finally understood, too late. Besides, she was pregnant now. There was no longer any doubt. The only thing more terrifying than raising Ralph's child under his law was raising it in a house with her cruel sister, Cindy.

Ralph smiled. A gentle, but hard smile all at the same time. He took her hand and led her up the stairs where they made love for the first time as husband and wife. It was as gentle and as hard as that smile had been and they both had been satisfied before they were through.

Afterward he had requested she make him dinner, though they had eaten at the reception, and she had happily agreed. But when his steak had been overdone, even though just barely so, he had thrown the plate against the wall, shattering the porcelain and splattering peas and baked potato every which way. His hand had reached out, so quickly that she hadn't seen it coming, and grabbed her neck so forcefully that her teeth chomped down on her tongue, causing a burst of iron-tasting blood to fill her mouth as he wrenched her eyes down close to the mess he had created.

"You must make my meals with perfection, as you must be perfect in all you do as my wife. I am worth more than dried out meat, wouldn't you agree?" Ralph enunciated his words by pressing her still sore cheek into the mess. Butter and sour cream smeared against her flesh and small chunks of potato stuck into her hair.

She nodded as she tried to hide the sobs and was terrified at what may come next. He let her go and she instantly started to clean up the mess, not daring to meet his gaze. His next plate had been to his liking, and she had eaten all of her own dinner, suddenly ravenous from the long day's many twists and turns. It was late by then, well after midnight, and she had earned that meal. She ate with potato in her hair and smudges of sour cream that the dish towel had missed still streaked across her red and swollen cheek. All the while they ate, she kept her eyes from meeting his. Again, Ralph had smiled. Again, he had reassured himself that he had made the right choice in Nadine.

Their time there, in that picturesque cabin in the woods, was spent full of love and pain and a mixture of both. They explored each other's bodies and their minds. He taught her how to cook and clean and please him in all the exact ways he felt she should and when she did not perform to his liking, whether in the bedroom or elsewhere in her wifely duties, she was punished in crueler and crueler ways. He would hit and curse and demean and let her know that it was her fault he had to do this. She was not a victim, for she could choose to do it the right way the first time.

And she endured the slaps and pinches and pulled hair. The twisted grasps and pushes. He didn't hurt in a way that would require a trip to the hospital and he made sure that his marks on her could be hidden. He was not a stupid man, no matter how cruel and harsh he could be.

7

By the time they finally moved into their new home, she was well versed on his idea of how a wife should be. The years went by, her doing her best and enduring when she failed. He leading his household and not sparing the rod on she or their children. He was the true master of his domain and of all who lived within it.

They grew older and their children moved away. They called her on Mother's Day, but they always had excuses when holidays rolled around that would normally require a visit home. She and he grew old together and Ralph's domain shrank to just they two and their home and their furry little companions.

But she had made him a very happy man even though he had made her miserable and bitter. He had stolen all of her good parts and replaced them with wilted shadows of what they had been. He had doused her hope with pain. But she had endured it all with as much grace as her broken heart could muster.

The only thing Nadine had found to take comfort in that differed from her tormented childhood life was the fact that Ralph wasn't mean to pets, as long as they didn't poop or pee where they weren't supposed to. This had enabled Nadine to find that lasting kind of love that came with no restrictions. It kept her going through the years after the children had all gone away. The love of her kitties was real and held no strings. Her gentle strokes along their soft-furred backs and her scratches under their fuzzy chins would be rewarded with purrs and rough tongued kisses.

That love was special to her. She wasn't allowed to have more than two cats at any one time, because Ralph didn't want to live in a home full of animals and the smells they brought, but he enjoyed them, too. He laughed as they ran around, chasing each other's tails and batting at balled up paper he would throw for them on those longest days in winter where it was too cold for him to go outside. Their love was special to him, too.

When their dusky pale orange cat Peaches came up missing, he was meaner than normal with his worry, and she was more anxious and liable to make mistakes with hers. Peaches had been a special cat. Orange cats were usually male, but that didn't stop Peaches from being born a girl. She was sassy and loving and generous with her purrs. She had loved Nadine more than any cat had ever loved, or been capable of loving their master, and the worry of her absence ate away at Nadine's tired old soul.

"I think it's that neighbor girl. That Emma!" she told Ralph at dinner the night before she finally went to speak to Sarah. "I've seen her in the backyard staring at our Peaches. The look on her face about made me die of fright right there on the spot. And I'm not a woman who frightens easily as you yourself know more than anyone, Ralph."

"I've seen her, too!" Ralph leaned forward in his dinner chair, a small drip of dark brown gravy dripping down his chin from his mouth as he spoke. His coffee-stained teeth from years of neglect shone out yellow through his wrinkled and twisted lips. "She's a wild one, that child is! No father in the home to guide her, the mother just letting her run amuck. Not like our kids. No, they knew how to behave in this world."

She nodded, and for a second her heart grew heavy at the thought of her own children now long gone, scattered across the globe. She knew they were still close with each other, and that gave her some solace, but she ached for their company and for their love. She had been the best mother she could be under the circumstances of having Ralph for a husband, but she wished she had had the strength to leave him. Or the foresight to have never married him in the first place.

"She's an evil child," Nadine whispered conspiratorially after a few seconds where only Ralph's sloppy chewing could be heard in their small kitchen. "I saw it in her eyes when she looked at Peaches on the fence. I took her in, then, to play inside with Georgie, but you know how Peaches loves it out there. She ran out when you came in from the grocers and I haven't seen her since."

"Don't you blame this on me, you spiteful bitch of a woman!" Ralph spat at her from his place across the table. This time chunks of meatloaf flew and dribbled down his face. He slammed an old and gnarled fist on the table, and she jumped at the sudden loudness in this quiet place. "I shouldn't have let you get that goddamn cat in the first place." He sighed then, his love for the cat softening his quick anger. "But don't you blame this one on me."

"No, of course it's not your fault, Ralph. That isn't what I meant at all. I was just saying that she must have taken her that night, that girl from next door. Emma. She must have taken our Peaches and… and…" A few tears fell from Nadine's eyes as she thought of the horrible possibilities that may have befallen their beloved pet at the hands of that wretched child.

But there was something else about that girl, Nadine thought. Something dark and sinister. She could feel it oozing out of the child when she watched her staring at Peaches on the rickety wooden fence their properties shared. It was in the girl's eyes, as well. In the way they had sparkled and changed. They had seemed to *glow* this too-bright green as they considered the cat. Peaches had just stared back, as if stunned or lost in thought. Or as if she were a deer who got stuck in the brightness of oncoming headlights and so couldn't move even if it meant saving her own life.

That was the thought that had sprung Nadine into action. The thought of that little girl's eyes being the beams of some oncoming thing that carried death in its grip and her hands reaching up as if they were the vice of some hunter's trap. Her mind's eye could see those little fingers digging into the soft plump flesh of their tame little Peaches and she had jumped with a gasp and ran across the long dead grass of her unkempt backyard. She had reached up and grabbed her baby off of the fence railing, which was on her side, thank goodness for that, and pressed Peaches hard against her beating chest as she carried her back into the safety of their home.

The cat had sat motionless inside of Nadine's loving embrace for a few long minutes and all that time Nadine had whispered small loving words in the hope that by showering Peaches with them it would soothe the cat and break it from its spell. Finally, the cat had shook its head as if to clear its mind and mewed up at her master. Her soft orange fur only broken by softer white tiger stripes. Peaches' bright yellow eyes shimmering at her master's dull blue ones and her whiskers long and white popping out beside her small pink nose.

Nadine's heart melted with happiness inside of her chest and she smiled. "I'm just being silly, aren't I, precious Peaches?" she said as she stroked her kitty's long back, causing the animal to arch her spine into her owner's pressing palm as it stroked, her tail popping out the end of the passing of her hand like a fluffy striped question mark.

Peaches knew she wasn't just being silly because Peaches was a hunter. For a moment there, Peaches had been the prey and she knew that this human who she loved had saved her life. A fact she would soon forget as the call of the outdoors again took over her little cat brain. But for now, all was right in the world of Peaches the cat. And so, Peaches had purred.

Nadine had not been wrong in her suspicions regarding Emma and the missing cats. Aside from the fact that it hadn't really been Emma, herself, but instead the child which held her hostage inside her own body. The child hated cats. She always had and always would. It wasn't a hate that had a purpose or any reasoning the child could even understand. She just loathed them. Perhaps only for the sake of having something to loathe. More probably, though, it was because her overwhelming dislike for the small, sleek creatures gave her an excuse to murder and devour them. Oh, how she loved the taste of a frightened feline on a lazy Sunday afternoon.

Peaches had caught her eye almost immediately after the child had come to live inside of her new host's home. She was always sitting on the back fence, licking her paws or looking up into the treetop as the sunlight slowly drifted through the branches and the leaves that grew there all year. Watching as the local birds bounced around and flittered from here and there, singing their soft melodies.

It was a view that the child could see directly from Emma's window, and she had sat there in those first few days almost constantly, her small legs curled up on the ledge of the wide shelf that ran the length of that wall which was designed for children to sit and gaze out at the world on rainy days. A place to make up adventures and what ifs and watch as the moon began to rise into the darkening sky with its cheesy Cheshire grin.

Sarah had been beside herself with worry then. It was the beginning of the change and she hadn't yet known that something evil lurked within her Emma's small frame. She would feel the child's cheeks and forehead with gentle, loving hands. Checking to make sure that the child wasn't sick because she most certainly wasn't her normal bouncy self.

Those first few days when the child was properly locking up her prisoner and completely stretching into her new digs, she spent a lot of time watching and resting and waiting. Taking in her surroundings and developing an understanding of how things worked in her new home. Coming up with a strategy of how and what and where. It was the calm to the chaos that would follow.

In that time the child had developed a need to know what that particular orangey cat on that rickety fence in the yard tasted like. She needed to know what the snap of her bones would sound like in her jaws. What the feel of her warm blood across this new flesh of hers would feel like. And so, she sat. And watched. And waited. And a very un-Emma like smile played across her lips as she did so. The reflection of her too bright green eyes danced on the window where her gaze drifted through the glass.

It got to be so that the child liked the anticipation. She let it grow and grow as the days went on. She let it build and become almost a living thing inside her mind. The want to tear the flesh from that softly striped, mewing fuzzball on the fence. The child waited and nurtured the bloodlust she held for that cat.

There had been other felines in the meantime. Random strays that had gotten too close and were lost into her hunter's gaze. Fulfilling her need to feed in between the larger times where she was forced to slip away and roam the city for her human prey.

When the time finally came that her lust for the taste of that kitty's salty insides was too great to wait any longer, the neighborhood had already been whispering about their missing cats and kittens and wondering if perhaps there was a cult nearby, using them as sacrifices to some unnamable god or to Lucifer, himself. But there had only been the child and she was good at what she did. Never being seen or raising suspicions. Until, that is, the day she went for Peaches.

The child had put the sleeping wish on mommy and then snuck out the back door as quiet as a mouse, so as not to disturb the cat who had been resting in that same beloved spot, busily licking one peach colored paw and then the other. A soft purring sound was coming from somewhere deep inside Peaches' chest as she performed her after nap ritual, a sound that made the child's mouth water with anticipation for the snack to come.

Emma's small body had crept slowly across the yard an inch or two at a time. She didn't want to disturb the cat because if the cat looked up too soon it would sense the incoming danger and flee. The thing she hated most about cats was their ability to sense the monster inside the child. They hissed and swatted tiny razor-filled fists if they were not carefully caught inside of her gleaming gaze. They ran if running was possible at the first hint of her coming toward them. So, she had to be careful when entering their presence. So very careful not to disturb the small beasts.

Her want for this particular neighbor's pet was so great that the child's concentration on what she was doing overtook her mind completely. Inching ever closer until finally she was within distance of her hypnotic too bright flashing gaze. Then she moved, a little quicker. Now it was okay for the cat to stop and look. Now it was what she wanted.

The child's shoe snapped a small twig that had fallen from the leafy canopy above and Peaches instantly jerked her head to the side, her eyes suddenly being held and then lost in the eyes of the child. The child had been so full of electric anticipation that she hadn't heard the neighbor's door creak softly open as Nadine walked onto the back porch of her house next door. She had raised her hands into vice like claws and had continued walking toward the poor, caught prey on the fence, and that is when the woman took action and intervened.

The child had been livid at the loss, for she was not used to losing and had made herself a vow that she intended to keep. That cat would be her dinner and there was nothing that would get in her way. Even if that meant she would have to track it down inside that old lady's house, she would taste its blood before that day was through.

But she hadn't had to wait around very long. Peaches had returned to her most beloved spot on the fence that divided the property, licking its paws without a care in the world. As if it hadn't almost been lunch that very same day from that very same spot. This time the child was more careful not to be caught. And this time the child was successful in her capturing.

The child had taken the shock-frozen Peaches after snagging it from her usual space atop the beam and brought her to the storm cellar, a place Sarah never went, and that Emma was not supposed to go. Down here was the child's secret place. The place she brought her animal prey to be devoured in peace. Away from the people who would try to stop her. Away from the people who wouldn't understand her need to feed.

This place was dark and dank and smelled of old blood and death and decay. The floor was littered with broken collars here and there. Silvery, blood smeared name tags glinted from the dirt floor in the light that drifted in through the cracks in the wooden door that lay just above the ground outside, setting atop a cement base. The door had once held a lock, but that had not been hard for the child to take care of. She was strong beyond her body and one quick yank had pulled the rusty screws which held the latch easily out of the rain rotted wood.

It was a small room, no larger than ten feet by maybe fifteen. There were no shelves or storage boxes down here to clutter up the place. It was just an empty concrete room with a floor made of earth and there was something about this place that called out to her animalistic side. It comforted her more than the soft bed upstairs. It was the child's real room. Her safe space. The only place around, aside from the sewers lurking below the city streets, where she could be her true self without fear of spoiling her disguise.

She held the softly breathing cat close to her body as she carried it down the stairs, making sure to close the wooden doors before descending. It would be lost inside its mind for just a few more minutes as her mind's grip on it slowly faded. Just enough time to place the fragile body in the middle of the room and then back away to sit in the shadow of the staircase.

Peaches lay there on her side in the middle of that dank, dark place. Her tiny diamond-shaped nose puffing up small bits of dust into the broken rays of light shining dimly down from the doorway above with each rise and fall of her pale orange chest. She was lost to the world around her. Her eyes only seeing a sea of bright green rings spinning and swirling and she was caught in it, unable to move even the tiniest bit. Aside from the steady buh-bump of her heart and the intake of air into her lungs.

Slowly, so slowly, the rings faded. From bright green to a duskier color until finally the world began to regain its solidity once again. Peaches lay still a moment longer. Confused at where she was, but not confused at all by how she got there. She could sense the predator nearby. She could smell the rankness of the other that lived inside the body of the child.

She had once loved the little girl next door. Had once rubbed up against her tiny legs and meowed and purred with every stroke and scratch from those tiny child's hands. She could feel that Emma still existed within the shell of her flesh and bone, but deep within. Unreachable at the moment. This other thing was closer to the top and encircled the real Emma in a cell built of an evil will too powerful for the mind of one so young.

Peaches couldn't understand how the humans couldn't see or smell the difference. Peaches was afraid for the little girl and for her nice mother who often gave her bits of chicken or tuna salad when they ate lunch in the yard, picnic style on a blanket. That was before this thing had come and stolen the child away. Peaches missed those days and longed for the time when this thing would leave them be. If it ever would.

The poor cat lay still a moment longer, trying to find its bearings before alerting the child to her awakeness. Searching the room desperately with her night-visionesque cat eyes Peaches looked for any means of escape. She could almost *see* the smell of death in this place of darkness. She knew the door must have been how they came in, but it was closed to her now and so there had to be another way. Her life depended on it.

The child sat watching the cat like an animal would watch its prey. She breathed shallow breaths while waiting, knowing that Peaches was feigning sleep in the hopes of finding escape. The child smiled and suppressed an evil laugh. She wanted the cat to have hope until the very last moment. She wanted it to think that escape was possible, though she knew it was not. The cat would die in this lovely room and there was nothing it could do to change that. The only thing the cat could do is make it more fun. The child loved the chase almost as much as the catching. The chase made the catching so much more delectable. The chase made it so much more enjoyable.

Peaches slowly tilted her head up and off the gritty floor of the cellar. Sweeping her gaze around to scope out the entirety of this underground fortress. Hoping for a crack she could squeeze through that the child could not follow. A vent or an opening just the right size for a housecat and nothing bigger. The poor beast's heart sank as she realized there was nowhere to go. Nowhere to run. Her only hope lay in the unbreachable door and so she would have to dare the stairs, though she knew that's where the child lurked. Somewhere in the shadows that were unusually black and bleak and unbreakable, even to her cat's special vision.

The child tensed and stopped her shallow breaths. She saw the cat bring up its head and sweep the room for escape. She could sense the moment when Peaches realized that the stairs were her only option, though they really were no option at all. When the cat smoothly regained its feet, her back to the wall farthest from the stairs, the child's fists clenched quietly. Peaches backed up a little, her stealthy feet making almost no sound in this place where time seemed to stop ticking. Her yellow eyes searching the darkness for the child, though being careful not to meet her gaze.

Peaches acted then, as fast as she could. She was a little bit plump but still could be as quick as liquid silver through a heated tube on the hottest of summer days. She leaped toward the staircase but as far to the right of the steps as she could, sensing the child somewhere to the left, and thought she had made it for a second before the child's twisted fingers swiped out of the darkness and batted her back through the air and into the wall.

Peaches hit the rough and blood-stained cement and bounced back into the middle of the room, almost to the very place she had awoken. Pain joined her fear and hope of escape drained away. Her left shoulder cried out with every move she made, though she pushed that deep back inside her mind. Survival had no time for the aches of the wounded if the wounded wanted to make it out alive.

The child laughed then. A cold and bitter laugh. Bitter, but happy, if those two things could coexist. She stepped out from the darkness that lived aside the stairs as if she were stepping out of a cloud of blackness. Small whiffs of it trailed around her feet as they came forward from it and Peaches watched with ever growing terror as the child took a form other than that of sweet little Emma.

The child's head jerked quick and hard, first one way and then to an entirely unnatural angle in the opposite direction. As it jerked it seemed to grow and stretch. The neck thinning below it as it raised up higher toward the hairline cracks in the ceiling above their heads. The child's skull growing taller and taller and its grin stretching as far as it possibly could before finally stopping just below her ears. Ears which themselves were changing, growing more and more narrow and pointy on the ends and they moved as if to focus in on the sound of the frightened cat's quickening heartbeat.

The child's eyes grew larger and more round. They seemed too large for the head to support, and still they grew and grew until they lay like saucers shining out into the room. A green glow so bright that Peaches had to squint her eyes to still see filled this little place where the cat and child were caught in a dance as old as time itself. A dance of predator and prey.

A frenzy was growing inside of Peaches' almost broken mind. A need to escape and live and not experience a painful death in the grip of this monster's twisted claws. Claws that had started out as short pink digits extending from a tiny hand and had grown and sharpened and twisted into things so inhuman that they were unrecognizable as fingers anymore. The nails were sharp as razors as her stretching arms grew down from the growing body and scraped against the floor.

Even the child's legs grew longer and longer. Bonier and bent at odd angles so that the elongated form could fit crouched in this tiny room. A room that seemed to grow smaller and smaller as the child grew taller and lankier and more terrifying by the second. Drool dripped down the child's now narrow chin, escaping through her thin lips in rivulets.

"Here kitty, kitty, kitty!" The child rasped in a creaky voice out into the room. Spraying drops of putrid smelling spit into Peaches' now dingy fur. Dingy from the dust and grime of this under place it had been brought to against its will. "I'm going to eat you all up!" she croaked, and then a laughter bellowed out of her in wheezy gusts.

That was all it took to splinter the poor kitty's mind. It no longer had control of thought and frenzy steered the wheel. She ran toward the stairs, even though it was toward the monster, and the child watched as it took each step quickly and with a feral agility. When it reached the top it scratched and scribbled, looking for a weakness it would not find and again the child's wicked laughter filled the poor kitty's ears.

Peaches clawed and clawed until pure instinct told her to run another way. Just in time she evaded the bony claws of the villainous creature in the room as it swiped for the furry hind quarters of the sad and frightened cat. She ran as fast as she could, her tail a poofy blur as she sprang from one corner to the next. Panic controlling her mind as she pressed her nose into every crack and cranny she could find and still the child laughed and laughed and laughed. Fueling the discord that caused the cat to flee from wall to corner to wall again.

Finally, the child gave chase. Hunched awkwardly forward and using the palms of her hands as well as the pads of her feet to run after the cat. She stayed just one step behind, letting the cat think it had a chance to get away, even though the cat knew somewhere deep down inside her tangerine-sized brain that it was no use to run. There was nowhere to go.

Eventually Peaches gave up. Her heart was beating too hard in her chest. Her lungs burned with the effort of trying to evade her evil captor's razor-sharp grasp. Her shoulder ached with the sharp pain of the impact of being flung into the wall and then the running and scratching she had done. Her claws bled from the effort of trying to find purchase in the wooden door and purchase in the cracked cement walls. Some had even been ripped cruelly from her furry swollen paws in her effort to survive this horrid inescapable ordeal.

Peaches stopped, back in the middle of the room in the same place in which she had awoken from her green and spinning nightmare. She lay back down on her side and curled into a tight ball of fur and blood and ache. And then she waited. Willing it to be over soon and not to hurt too much. She had been a killer of birds and mice and bugs and so knew what was to happen next. And for the first time in her short feline life, she felt a sense of empathy for all of those tiny lives she had taken. She knew now what it must have been like for them just before she pounced. Sometimes she had toyed with them, too. Letting them run with broken limbs or wings that could no longer fly. But always, the ending was the same, as it would be now. But it wouldn't be her jaw doing the tearing of the flesh. Instead, it would be her flesh that would be torn.

The child in its new and stretched out form scuttled across the floor, not unlike a spider would. It hovered over the huddled body of the cat and reached its long neck down to sniff deeply of the fur. The smell of fear was like ecstasy to the beast that lived inside the body of the child. It fed her deeper darker soul and enlivened her mind. Sharpening the colors of the world around her and making the sounds more crisp and clear.

Her long tongue slipped through those nightmarish lips and drenched the fur with stinking spit as it ran up and down the poor cat's body. A body that shook with fear and horrible anticipation. The tongue stroked up and down the entirety of the cat, again and again, until the fur was matted and wet and Peaches looked like something almost drowned.

The child soaked up as much of the fear streaming from the cat and when she could no longer take the anticipation of something more, she held up a single claw like finger in the air above the cat's still body, hovering there above it as if searching for the exact right place to stop. A few moments passed as the child's blazing green eyes considered, and finally it lowered its talon in a lightning-fast jabbing motion. Piercing through Peaches' body just below the shoulder, and through her ribs, expertly missing her panic-stricken heart in the doing. The child's sharp nail went through the soft flesh and muscle and between the bones of the cat with so much force that it planted itself three inches into the hard-packed dirt floor beneath them.

The pain caused Peaches to flail and try to break free from the child's claw, which had the cat pinned firmly to the space below her body. She scratched and bit against the boney finger that bound her there to no avail and howled a sound so full of agony and grief that any who happened to hear it would have had their blood run cold. But there was no one to hear that shriek of horror and pain. The sound belonged just to them, and the child fed on it.

Peaches bled from her wound and a puddle began to grow around her flailing body. The child then brought her other hand close and with an expert twitch of a too-long finger, the scalpel like nail cut the drenched flesh of the cat from her chest all the way down to where her tail met her torso. Peaches jumped one last jump and then lay still. Panting as she watched through helpless eyes as the lizard like tongue stretched back down and inserted itself into the slice. It slowly pried open the flesh, it's tough and bumpy tongue working its way between the layer of fat and muscle and bone.

The child inserted a fingertip then, as if a sharp hook into the mouth of a fish and snagged the skin an inch away from the slit she had made in the cat's soft underbelly. It pulled the flesh up and away, letting loose long noodle-like ropes of intestine out onto the floor, and a small mist of steam began to rise up from the pile that had just been snug and warm inside of Peaches' body. The bright white of the cat's rib cage shone out in the green light that emanated from the child's oversized eyes. Her tongue had cleaned it free of blood and sinew as it separated the flesh from bone just moments ago. The sound of the feline's rapid heartbeat seemed to grow louder as her ribcage was exposed to the darkness here.

Peaches lay there in a universe of pain so great it seized her in a motionless grip as shock tried to take her to another place. A place where this would all just be a distant thing, irrelevant to her. A place where she could peacefully wait to die. She could feel the pain and the tugging as the child opened her up. She could feel her flesh being folded back away from her body as her insides were revealed to this dank air. She could feel the burn in her chest as she tried to breathe through the blood that seeped around her nose and through her mouth, but it was thankfully all a faraway thing. A thing that belonged to some other Peaches. A Peaches that was almost her but not quite so.

The child bent then, closer to the exposed insides on the floor below her and lowered her face toward the iron rich smell that was pouring forth from Peaches as if in one long wave that had no end. Her long, thin lips widened and settled over the muscle and bone. A squelching slurping sound began to fill the air as the child fed, slowly, so as if to prolong the death of the tired kitty caught in her grasp like a fly in a spider's silky web. The child suckled the cat almost to the point where the cat's life was sucked away and then stopped, almost too late, but not quite.

Then the child that was not really a child at all removed the claw that held Peaches pinned into the blood muddy floor and gently picked up the dying body. Its intestines pouring all the way out as the cat was raised into the air, and they hit the ground with a sick and low slooping sound, trailing to the floor from the body as if a marinara-drenched noodle hung over the lip of a dish. She cradled the dying cat gracefully inside of arms that should not be capable of grace, with their length and uneven bends, and then brought it slowly closer and closer to its opening mouth.

The cat was no longer capable of thought, rational or irrational. It existed in a numbness as it floated closer and closer to death. Even as the child slid it into a mouth that stretched and grew to fully house Peaches' eighteen-pound body, it floated farther and farther away. Just before the shark-like teeth chomped down and crushed Peaches' skull and shoulders and hips, the cat drifted off into the peaceful darkness of death. It was spared, at last, from the child's evil feast.

The child could taste the change as the cat passed over from living to dead and she smiled. She liked it when they died inside of her, made incapable of true escape. She liked to imagine that their souls were being devoured as were their bodies, and she crunched merrily on the broken bones and squirting stomach and kidneys and liver and eyes. Finally, all that was were the fallen intestines, somehow still trailing from the ground on up into her mouth. She giggled as she remembered a cartoon she had watched once with animated dogs eating spaghetti.

Spaghetti was one of her favorite human meals and so she slurped this last remaining proof that Peaches had been here, just as she would spaghetti. She slurped and slurped and slurped. She loved the feeling of the thick, stringy guts being forced up and into her lips and filling her cheeks with ooey, gooey deliciousness. Finally, when her mouth was full and the floor was empty, she chomp chomp chomped them up, too.

Peaches was gone, but the child was happy and with that happiness she let her body shrink and change back into Emma's small form. The child looked around to make sure that she hadn't missed an ear or tail, and then with a congratulatory nod she skipped across the floor and to the stairs. Her dress and face and hair were filthy, and she would need a bath. What a wonderful end to a tiring day this had been. She yawned as she let herself out into the darkening world of their backyard. After her bath with a tub full of bubbles she would go to bed with no supper. She wasn't hungry, but she was getting tired, and the moon was starting to peek out over the tree above.

8

Next door, Nadine was scraping some leftover scraps of the fried catfish she had made for supper into Peaches' and Georgie's bowls. Georgie was there, happily and greedily eating what she offered, but Peaches was missing. That was when she had started to worry. As the girl next door silently crossed her own yard's dying grass and let herself into Sarah's kitchen door, Nadine had started to wonder where she was. Not knowing that Peaches would never come home again.

Later, Georgie would sneak over to Peaches' bowl and greedily lap up the cold catfish that he knew was not meant for him. The empty bowl would give Nadine a little hope, and what harm was there in that? None that Georgie could think of.

The child would have let the old woman be had she not gone over and made it clear that she thought that Emma was to blame for the missing neighborhood pets. It was smarter to keep suspicions away from the home, so now she would have to take care of this problem. But carefully, in a way that aroused no more attention at the door of Sarah's house.

That was okay, though, the child was good at spreading chaos and misdirection when she needed to be. It was more than just survival instinct in her case. In her case, it was a hobby.

The back door to the MacGregor home was atop a cement block about four feet off the ground. To get there you had to go up five cement stairs. Once there it offered you a fine view into the neighbor's yards on both sides. The tall maple that called their backyard home was expansive and blocked the view of the neighbor's house behind them. The child took a second at the top to look over at where she had stood that day that Nadine had caught her sneaking up on the delectable kitty and smiled. Glad it had happened the way it had because it had brought her to this. To play a game that wouldn't end in a feast, perhaps, in the traditional sense, but oh boy! Would it be fun!

The back door was locked when she tried the knob, but it twisted, anyway, in her child's small grip. The door opened on quiet hinges as Ralph prided himself in a well-kept home, and the child let herself in without notice, closing the door behind her as she went. This room was where the laundry was done. It smelled of summer breezes and soap, which made the child scrunch up her nose in distaste at the strength of it.

The kitchen was next, and there she could go into the living room through one doorway or down a hall that led to stairs in another. She waited for a while in the somewhat darkness of the laundry room. It was still morning, and the sun was shining happily down on the other end of the house. This gave her comfort in the shadows while she waited and watched and listened.

She could hear a TV in the living room and Ralph's heavy breathing as if he were asleep. Probably laid back in a recliner with his slippers barely on his feet, a small bit of drool snaking out of one side of his old man's open mouth, his head askew to one side where it had gently rolled as the sleep took him. His belly full of a well-cooked breakfast from a wife whose idea of what love was was twisted by a lifetime of pain.

Upstairs she could hear a soft whirring of a sewing machine as Nadine mended this piece of clothing or that. The child felt safe to wander now and she slowly walked through the sparkling kitchen and into the well-cared for hall. Her shoes made soft clicking noises against the hardwood floor, unheard by the two human inhabitants of the home, as she moved from one room to the next.

The hall was lined with pictures, carefully hung. Displaying memories from times long gone. School photos of children with forced smiles and perfect hair and crisp, clean clothes. She could see how haunted their eyes were and a smile played her lips.

She ran her hands along the brightly painted wall and the memories hidden within reached out to her. She saw the sad children that had lived here. The way they had tried and tried and tried and still had never been good enough. The times their father

71

had beat them for being too loud or cursed them for being too soft. The belongings they had lost to his tearing hands and the fright they had felt when they watched him beat their mother or felt his fists upon themselves. Their blood sometimes spraying out from their bleeding noses or busted lips and decorating each other's skin, which they could feel for hours after having it carefully scrubbed away in the tub.

The child could sense the pain and hurt and anguish that had gone on here. The wood cried out with it. The foundation creaked with the weight of it. The windows almost bursting outward just to get away from the echo of it all that forever reflected in their shiny panes. And so, the house gave her everything she needed. It wanted them to pay for the pain it had forced into its very essence as a home. A house's job was to protect and be filled with love. These people had filled it only with bitterness and regret and blood.

The child walked down the long hall, her hand dragging along the wall as she went. Her fingers trailing and changing as she grew closer to the stairs. With each step up she changed a little more, this time not into a giant scary monster, but a child not much smaller than Emma. A blonde with bright blue eyes and a little button nose and a naturally rose-colored smile. By the time she reached the top, it was like she WAS that child, from all those years ago. Not the woman version who lived somewhere out there in parts unknown, but the long ago four-year-old little girl who had been taught in this home that love meant pain instead of kindness.

"Momma?" the blonde girl called. A soft voice different from Emma's. Higher pitched and kind of shaky. As if afraid that the act of speaking was going to get her in trouble.

Down the hall, the rhythmic song that the sewing machine made paused as Nadine listened. Thinking she heard her baby girl's voice, Katy, the youngest, calling out to her. But no, that was silly, and she began to sew again. The noise a rhythmic burrr in the otherwise quiet upstairs.

"Momma?" this time louder, and this time Nadine was sure she had heard it. She stopped and stood and stared toward the door. Terrified and yet elated.

"Katy?" she called out. "Is that you, dear?" She straightened her apron as she took a step toward the hall. Wiping the sweat that had sprung up on her palms and between her fingers as she did so.

"Yes, Momma." came from the little blonde girl's mouth. Her eyes shiny and full of tears threatening to fall.

"Oh, Katy!" Nadine called and rushed from the room. Then, she froze. She had expected to see the full-size version of her youngest child standing there. Her Katy that was traveling around in the back of a van with a man who was very much like Ralph in temperament, but not so much like him in the need to support his family.

She stopped and stared and gasped at the child. "But, how?"

"Momma, how could you?" the child asked. The tears now beginning to fall as her sad blue eyes searched Nadine's, as if demanding to find an answer there.

"Katy?" she uttered in disbelief again at what she saw before her.

"How could you let him hurt us like he did?" Katy's voice grew cold and cruel. "How could you let him teach us his wicked lessons and make us cry and break our bones?"

"Oh, Katy, I-" But Nadine had no excuse to give. The child was right, even if there was no way she could be here in this small form. In the long-ago body of her youngest babe. Then suddenly an idea of what must have happened occurred to Nadine and she dropped to her knees in front of the four-year-old girl and wept.

"Oh, Katy." But this time a quiet wail. She did not want to disturb Ralph in his morning nap. She needed to keep her Katy safe from him even though she must really be out there, somewhere lying dead in order for her to be here as the child she was so long ago. She needed to finally keep her safe from him to make up for all of the times she had failed at that before. "I'm so sorry."

"It's too late for sorry, Momma," the child squealed and Nadine jumped, placing a finger across the child's very real lips.

"Shhh, Katy! You mustn't wake him. He'll be angry if he's woken." Nadine's voice a desperate whisper now.

"You always only cared about making him happy, Momma. But what about us?" Katy had placed her hand on her mother's finger and gently removed it from her lips. "What about Tommy when

Daddy broke his arm for spilling his milk at the table when he was six? He had tried to clean it up, but Daddy didn't care. He screamed at him and made us all cry and Daddy had jerked him up so hard that his bone snapped so loud we all could hear it. You protected Daddy from the doctor who asked what had happened. You lied and blamed it on Ralphie. But Ralphie would never hurt a fly."

"Oh, honey, I'm so sorry, but you just don't understand. You just can't see what it was like. How much worse it could have been," Nadine pleaded with the child that shouldn't really be there but who was there just the same.

"But can't you see how much better it could have been?" Katy replied. "How much happier we all could have lived had you taken us away to stay with one of your sisters or your uncle or your mommy? We could have been happy and become happy grownups if it wasn't for you. If it wasn't for *him*."

"I couldn't. I couldn't leave him. What would I have done for money? How would I have clothed you all and fed you? And the law would have been on his side, no matter how many black eyes or broken bones we had." Nadine began to cry now, in self-pity and self-doubt.

"Ralphie's wife cheats on him. They have three kids, and he doesn't know if any are even his," Katy whispered. "He drinks too much at night and falls asleep crying. He doesn't think he's man enough to stand up to her, and he loves her even though she loathes him," the child spoke, her voice a child's voice, but her words well beyond a small child's reach. "Tommy is in debt so deep that he looks behind him when he leaves his house. He's in debt to the kind of guys who you don't want to owe money to because they take out their interest in body parts and his interest rate is sky high." Nadine started crying harder then, sick with worry now, and grief.

"Emily's husband beats her, too. Just like Daddy beats you. Only Emily hits him back. They drink and do drugs and hit each other and hit their kids when they get too close. All because she thinks that hitting means love, because that's what you taught her. What you taught us all." Katy's voice was so accusing and hateful when she spoke that Nadine was filled up with it. She felt like dying just as Katy must have died to be here now this way, and she lay her head down on the child's tiny feet.

"Katy, tell me, what can I do? How can I make up for it? How can I take it all back?" the mother begged the child. Her wrinkled, liver spotted hands clutching the girl's thin ankles in a grip so tight it would have surely caused pain, had the child been capable of being hurt in such a way as that.

Katy knelt and placed a gentle hand atop the old mother's silver hair and ran it slowly down across her pain-stricken face. "There's only one thing you can do, Momma. What you should have done years ago."

A look of understanding slowly dawned in Nadine's eyes. She lifted herself up into a sitting position on her knees, her hands resting casually on her upper thighs. A single tear slipped from an eye that seemed almost entranced with the thought of the chore that lay before her, and for the first time in decades the woman smiled a pure smile that reached her eyes and down to her heart. She felt like she could finally be free. Free of the shackles she had tied herself to when she had agreed to be Ralph's wife. And free of the guilt she bore every second of every day for the pain he had caused her children by not standing up to him when they needed her most.

Nadine was so lost in thought at what must be done and what it would mean that she didn't notice as the child slowly slipped away. Back down the hall and down the stairs. Leaving the woman in silent contemplation, for the child had more work to do and not much time to do it in.

"Hi Daddy!" A familiar voice drove Ralph from the hazy dream he had been having. Something about fishing at the lake with the kids when they were young. He had always enjoyed those trips, thinking himself the good father, even though he always held new forms of abuse by his hands for his family.

"Did you miss me?" the voice came again, and Ralph opened his eyes with a start. The first time he had heard her he had thought it a voice from the dream. A long-ago remembrance of his Katy-Bug drifting to him through the years as he slept. But, no, it wasn't a dream. She was there, standing just beside his chair. A happy smile across her beautiful child's face.

Only, it couldn't be. His Katy-Bug was all grown up and had attached herself to some hippie loser as if he had taught her nothing of the world at all. He knew he had spoiled her, but to have her life become so horribly embarrassing for him had been such a disappointment to his heart.

"It's Momma's fault, you know. She always worked against your teachings. Making us soft. Making us resent you. If it weren't for her, I would have grown up fine and made you so proud," Katy's young voice said so solemnly that Ralph's chest hitched with the threat of angry tears to come. Which was even more absurd to him than his grown-up child appearing here as the four-year-old she once had been, the idea that he, Ralph MacGregor, could cry over the choices of others.

But it was true, what she said, was it not? It had to be Nadine's fault. She was always trying to undo his hard work. To kiss away the booboos when the booboos were meant to teach and guide them into knowing not to make the wrong choices. All of his children had grown to resent him, and he had never considered it before this moment that all of that had been because of his wife. The woman who was supposed to love and honor and obey had taken from him the one thing that should matter most to an old man like himself. The love of his children.

Katy reached out and placed her small hand against Ralph's aged face. It burned cool on the warmth of his skin and as she slowly and gently caressed the father's cheek he could feel it leave a trail of ice as it went. And with that trail, the anger inside of him was awakened and grew hungry. He knew he must feed it, or he would go insane with it.

"It's okay, Daddy. You can make it better. You can make it right. We're all back now and you can have a second chance. But first…" Katy started but didn't need to finish because Ralph already knew what needed to be done.

"First I must teach her a lesson," he finished, but the child didn't mind. An innocent grin bloomed on her face, but her eyes were ablaze with some other emotion. An emotion that said that she was anything but innocent.

Ralph leaned down and pulled the handle on the side of the

chair. His grip was strong with the hatred he felt building inside of him and the chair swung closed too quickly, causing him to yank forward and as he did the wooden lever broke free inside his grip. He looked down at it with thoughtful curiosity. A wooden chunk about eighteen inches long. About two inches thick where it started in his palm, but it grew and thickened to around four inches where it had attached to the side of the recliner. But that is not what caused the gruesome smile to spread across his doughy face. A smile that resembled that of a Jack-O'-Lantern past its prime. A little squishy at the edges of the lips and just below the eyes.

It was the bolt that caught the attention of that evil part of him that lurked just inside. A bolt that tapered into the sharp edge of a screw, about half an inch thick that jutted about three inches out from the oak finish of the wood. It looked like the perfect tool for teaching a lesson that Nadine may actually remember and never be able to forget.

"I can have a second chance," he whispered, to himself more than to the impossible little girl now standing at his side. "And this time, I can get it right."

"Yes, Daddy," she nodded, and he delighted in it. He craved his children's love and acceptance as much as did his wife's, though neither of them had ever talked about it with the other. Perhaps had they shared that secret before this day, it may have ended differently for them. But, more than likely, it wouldn't have mattered at all.

Nadine stood after her youngest child had disappeared down the stairs, but slowly, as a frenzied daze crept through her limbs. She stared for a moment at the place where the child had been standing, as if wondering how it could possibly be true. But no thoughts were racing through her mind at that moment aside from one. One rage filled thought that had been there since that very first slap in the cabin that day so many years ago. A thought that had grown old as she did, but never really left. It whispered to her over the years, sometimes more loudly than others, especially so when their children had been his victim.

"I need to stand up to him." She whispered it as it echoed through her mind. Again, and again the words came quietly from her lips. Over and over and over. And each time they fell from her chamomile tea-moistened tongue, they grew brighter and brighter in her mind. More and more pregnant with rage and hate and anger. A lifetime of abuse had created a Gollum and as it was being born inside of her heart, she allowed it freedom to stretch and fill her limbs. She welcomed its strength and as she grabbed her special fabric shears from the desk in which she kept her sewing things, needles and patterns and a rainbow of threads of all colors, she took comfort in the feel of their hard cold handles as they settled around her thumb and fingers. They were as cold and as hard as her heart had just recently become.

She stood there listening. A haggard duplicate of her normal self. An angry scarecrow in a blue dress with dots of yellow flowers. Her hair up on her head in a tight bun and her crisp white apron with the deep pockets tied around her narrow waist. Her face was wrinkled around her eyes from years of worry and fret. Her nose was a little bit crooked from the breaks it had sustained over the years that had been clumsily set by Ralph's rough hands.

But it was her smile that would run your blood cold if you were confronted with it at that exact moment in time. It was thin and stretched nearly from ear to ear. A wild grin which screamed insanity out at the world with just the way it spread and sneered. Her teeth were shiny with moisture, and unlike his were clean and white with the care she had put into them. But they were almost too white in the light of the room as it drifted in through the lacy pale curtains covering the window. The gums that held those shiny teeth in place were a pink similar to the shade of those sheets on that oyster bed and a clear ribbon of saliva poured out over one of those stretched lips and ran down her chin. Welling up and at the same time it finally could take the weight of itself no more and dripped, she moved.

It was time. She would stand up for herself and her children and be damned the consequences. He would never lay a hand on any of them again. She was through taking his abuse and she would get revenge and make it right for what she had allowed her children to go through. In her mind, this day was long overdue.

She raised the scissors high in her hand, their sharp end

glistening as it stuck out of her tightly closed fist. A fist that held those scissors in a death grip, the fingers clenched through the handle in a way that would ensure they weren't knocked loose or grabbed away. They were as if an extension of her very body. Grown there through the animosity and bitterness that now filled her heart and mind and soul. Their dagger like point stuck out in a defensive way, as if her fist were the head of a poisonous snake and they were the fangs. It was poised and ready to strike.

So, Nadine left the room. Headed through the house that had kept their secrets and borne their pain. It had soaked up the blood and the curses and the strife and it readied itself now for more. It could sense the turmoil growing in the air. The white-hot electricity that sprang out from both its masters. Its walls creaked in a lonely call of despair and revulsion for what was about to happen. A home was meant to keep you safe, and this home had been misused. It had been forced to harbor anguish and misery, not happiness and love.

Ralph heard her enter the room and he turned his massive body toward her tall and thinner frame. The child, now blonde and just a bit smaller than the red headed Emma from next door, stood behind him, peeking around the father's giant form. A look of despair on her tiny, upturned face.

"Please, Daddy," the child shrieked in Katy's voice. To Nadine she sounded like she was begging him not to hurt her with the club he held in his raised fist. A piece of wood that looked familiar to her in some distant way, but she couldn't place it in her frenzied mind. To Ralph's ears he heard the child begging him to not let their mother make them soft and spoil them for adulthood like she once had done in his way of thinking all those years ago. To both, those two little words, shouted into the air in a tone of dreadful panic, had the same effect as if a starting gun had been shot off in their small, but fanciful, living room.

Nadine opened her eerily sneering mouth and screamed. A battle cry filled of decades of pent-up sorrow and rage. It grew and grew in the room in which they stood until it filled the place in its entirety and started seeping into the light cream painted walls. A guttural sound that as it left her lungs it filled her soul with strength and when it finally began to peter out, she raised her fist, pointy end of the scissors held out toward him, and ran.

The sound of her agony, finally unleashed after all of their long lives together, enraged Ralph in a way he had never felt before. All of his hard work and years of careful cultivation seemed undone and that wouldn't do at all if they were to get a second chance. A chance to fix the errors in their children's' lives by ensuring their strength and digging out their weaknesses. He needed Nadine to lose her softness and to stand hard by his side. He needed her to have the same stern resignation that bloomed within himself for it to work this time. Otherwise, they would fail again, and he couldn't take the thought of it.

So, as she raised her weapon and began her mad rush toward him, so did he follow suit. The handle from the old recliner swept up as he ran the short distance to meet her in the middle of the small space, the sharp end of the screw poking out reflecting tiny rays of sunshine as it moved swiftly through the air.

As if they were dancing a well-rehearsed and choreographed dance, they met and swung their weapons in a graceful arc, both perfectly in time with the other. She buried the stainless-steel end of her shears deep into his right shoulder and he whacked the screw end of the bludgeon crudely across the left side of her face, where it dug in just below her left cheekbone and tore a ragged opening that extended down into her lips.

His blood gushed out at her from the artery she hit as she brought the shears back out in one hard yank, spraying it across her face, speckling the already gruesome sight with red pinpoints of gore. Her blood oozed from the gaping wound he had created and again, she screamed that cry of pent-up rage, only this time directly into his anger furrowed brows. He could see her jaw where it met up near her left ear, and all of her teeth that she had carefully tended over the years now were painted pink as her wound seeped over them. Blood mixed with spittle showered onto his flesh and again his outrage with her bloomed as a black rose inside his heart.

They raised their weapons high, again in perfect unison, and again they brought them down. The scissors this time finding purchase in the soft part of his neck, and this time blood flew without them first being yanked away. A bright crimson burst shot out across the room and painted a family portrait from long ago. Misting the picture of perfect family values, leaving a leery film over it that seemed to reveal an image which was closer to the truth.

His bludgeon this time around had dug its crude metal spike into the base of her left ear and as the force of his swing caused it to continue its dreadful pass, it tore the ear lobe away from her skull with a sickly wet tearing sound, ripping flesh from bone as it knocked her head sharply to the right. The tear extended, exposing the pointy bone in her left cheek and the purple-red fibers of muscle just below her left eye before he yanked it back and the chunk of ear came back with his deadly tool of destruction. The flap of skin now folded and hung before her lips and as she screamed one last misery-filled scream, it rustled in the hot wind of her excited breath. She looked like a horror show zombie fresh from the grave and he was being drenched down his neck and shoulder and side in his own life's vital fluid.

Nadine abandoned the scissors now and reached her clawing fingers up to his face. She wanted him to feel what she now felt and so she dug her forefingers behind his ears on either side and then inserted her thumbs as hard as she could into his eyes. At first there was no give, but then they sunk deep between the balls and the sockets on the outside edge of each. She pushed them in as deep as they would go, relishing the sound of his own pain filled wails and as he brought the club up for one last blind swing, she popped her thumbs backwards and out, pushing the eyes themselves out first and leaving them dangling from dripping red and blue cords on either side of his thick old man's nose.

Ralph tried to blink to clear his vision, but all it did was cause a rush of agony to fill his face, and as he brought the club down onto her temple his eyeballs swung, and she reached up and snatched them away as if picking summer ripe cherries from a tree. He squealed a high-pitched squeal as he felt the fibers that connected his eyes to some deeper part of him tug free and the darkness enveloped him fully now. His terror grew along with the hateful indignation that poured through him then and he swung and swung and swung. Each swing found purchase on her head and temple and neck, and each swing was accompanied by a crack or squelch or slam.

One final time they danced in perfect, horrible unity. His body stepped around her and she twirled in the same direction, not on purpose, but in a daze of dying confusion. They both fell to their knees before the other and sat there, stunned and broken. Their bodies finally crumpled to the floor. Their faces each a repugnant abomination, both in their own gruesomely special ways. Her skull was caved and crushed, and her teeth and tongue were exposed to the world in a way that they never were meant to be. His eye sockets were gruesome empty holes that in the shadow his head made as the sunlight came in from behind him, they looked endless and black and otherworldly.

Ralph and Nadine lay there together as they died. A slow circle of thick blood grew around them. Their chests rose and fell slower and slower as their hearts beat with less and less regularity. Their lives both flashed before their eyes, and each were reminded of their deepest regrets and their most vile memories. As if they were already cast down into their own personal hells.

The child stood two steps away from where she knew the blood would stop its creeping journey across the polished hardwood floor. It was Emma's eyes she now looked through once more. Emma's hair lying bright red softly down her back. Emma's lips turned up into an evil and most satisfied looking grin. She watched them until they took their final dying breaths and then watched them for a few moments more. She was happy in the way a child is happy. A simple joy spreading through her in some way that grownups can rarely experience. This had been a fun game and now it was time to feed.

She had soaked in what she could from the hate filled couple as they had danced and died. Their emotions had been raw and delicious to her mind's ravenous mouth, but now she wanted more. She carefully stepped around the beautifully ugly scene at her feet, so as not to leave any trace that she had been there and walked giddily down the hall. Underneath the stairs was where she had felt the heart of the home beating its tireless life away, and that is where she went to feed.

The child stood where she sensed the house's heart beat the strongest, below the tallest part of the stairs. She turned and placed her back against the smooth cool wood and slid slowly down and into a criss-cross applesauce position on the floor. She leaned forward and took in a slow deep breath, letting it exhale as she splayed her child's fingers, palms down, against the floor.

For a moment there was just the sound of low creaking from the walls around her. She could sense the house deciding if it wanted to fight or just give in. It knew what she wanted from it in the same instinctual way as Peaches had when she had caught the kitty in her stare. But it didn't know at first if it should give.

It thought back over the memories it had stored deep inside its wooden bones and considered what the child wanted. The house had had only the MacGregors living within its tired walls. They had been the ones who won the bid after it first had gone on sale and the house had been excited to be a home when first they came to stay. A husband and wife and two small children with a third on the way. It had taken Ralph a little longer to get exactly where he wanted to be when they bought a home of their own, but the house hadn't cared about any of that. The house was just glad to have a family to give it purpose and at first it had rejoiced.

The house had been a lovely two-story home and had been painted a soft periwinkle blue with white trim. The inside walls all started out white and the kitchen had all brand-new appliances for the time and even housed a double oven so the mother could bake cookies for the little ones who always seemed to be clutching at her apron. There was the living room off the kitchen downstairs, as well as a den off the hall on the left, the stairs on the right. The den was only for Ralph, and the children shared two of the upstairs bedrooms, one for boys and one for girls. The third bedroom was the sewing room where Nadine made and mended their clothes. The fourth was the master where a double bed sat centered on the main back wall, under a window where Nadine would lay and dream up at the moon and stars at night. Also, there were two bathrooms, one upstairs, and one down. Both had giant tubs where the house had imagined kids would play and splash and become scurvy pirates on a rough sea, looking for golden treasures, or become beautiful mermaids who swam the ocean blue in search of adventure and jewels.

But these children had been very quiet and very neat. There was no running up and down the stairs, as the house had been longing for after it was built. There was only hushed laughter behind their closed bedroom doors and only then when the father wasn't home to hear. The children played outside but only in the farthest part of the yard where their voices wouldn't drift so easily back in through the window of the den and when they played, they were very careful not to dirty their clothes or track in mud when they were through.

The house had loved the children, anyway, and it did its best to protect them from the cold and rainy days or the harsh beating down of the sun's sweaty rays. It was a good home. A proud home. But also, it was a sad home. Because though it protected the children from wind and weather it couldn't protect them from the abuse they had to suffer at the hands of their own father. The man who was supposed to keep them safe was the one thing they needed to be kept safe from and it was something that the house was powerless to protect against.

It had tried, once, to slam a window on Ralph's body as he leaned out from the den to give a harsh warning when the laughter had reached his ears. Children, to Ralph, were expected to be seen as little as possible and never ever heard unless spoken to first. As the man had bent forward, his fingertips grasping the edge of the wooden windowsill, the house had willed with all its might to drop the window down hard and fast enough to lop Ralph's head straight off his neck. A clean slice that would kill the bad man quickly and end the suffering inside the home as fast as his head would roll across the dark green grass.

But it had stopped itself in the last second. Seeing the four MacGregor children staring up at their father, a look of hushed fear across their tiny faces, the house had not let itself go through with it. It would have scarred the children for the rest of their lives had they seen such a thing. It would have made the house no better than the horrid man himself.

Like Nadine, the house endured. It sat and soaked it all in, unwillingly so. It did its best to be there for the children when they cried. It never made any noises at night to scare them as they slept, and it always creaked extra loud when their father came or went, no matter how softly he tried to tread. It wanted them all to have a warning of the beast that lived with them within the house's walls. It was the only true comfort the house could offer, and it gave the house a little solace, which at least was something.

The child felt the house begin to ponder, and the child waited patiently. She could take what she wanted with little effort if the house denied her, and they both knew it, but the child felt an odd kinship with the house. It was a thing often misunderstood by mankind. An item taken for granted and often abused and mistreated. Houses had spirits, just like anything else, even though man thought they were the only creatures who did. It was laughable, really, about how little man knew of the world in which it believed it had conquered.

You couldn't kill a house like you could a human. The house's heart beat in a place beyond the physical scape and so could not be reached by hammer, or nail, or gun. You could try burning it with fire, or ripping it apart, but you would have to be completely thorough in your doing so and there could be no structure left, or beam, or floor. But a house's soul could be siphoned, if you had the capabilities to do such a thing.

It was made up of the memories it had created in the lives of those who lived there. The good memories, and the bad. There were good houses and there were evil houses, but most started out with the simple need to protect those who called it home. To love them and care for them and be strong for them, even when they couldn't be strong for themselves. It was the actions of the people inside that could turn a home dark and evil. If enough blood had been spilled or curses made and kept inside the house's walls, it could turn bitter and cold against humanity and those who passed over its threshold.

This house had been a better house than most. It had suffered through countless crimes by father to son and daughter and wife. It had wept when they had wept, and it had felt their pain through its floors and walls and wires. It had somehow kept its dignity when it felt so guilty at being so useless.

Now it saw it had a chance to be free. It could, through the child, erase the dark parts of its soul. It could set empty for a while. It could not know who it was or why or when. But eventually, as always happens, or so it had the understanding, a new family would come. It would awaken the house and hopefully be happy there. It would forget all of the misery it had witnessed and all of the hurt and pain would be washed away as if it never had happened at all. There would be months of confusion, and possibly of terror in the not knowing, but, in the end, it would be better off than this.

The house decided that it would do anything to be rid of the overwhelming guilt of its failures and so it relented. It opened up to the child and gave it all she wanted. It gave it all it could. It kept nothing back, knowing that it would almost die, but taking comfort in the fact that with a new family it would be reborn.

The child felt the give and her fingers began to tingle. She closed her pale lids over those dazzling too-green eyes, but still, the shine of them came through as she began to feed. Memory after memory was offered up to her and she absorbed them all. Christmases and birthdays past, graduations and goodbyes as the children left, grown and ready to be free of this place. The child seemed to relive each and every one as they were transferred from the smooth floor and into her darker place, where they would be absorbed and digested and feed the child's will and mind. It would be a blessing for the house, really. A good deed from one whose actions could ever hardly count as good.

The child smiled as the memories washed over and into her. She saw a young blonde boy around the age of eight drawing quietly at the kitchen table. A happy drawing of a happy house, for the children loved this house very much and could feel in the magical way that children have that the house had loved them too. The drawing was slow going as the young boy did not want to make any mistakes. He had been trained since birth to be perfect in all he did, as perfection was expected and if not produced there were consequences.

He slowly drew the children playing in the front yard. Two

sisters, a brother and him. The oldest brother held a bright blue ball and was getting ready to bounce it to the sister next in line. None of the crayon children had little waxy smiles drawn on their careful round faces. Instead, their lines for mouths were straight across, not happy, and yet not quite showing the sadness that lurked just beneath. The mother was drawn next, on hands and knees, scrubbing the walkway that ran up to the stairs, her eyes were wide blue dots, and her red line mouth was a zigzag of worry.

The father was drawn bigger than the rest. He towered over them, standing on the porch. He was composed so that his body stood as tall as the second-floor windows. His crayon mouth was a circle and his eyes were two letter V's on their sides. One small, crayoned fist was holding a brown loop of belt that was made obviously so by the grey buckle on the end. The other flesh-colored hand was in a fist as well, but this one had a long and accusing pointer finger extended out at the stick figure mother in her light blue dress.

The child stopped and looked at the picture. Something was missing and he couldn't think of what. But then in a flash that brightened his face in the realization that made him look almost like any other child, happily drawing away, he smiled and picked up the red Crayola and added drops of blood from picture-mommy's nose. It dripped out and down onto the patch where she was scrubbing away with her small and tediously drawn hands.

The child had been proud of his drawing. He took the time to write his name all neat and cursivey like his teacher taught him to at school. He knew it captured his family exactly how they were and thought his Daddy would be super proud. Maybe he would even pat him on the back like he did when they did something he really liked and say in his gruff Daddy voice, "Now that's a really fine piece of art there, son!" And, oh, how his little boy heart would fill with happiness and love for the man who he hadn't learned just yet he didn't have to love.

The little blonde boy carefully replaced each crayon in their box and closed the lid. Then he carried the extra paper and the yellow box with green stripes across the kitchen and placed them neatly in the bottom drawer of the cabinet by the door to the laundry room.

That being done he grabbed a rag and rinsed it with the hottest water his little boy fingers could stand from the tap and wrung it out until it was almost dry. With a tongue sticking out just a bit on one side, he thoroughly cleaned the tabletop so as not to leave any trace of the tiny bits of colored wax that seemed to stray when coloring took place. He was a good boy, and this is how good boys behaved.

When the rag was rinsed and rung and then hung on its metal arm below the sink, he proudly took the picture and brought it to the closed door of the den. This room was a dangerous place. It had the feeling of a troll-infested bridge. The children sometimes whispered in the furthest corner of the backyard that great and ugly monsters lurked within. And that the monsters whispered to Daddy as he worked, creeping inside his brain and making him angry and mean. That's why he wasn't like the nice daddies at the park, who pushed their children on the swing or swung them around way up high in the air.

The boy stood before that door that seemed to grow in height and width in front of him. The knob shone out in a brassy glow as his fear struggled to overtake his bravery. There was a battle fighting within the small child's mind between what would keep him safe and the thought of making his daddy proud and maybe he would even pick him up into a giant's hug.

In the end, he didn't have to decide at all. Despite being well oiled, the knob twisted squeakily open as the house wanted the boy to be aware that danger was coming. The boy jumped as it swung back and the father was suddenly there, standing before him so tall and so imperious that the boy, for a moment, forgot all about why he was here and his hopes for fatherly acceptance.

"Yes?" Ralph's voice had been hard and agitated. He hadn't expected this pint-sized interruption to his busy day.

"Uhm," was all the boy could say as he handed up his work. Forgotten was the fantasy of love and pride and acceptance as it suddenly seemed an impossible wish.

Ralph roughly took the paper from the small hands that shakily held it up to him. He was curious to see what his boy thought was so important to stand outside his door for God only knew how long on such a bright summer day as this. But when Ralph's eyes took in the drawing, it wasn't pride he felt for his son's hard work, but instant and bright hot rage.

"Is this all you see me as? A man who beats his wife? Not a loving father like the other kids draw and hang on their fridge?" Ralph would never permit a child's sloppy drawing to hang on his fridge. Only perfection was allowed to be displayed in his home. He sometimes had clients over, or friends from work or church, and when he did, he needed them to see no messes or mistakes. He wanted them to be jealous of him and what he had and what he had built. But sometimes when he was at their houses, he would see the love the children of these other men had for their fathers. He would see the crudely drawn families on food speckled refrigerators and find himself the jealous one. He couldn't understand why his own children didn't love him the way that these messier kids loved their dads. Couldn't they see that because of Ralph his children were superior to theirs? Couldn't they appreciate all of his hard work in making them perfect?

His rage built at the indignation of it all and he seemed to grow in it before his child's eyes. Suddenly the boy had wished he had never tried to please his father and wanted only to sink away into the floorboards and escape. But he knew that escape was impossible, and he began to cry. His tears were from fear as well as from the heartbreaking realization that this man before him would never be like the other daddies. That this man before him would always be hard and cruel and void of love for him. That was the moment that the boy started to realize that just because you had a father did not mean you had to love him.

"Is this what I look like to you? But wait, something is missing, isn't it?" Ralph bellowed down in a giant's roar. He crumpled up the paper and threw it at the boy's terrified face. It hit his nose and bounced away, landing back in the den, and rolling deeper into the room, forgotten. His hands now free, Ralph undid his buckle and as Nadine hurried down the stairs, screaming at Ralph to stop, he swooped the shiny leather out of the loops that bound them to his pants and grabbed the tail end and the buckle in one mammoth fist.

"Is this what I do? I beat and hit for no good reason?" Ralph screamed, tiny bits of saliva misting out before him as he raised the leather loop high above his head.

The boy tried to raise his hands above him before the belt came down but was just a little bit too slow. The leather bit the back of his upturned face and instantly a red welt striped across his cheeks.

"No, Ralph! Stop!" Nadine had yelled as she finally reached the bottom of the stairs, but Ralph wouldn't stop and he brought the strap down, again and again.

The child had no course of action but to huddle on the floor, his arms wrapped around his head, and before Nadine could reach them, he had been hit six or seven times. Nadine had tried to snatch the belt away, but Ralph smacked it across her face, blood dripping instantly from her nose, and instead she covered her child's trembling body with her own. Together they were his whipping post as he hit them again and again and again. He hit them until all of his rage poured away and when he was finally done, he saw the pain and blood and torn clothing on those two that he loved in his own twisted way and the kid's apt drawing exploded in his mind as he saw its truth. He backed back into the room and slammed the door with a trembling hand.

Only when the lock twisted and clicked did the other three children come slinking down the stairs. They helped their bloodied mother up and aided her in taking her beaten son into her arms. They guided them up the stairs and into the bathroom, making sure to be as quiet as church mice as they went. Once upstairs they drew the bath for the mother and the oldest daughter shooed the two youngers out and helped her mother out of her clothes.

The girl winced at what she saw and once the mother was in the hot tub, she helped the brother join her. He was silently weeping in the mother's arms, unable to stop the flow of his tears and he lay his head against his mother's bosom and finally fell asleep in her mother's grasp. There was nothing crude about this gesture. It was a mother and son in pain and taking comfort in the innocent and pure love they shared, each for the other. The oldest daughter got the stinging medicine from the drawer beneath the sink and began applying it to their wounds with puffy white cotton balls.

The smaller two children huddled terrified in the girls' closet.

They held each other in a grasp so tight that later the mother would have to gently separate them and whisper that it would all be alright. Ralph had stayed locked away in his den for almost a week. Leaving only to use the downstairs bathroom and to go to work. He came home late those nights and then locked himself away before disappearing again, in the morning's new light. He grew even harder those days as he sat in his linen-covered office chair and stared at the crumpled paper he had smoothed out on his desk.

That was when he first realized just how soft his children really were and the fact that Nadine had intervened had made it even worse on everyone. He vowed to harden them up and straighten them out and he used that time away from them to board up the cracks in his heart that picture had made. He wouldn't let them turn him soft. That would be the devil's work, alright.

The child saw all of this in an instant, but also as if she had been there lurking in the shadows, and as soon as it was gone another memory was offered up. This time it was the girl, Katy, the youngest of the four MacGregor children who she saw at the same kitchen table but a few years after the age that the child had worn her as disguise.

"Please, Ralph, can't you see that she's -" Nadine began. *Smack*, the sound of Ralph's giant opened palm coming down hard across her face.

"How many times, Nadine, must I remind you that you're my wife? You must do as I say and stand proudly at my side. You must obey me in everything and never disagree with my words, for they are law!" he spoke, his voice low and threatening.

"I'm sorry, Ralph," Nadine's response just above a whisper, her hands clenched in her apron and her cheek ablaze where his hand had met her skin. "It's just that she's sick. She's not feeling well enough to eat, is all."

He glared at his wife, and she tried to back away, she knew she shouldn't have spoken out, but her heart hurt for her baby girl who sat so tiny in the chair. Katy's small face burned with the fever the chicken pox had brought along with the tiny red dots and itches. A plate of food sat before her barely eaten and a troubled frown stretched across her face.

When the hit to her mother came again, only this time with closed fist instead of open, the girl jumped in the chair and once again picked up the fork. To the small child's defense, she had been *trying* to eat the meal, it was just that her head swam, and her stomach threatened to reject anything that she was able to chew and swallow without gagging first.

Poor little Katy tried again. Spearing a small piece of parboiled broccoli, she brought it to her lips. The smell was instantly overbearing and as the husband hit the wife a third time with one hard closed fist, Katy lost what little had actually made it into her sickness-weakened tummy. The adults both paused at the sound that Katy's retching made, and the smell of half-digested roast chicken filled the air.

Ralph stood there above his wife staring down at her and his anger twisted into something that seemed almost gleeful. His grimace softened and he actually smiled as his fist relaxed and turned into a gentle helping hand.

"Okay, Nadine. Let's have it your way. If you're okay with the girl wasting food that I work hard to put before her, then you can eat her supper." He offered her his hand as she had fallen to the floor during her struggle with his fist. She slowly reached out and allowed him to help her to her feet, which was something she wasn't sure he had ever done before.

Nadine said nothing as she stood and considered the truth behind the task he sat before her. Her own stomach lurched at the sight of the child's plate. A spew of bile had been released and coated the food that had sat untouched. A yellow looking film glistened over the chicken thigh, only partially eaten, and mixed in with the gravy floating in the mashed potato moat.

Then her gaze softened as she took in the poor child. Katy was staring at her mother. An exhausted look of apprehension and sadness and regret filling her poor little upturned face. Silent tears ran down her fever flushed cheeks and at that moment Nadine would have done anything to let the child escape from this room.

"Katy, dear, go on up and have your sister bathe you and get you ready for bed." Her voice was tender and full of love and resignation as she wiped away a bit of blood that had escaped from an opening in her lip.

The child's eyes were instantly full of gratitude for her mother, whom she loved more than anybody else in the whole wide world. She knew she did her best to protect them from their father, whom she also loved, but in a way she didn't understand.

"No," Ralph stated. His voice was flat and firm, and they both looked at him. "She has to stay and watch you eat it. She needs to know that there are consequences to her actions." He walked around the table and pulled out a red vinyl covered chair. "Sit here, Katy-Bug," he instructed, and the child instantly obeyed, a fresh flow of silent, salty tears beginning to cascade down her cheeks.

Nadine nodded in resignation and smiled warmly into her daughter's face. She knew she had to do this with as much grace as she could muster, or it would hurt her daughter's heart even more. She didn't want Katy to feel guilty for this and she really didn't want Ralph to have the satisfaction of her gagging it down.

And so, Nadine sat in Katy's normal seat. She tried not to think about the chunks floating in the amber colored sludge that filmed the meal like a chicken gravy that smelled of wretchedness. She picked up the fork that had been clutched in Katy's small hand and began to eat the meal she had lovingly placed there almost four hours ago that night.

She didn't meet his eyes as she scraped the utensil across the plate. Into the cold and congealed potatoes with the new gravy Katy had so tragically provided she dug the fork's cool, hard side. She brought the forkful to her mouth and the air in the kitchen grew tense. An electric surge began to run between the father, the mother and the daughter and everyone, including Nadine, was on the edge of their seats to see what would happen next.

Poor little Katy clenched the cushy seat on which she sat so tightly that her knuckles turned white from loss of blood flow. Her tears continued to course down her face and her heart was hurting, heavy with the guilt of what her mother must do because of her own inability to finish her meal. Ralph stood tall with his arms crossed across his chest, a cruel smile had covered his face and his eyes sparkled with happy anticipation.

Nadine paused, just for a second, and then opened wide and

brought the fork deep into her mouth. She closed her lips and scraped the food away from the metal spines, beginning to chew as soon as it had cleared her teeth. The food was cold, but the bile was hot. Congealed gravy mixed with a thick acid flavor that made her stomach churn and threaten to add its own mix to the entree at hand.

She told herself it would be okay and that she had to do this as she chewed slowly, allowing time for her taste buds to adjust and her tummy to settle. Then she swallowed. Her face was unreadable as the horrid food slid down her throat. She gagged only once but was able to catch herself in time not to add to the mess before her. She could feel Ralph's happiness beaming down on her, a look she had not seen since their wedding vows. A tear of her own fell down one cheek, but she refused to give up.

Again and again, she scraped up forkfuls of rancorous food and again and again she chewed and swallowed. She had to stop at times to will it down and others to swallow what tried to come back up, but eventually she was successful, and the plate sat empty before her. She placed the fork down with one last grimace and then without meeting his gaze, she asked if she could please put Katy to bed. He had nodded his agreement and turned and left the room, convinced that he had done his duty and that his youngest child would from now on respect the food in which he provided, and her mother prepared.

Nadine slowly stood up, smiling as bright as she could muster into her daughter's eyes and scooped her burning body from the seat in which she sat.

"Do you want a bath?" she asked her, and sad Katy could only nod as her voice was for the moment stuck inside her throat. "Yes? That does sound nice, doesn't it? I can even add bubbles, if you want." Nadine's heart was full of love for the child that only mothers can feel, and she held her tight as they walked into the hall.

"Yes, please," Katy managed a broken whisper as they went.

The child watched them go and then the memory faded into her mind's ravenous maw, only to be instantly replaced with another and another. Memories seemed to flood out of the house now, washing

94

over and into her as she sat there on the floor. Her palms were sticky with sweat, but unwavering as they pressed against the wood which grew a little warm, but not too hot, with the transfer.

She saw bleeding and torment and hate-filled love. She saw tears and laughter and a fear so great that it burned inside of her as an aftertaste. She saw Nadine's struggle to keep the children safe and she saw the sacrifices that a mother makes for her young. It made the child think about Sarah and how she cared for her even though she suspected that Emma was different now. It made her, in some twisted way that the child couldn't understand, have love for Sarah, because watching Nadine take punishment in order to protect she knew for the first-time what love was. She knew that Sarah loved her. Had other mothers loved her, too? The child wasn't sure.

As the house gave away all it had to give, its shiny chrome sinks grew dull. The carefully painted walls began to crack and peel. Even the floorboards on which she sat seemed to age before her eyes, though it had been carefully oiled and cared for diligently over the many years it had stood. With the last few memories the house let out a low and long creaking groan. A sigh of relief to be rid of all the darkness. It stood there now, an empty shell, its consciousness stuck in limbo, confusion of who it was and what its duties were. It felt somewhere deep inside the need to protect and keep safe, but who, and what and why? It did not know.

When the child finally felt that there was nothing left to take, she stood. She sensed there was another being here. A small one. A cat. A smile played her lips as she willed it to feast on what she had left for it. She made sure to leave the sink in the kitchen running, just a bit, so there would be water to keep it alive for however long it would be stuck alone inside. Then she checked the food dishes to make sure they sat empty, and when seeing they were an evil, giddy giggle escaped her.

Then she went back through the door she had entered hours ago and left secretly back to her own home, next door. For it did feel like home to her. It was where she felt safe, with a mother whom she loved and who she felt loved her, too. That was an odd new feeling for the child. The love of and for another. She was baffled by what it meant and also, a little afraid. But mostly, she was relieved. For the first time in forever she felt like she wasn't alone in the vastness of the world in which she lived. For the first time in forever she felt the curious attachment to someone other than herself.

She walked noiselessly into the mother's room and watched her for some time. Sarah was sleeping an unquiet sleep, her mind caught in desperate nightmares where she searched for Emma in dark caves full of ancient and horrible magic. The child walked over to her lying there and placed a calming hand atop her sweat drenched brow. She smiled at Sarah as she lay sleeping on the bed and then swiped a cool hand down one cheek. The mother instantly quieted. Her dreams drifting apart and dissipating, and she was finally allowed to slumber peacefully.

The child climbed up and underneath the soft and cozy bedding. She snuggled in next to the mother and Sarah instantly pulled her close. She cradled Emma's body in her mother's protecting embrace and together they drifted off into a slumber where dreams did not exist, and peace held them in its own motherly grasp.

9

It could have been hours or days that they slept there together. Mother and daughter both snoring softly as they lay in blissful harmony for the first time since the child had come to stay. Well, mother and surrogate daughter who looked and sounded like Emma but who was different in some strange way that the mother couldn't quite understand.

It was not an alarm that woke them but a noise from somewhere in some other part of the house. Sarah slipped from sleep all at once, startled but refreshed. This had been the best sleep she had gotten in the past many months, and she felt almost human again. She looked down and saw the girl wrapped up in her arms and she smiled. Had this all been some sort of horrid nightmare that she had finally awaken from? She hoped with all of her might that it was.

"Hi baby. Good morning," she whispered to her sleeping child's softly breathing form. The child rolled over then, her face pointed toward the sound of Sarah's benevolent voice and stretched her arms and legs as far as they would reach before opening her eyes and smiling brightly up at Sarah.

"Good morning, mama! Did you sleep well?" she asked, those fantastically bright green eyes searching the mother's face for recognition of the gift she had been given. The true sleep that she had withheld all this time. The deprivation of which was meant to keep the mother from thinking of a way to stop the child. The child trusted Sarah now and so had given her a little peace. The child had decided that Sarah was no threat and instead would always be there to protect. So now she wanted Sarah's recognition and gratefulness.

For a moment Sarah was taken aback. Her hopes that it had all been a dream came crashing down with the opening of Emma's too bright eyes and she knew that she had to play her disappointment close to the vest. It was an odd thing, waking up with the child in her arms. It had been a very Emma thing to wake up to and so, for a moment, the disappointment had been almost too great to handle. But she managed a bright smile and stretched as well. Her body making small popping sounds as she did so.

"I slept so, so good!" Sarah said happily to the child. "But, uh oh!" Her voice became creepy as she stuck her hands out like claws before her. "The tickle man invaded me in my dreams last night!" And with those mischievous words she jumped on the child, tickling her tummy and under her arms while making her best monster noises.

The child laughed and screeched with excited happiness. She loved it when Sarah played these games. It was one of the things that had differed between Sarah and all of the other mommies and daddies she had throughout the years and decades that had passed. Sarah was always trying to make the situation happy and fun. The child didn't realize that it was partly Sarah's way of distracting her so that the child didn't realize what Sarah was thinking. Searching her brain for the whys and whats and hows of this peculiar situation.

"Oh no!" Sarah bellowed, laughing as she did. "Now the potty monster has got me, and I've got to gooooo!" She extended the go as she pretended to be snatched off the bed and be pulled toward the bathroom. The child giggled in jubilation and delight and Sarah slid the door closed. How long *had* she slept? She wondered. She felt like she could pee for days and days. But she also felt like the fog that had taken over her mind had disappeared, which was good. Heck, it was *great*! It was just what she needed to try and figure this whole thing out.

Sarah flushed and then washed her hands as the child slid the pocket door open. A sudden look of worry had filled her face and an odd feeling of electricity seemed to be emanating out from her. Alarm bells began to ring and bang inside of Sarah's head, and she bent down before the child, wanting only to calm whatever storm had entered the room while she had been taking care of nature's call.

"What is it? What's wrong, Emma?" she asked, her voice

strained with worry.

"Momma, I heard a noise. Someone is in the house!" The child grasped the mother's hand and pulled her toward the door. "Is it a stranger, Momma? A bad guy like in the movies on TV?" Her voice was a little too excited sounding for Sarah's liking, although if there *was* a bad guy in the home Sarah felt like this pint-sized blood machine might just be the perfect houseguest. As soon as the thought came out, she regretted it. She would do anything to have her Emma back, and if that meant being murdered by some strange psychopath in her own home, so be it. It might be what ended up happening to her anyway, though it wouldn't be by the hands of some random street thug turned burglar. God help anyone who tried to fill that role here.

"I'm sure it's nothing, but let's go check it out, okay?" Sarah pulled Emma behind her, even though they both knew that the child was more capable at self-defense than she was. But still, if Emma was still in there somewhere she wanted her to have her body in one piece when she was able to return to it.

The child felt an odd admiration for the mother. She was very brave and put the child's safety first. She really was the best mommy in the whole world. The whole widest world. "Be careful, Momma," the child whispered as they left the room and walked slowly down the hall and to the stairs. The rooms they passed all had open doors and Sarah made sure to scan each one for signs of intrusion before moving on.

"What kind of noise did you hear?" Sarah asked in a whisper, just after making sure that Emma's room was empty of gun-toting gangsters or hairy one-eyed monsters. But then, before the child could answer, she heard a banging sound from downstairs, followed by a little girl's giggle and they both paused and exchanged a puzzled look.

"Shi- I mean, poop!" a woman's voice exclaimed from what sounded to be the kitchen below and Sarah knew instantly who it was, though why she would have a little girl with her she couldn't guess.

Sarah knelt down before Emma's small body and looked the child deep in the eyes. A serious look that caused the child to take notice because whatever Sarah was about to say, she meant.

"Emma, do you remember Auntie Jess?" she asked. The real Emma loved Auntie Jess, and this would be a test of sorts to confirm Sarah's worst suspicions about this not really being Emma at all.

The child stopped and thought for a moment. Searching Emma's memories for who this person down below must be. It only took a few seconds, but it was enough time for Sarah to finally be able to admit to herself that she wasn't going crazy and that whoever this was in Emma's body, it wasn't really Emma.

"Yes," the child said, but slowly, as if unsure of the reaction she should have. She didn't want any houseguests and the thought of having to play pretend when things were finally going so well here with Sarah did not make her happy at all. But if she didn't play nice with Auntie Jess, she would lose the bond she was building with the mother and she wasn't ready to abandon all of this just yet.

"Emma, I know that there is something different about you just lately, and that's okay. I love you no matter what, you know that, right?" Sarah kind of lied. She did love Emma no matter what this child did in the stolen body of her child and so the words sounded sincere enough to the child's ears.

"Uh-huh," the child said, nodding as she did so. Her eyes were wide and curious about what was to come next.

"I need you to please, please, please," Sarah paused and sighed before going on, "be on your best behavior, okay? I will try to get rid of her, but Auntie Jess can be a hard nut to crack when she wants to be. And we can't let her know that you aren't feeling yourself right now, okay? We love Auntie Jess no matter what. Just like I love you, no matter what, right?"

"Yes, but Momma, she won't stay long, will she? Not like all the other times before?" Emma's mind told the child that Auntie Jess had a way of popping in and staying, sometimes for weeks on end, before just as quickly popping out again. She could tell that Emma loved her Auntie fiercely and so she would have to play like she did, too, and the thought of it was just so exhausting. "I don't want her to stay." The child's voice was full of indignation. "You have to make her leave, Momma." Her emerald eyes began to sparkle as the electricity in the air around them again began to grow.

"I will try, Emma, but please, promise me that you'll try, too. Auntie Jess can't be like the kitties, okay?" Sarah begged, and the child jumped. She had known that Sarah knew something had happened with the kitties. But having Sarah admit that she knew it had been something bad that Emma had done but she had still protected her from Mrs. MacGregor made the child's heart soften just a little bit more.

"Okay, Momma. I promise that I will try, too," the child swore to both the mother and herself. Sarah's love, for some odd reason that the child could not understand, made her want to be good. The child didn't know because the child had never felt true love before, not really. When someone loves you, and you love them, too, you want to make them happy. It was as simple as breathing. And for the child, it was new. The house next door had caused this new thing to bloom inside the child's chest and mind. And if the house had been left capable of rational thought, it would have taken solace in the knowing.

"You almost said a curse!" the little girl's voice giggled from downstairs and the two redheads, with their hair all askew from the very deep sleep they had just awoken from looked in the direction of the stairs.

"And you'll play nicely with the little kid?" Sarah asked. She was going to try her best to get rid of whatever was going on downstairs, but she wanted them to go away her way and not in a flood of blood the likes of which she had had to clean from Emma's hair and skin and nails before.

"I love to play!" was the child's response as she turned and ran happily down the stairs. This could be fun, she thought. Playing didn't always have to end in death, now, did it?

Sarah looked after the child for a moment. A strained look upon her face. She was grateful for the sleep and chance to recharge her batteries. Her normal slumber when the child was up to no good was always filled with dreams. Dreams where she was looking for Emma in unimaginable places. Dark places with corridors and caves leading in too many different directions to follow with any logic or reason. And always there was the sound of

Emma somewhere, crying and calling for her desperately.

There were the other nights, too. The more normal nights when the little girl had gone to bed after a day of endless board games or cartoons or being pushed on the swing set in the backyard for hours and hours and hours on end. Days where the worst of her actions included squishing bugs or pounding lizards with giant rocks from the garden lining. Sarah would try to save as many helpless creatures as she could those days and would often end up with a swollen toe from a small boulder falling on her foot for the trouble. Emma would swear it was an accident and Sarah would play it off as one, but they both knew the lie for what it was.

On those nights, Emma would stay up late, begging for book after book to be read. Story after story to be told. In the beginning of it all, Sarah would try to get the child to go to sleep like normal. At a normal round time of eight o'clock. Just one story, okay, maybe two. But to no avail. And when she disobeyed, the child would throw a tantrum the likes Sarah had never seen. She would kick and scream and holler. She would bite and scratch and pinch. It got worse and worse until Sarah would relent and tell the stories. She would read the books over and over again if it pleased the child. She would do whatever it took to please Emma, and the worry grew and grew. The worry had grown so great, even, that Sarah had decided to make an appointment with a child psychologist. This was absolutely new behavior for her once well-mannered kid and she didn't like it, not one little bit. She wanted to know if something bad had happened to turn her baby into a monster almost overnight. Especially with all of those days of her just sitting at the window like that.

The phone had rang and rang each person she had tried to call, but there had been no answer. Not even an answering machine or message service. She kept trying and trying. New doctors and new numbers, but always, it was the same and it was curious. Eventually she forgot about calling out for help because eventually she had dark suspicions that maybe this wasn't her child anymore. That whatever had replaced her Emma was something with powers and great strength and a wicked sense of humor. She knew, then, that there was nothing for her to do. Nowhere to turn for help. She was

Emma's only chance and if she did reach out for help from anyone outside these walls they would likely think her crazy and incapable of caring for a five-year-old little girl.

By then it was getting harder and harder to think. The child would go to sleep so late, and wake so early, that for those nights where sleep was without nightmares, it was for precious too few hours. The nights and days where the child came back after some bloody escapade or other, she would try to sleep peacefully, but the nightmares were always there then. So, she was always tired and there had been a fuzziness to her thinking. It was all she could do to keep up the look of pretending that this was her normal Emma. It was all she could do to try and figure it out while at the same time being able to cook and clean and play. Always she was playing, entertaining a child who seemed incapable of ever getting bored.

But now she felt refreshed. She didn't know why the child had let her sleep so long and so deep, but she was grateful. Sarah sensed a change in Emma. It still was not her true Emma, but there was something softer about her. Something that wanted to please instead of just hurt and take. And what about Jess?

She loved her sister and she hoped that her sister would be able to sense there was something wrong with Emma, too. Oh, how much she would love to have another mind to figure out this problem with. But how would she get her alone enough to speak? How would she explain without angering Emma and getting Jess hurt, or worse. She didn't know.

Sarah stood and followed behind Emma. Not wanting them to be alone for too long. Not wanting them to get hurt by who they would see as just a normal little girl. They didn't understand the rules and that, in itself, put them in danger.

10

"Auntie Jess!" the child squealed and ran across the room to the woman who was just a bit taller than her mommy and had Emma's brighter red hair than Sarah had. The excitement to see the woman was what the child sensed that Emma would feel and do and so she play acted her best Emma.

"Emma Jane!" Auntie Jess said and grabbed her niece up into a giant bear hug and swung her around, lavishing kisses on her face and blowing bubbles in the hollow of her neck. "Ewwwww! Did your mother feed you beans again? You farted!"

Emma and the child sitting on the kitchen table nearby both giggled happy giggles and Sarah smiled at the sound as she entered the kitchen. She couldn't help it. It was a beautiful thing to hear. A pure sound. A sound that Sarah dearly missed.

"Sofie! What are you doing here?" Sarah asked the plain looking child with wild mousy hair that sat with her feet tucked under her knees on the dark wooden tabletop that was centered in the large kitchen.

"Oh! Your friend's name is Sofie!" Auntie Jess said, a sound of relief and a smile in her voice. "That frantic woman who dropped her off must have said it, but she was going a mile a minute. She said you wouldn't mind watching the kid and she would make it up to you anytime. I say she should make it up to me since I've been the one she's been laughing at all morning!" Jess tipped a playful wink at the girl on the table and another carefree giggle burst out of Sofie's mouth.

"Mommy had a 'mergency," Sofie said, the giggle barely getting under control as she did. "Mrs. P couldn't come, and she didn't know what to do. So, she said I could play with Emma all day!"

"All day, huh?" Sarah asked as she looked around the messy

104

room. "And what are you doing here, sister mine? Sneaking in and then allowing random children to come play?"

"I'm not random, you're random!" Sofie protested and then began to giggle again. Emma, still in the arms of the aunt, shot the child a hateful look that only Sarah noticed before it disappeared just as quickly from Emma's face.

"Oh, the mouth on this one!" Auntie Jess laughed. "I like her!" she said as she sat Emma on the table next to what was once her best friend in the whole wide world. Well, the real Emma, if she were here to say so, would still agree with that sentiment. Instead, she was locked away tight, and this new darker Emma didn't much care for the little girl sitting next to her at all.

"Oh, don't worry!" Jess playfully ruffled Emma's fluffy curly hair, making it poof out even more than the bed already had. "I'll always love you most! You're my Niecey Bear and I've only got auntie eyes for you! So, turn that frown upside down, missy, and let's make breakfast!"

"Sausages and eggs and bacons?" Emma's voice asked, suddenly happy and excited again.

"Yes, and yes and heck yes times infinity!" Auntie Jess agreed. "Especially since I remembered after starting the batter that I don't know how to make pancakes and this Sofie kid said they were gross like dirt. Her words, not mine."

Sofie giggled and nodded and put an arm amiably around Emma's shoulders. "They were dirt pancakes!" she exclaimed, and her voice was very much too loud in the child's more sensitive ears.

"Well, that explains the mess, but, Jess, really, you have to go. Emma hasn't been feeling well at all. She's had the flu all week and only just stopped puking," Sarah lied as she began picking up the bowls and measuring cups from around the room and rinsing them off in the sink.

"Aw, nonsense, sis! I'm not afraid of any germ factory! Especially not one as cute as my little niecey wiecey!" Jess said from inside the fridge that she was leaned way too far into for comedic effect for the benefit of the two children who sat behind her. "Jeezus! How much meat do you guys eat? It's like a slaughterhouse in here!" She came out with packages of bacon and sausage and on top of the precarious pile, somehow not falling to the floor, an eighteen pack of eggs. "You got a man around here, hidden in a cupboard or something? I thought you guys were more into berries and shit."

"Language! Language! Language!" Sofie shouted and then erupted in giggles once more.

"Seriously, you shouldn't talk like that in front of the kids," Sarah sighed as she tried to figure out how to navigate this minefield.

"Aw, c'mon, Sare." Jess made her best monster face at the girls before setting all of the items down on the counter. "You know I can't control this thing. Besides, how am I going to be the cool aunt if I can't keep it spicy? I taught Emma her first bad word, you know."

"Yes," Sarah agreed. "And we had to take her out of daycare, thanks to you. Apparently they frown on little girls running around dropping eff bombs like they're hot at those places."

"Huh. Who knew?" Jess asked playfully and grabbed a clean bowl from the cupboard above her head.

"My mommy knew!" Sofie offered. "She says swearing is for losers and atter knees."

"Atter knees?" Sarah asked, perplexed.

"Yeah. Like when my grandma ran over that man's dog and the people took her to the courts to pay," Sofie explained. "My daddy had to hire an atter knee."

"Oh! You mean attorney," Sarah laughed and pinched Sofie's chin playfully before turning back to Jess.

"Well, your mommy just has a stick stuck somewhere," Jess said with an over-the-shoulder smile as she began cracking eggs into a bowl.

"What kind of stick?" Sofie asked. Her soft girly voice full of awe at the thought of it. "Does it hurt?"

"Only everyone else in the room," Jess said conspiratorially and Sarah was unable to stop the laugh that escaped her.

"Well. You're not wrong," Sarah added before grabbing out a pan for the bacon and one for the sausage. "You have to cook the meat before the eggs, here let me." She placed them on the stove and turned on the burners.

"Sofie and Emma and I are all three capable of making breakfast, thank you very much," Jess retorted. "Or do you have a stick inside of your tooshie, too?" Sarah rolled her eyes at that and gave her sister a fake dirty look.

"Ouch, Sarah, you could kill some bitches with that glare. Is it registered? Because people shouldn't be allowed to go around with something so dangerous," Jess asked as she plopped the sausage free from its greasy package and into one of the preheating pans. It began to sizzle after a few seconds of the silence that had fallen in the room.

"Your auntie said bitches," Sofie whispered, and then the two women laughed. It really did feel good to not be alone after all of this time and Sarah was terrified of what the outcome of this day would bring, but also kind of relieved to have her sister here.

"Emma are you feeling well enough for Auntie to stay for breakfast?" Sarah asked the red headed child who looked almost like a clone of the kid that Jess had once been.

The child seemed to consider and decided that she kind of liked this aunt. She could sense it made the mommy happy and why not? If she changed her mind there were things she could do to get rid of her. Nobody would even have to know. She could just put a wish on the auntie to go away and the auntie would. She could have her drive her car going really super-fast and then run smack into a tree. Or go to the city where the buildings were so tall that clouds whispered around them. She could take the stairs, one after the other, and when she got to the top she could throw herself off, thinking she could fly, but of course she would fall. There were a million and five other ways she could get rid of this auntie, but for now she liked her enough to see where it went. This was something new and it could be fun. Unlike Abraham, the child liked new sometimes. Unlike Abraham, the child was a doer.

"See, the germ factory is closed for the season and all that's there is my Emma Boo!" Jess said as she gestured with shiny oil covered hands and then dumped the entire package of bacon into the sizzling hot pan. "Oh yeah! Listen to those puppies sing!"

The children laughed in unison again and Sarah resigned herself and also looked forward to the day before her. Hopefully nothing bad would happen to Sofie or to Jess before it was through. She would have to play all of their cards carefully for them and be sure to keep Emma happy, but she thought it could be done and she looked forward to this time with her sister. Plus, maybe it would do Emma good to have a playdate with Sofie. Emma had loved Sofie and her giggly nature so much that maybe the sound of her best friend's laughter could be a beacon she could use to find her way home.

They finished off cooking breakfast together. The women handled the stove, and the children made the toast. Carefully pulling the hot pieces out after they popped up and each time they did so both girls would jump and fall into innocent giggling fits. Then they would slowly add creamy whipped butter from the dish with Emma's special colorful plastic knives that matched the forks and spoons and couldn't cut through skin, no matter how hard one pressed.

The women laughed as well at the sound of the kids and the jokes and stories they told and for one second the child knew what it felt like to actually be a part of a family. Taking the house next door's memories had not been meant to give the child empathy for these people, or a longing for happy times, but it had. She had felt the house's want for the children it had housed to know times like she was sharing with these people in this kitchen now and it had made the child want that, too. It confused the child but made her happy, as well. Maybe she could have what that home wanted to give. A happy safe life here with Sarah and Auntie Jess and best friends on play dates. Maybe she could be as a real child and laugh and play as real children did. Crazier things had happened, right?

At breakfast they all ate heartily and talked about silly things. The many adventures of Auntie Jess seemed to be the favorite topic and the girls listened with awe in their eyes and their mouths open as she spoke, enthralled with her words. Sarah only had to kick her under the table a few times to get her to take the rating back down to at least PG instead of the steamier places it was going. Jess meant well, but she just got so excited at the stories she would tell that she didn't always think about children being around since she had none of her own and was happy just to be an aunt when it came to the thought of kids.

Afterward the girls ran off to play as Jess and Sarah cleaned up. Sarah, for the moment, had been lulled into a weird sense of normalcy for the first time since Emma had changed and she didn't even consider the dangers Sofie would be in, alone with Emma in the little girl's room upstairs. Later she would regret that decision, but not just yet. For now, she happily did the dishes with her sister at her side, and they stood in happy silence as they worked. An easy familiarity between them.

"Okay, spill the beans, little sis. Why haven't you called mom? She's worried sick. And since when do you try to kick me out? When you gave me that key it was well understood between us both that I am always welcome here, no matter what and when?" Jess finally broke the silence.

"Jess. It's. It's complicated," Sarah said, but offered no more than that.

"Nothing has ever been too complicated for you to talk to me about. I'm your big sis. I'm here for you always and you know that." Jess's voice was soft and comforting. "Whatever it is, spill the beans. I can help you. Neither one of you seems yourselves. I'm not blind, you know."

"I know," Sarah said and then burst into tears she hadn't even felt were there.

"Aw, honey, come here." Jess wrapped her little sister up in her arms and gently tilted her head against her soft shoulder. Sarah cried for a while, soaking in the comfort of her sister's embrace and then she backed away from Jess and opened her mouth to speak.

She was going to tell her everything. Let it all out in one big gush and hope that Jess wouldn't think she was bonkers and out of her mind. She hadn't realized how badly she had needed another human to know and understand her situation until now, and Jess really would be the only one in the world who might believe her. They had been the closest of sisters ever since Sarah had been born and had over the years told each other all of their secrets. Until now that is. And Sarah was tired of holding back.

Sarah opened her mouth and started to speak but before she could get a word out, Sofie's frantic screams from upstairs broke the moment they were sharing and both of the women instantly began to run toward the sound, as mommies and aunties are hard wired to do.

11

"Let's go play!" Sofie announced as she grabbed Emma's hand after breakfast. She pulled her down the hall and up the stairs and Emma trailed obligingly behind. Thinking of how much fun having a best friend could be. Someone to keep your secrets, no matter what. "I forgot to bring my dollies," Sofie said as they walked.

"That's okay. You can play with mine," the child responded good naturedly right back.

"You're the best friend in the whole wide world!" Sofie told her with pure love that only children are capable of filling her voice.

"Thank you," Emma said, liking the sound of it.

They played for a while, but Emma got bored too soon. Playing dollies wasn't fun at all.

"Do you wanna see something neat?" the child had asked in Emma's voice.

"Sure," Sofie had responded as she shrugged her shoulders and sat down the dolly she had been feeding pretend mushy peas to. Babies always ate mushy peas, she thought.

"I can do magic!" Emma's voice confided in her best friend for always.

"Wow! No way!" Sofie said in awe and admiration. She had missed coming to Emma's house. Emma was the nicest friend in the world, to Sofie's mind.

And that's when it happened. The child reached out one small fist and tapped Sofie right in the middle of the forehead. For a second there was nothing but the feeling of some weird vibration in the air. Then Sofie seemed to get lighter and lighter and slowly she started to float up above the hardwood!

"Oh my gosh! Wow!" The little girl from down the street was

so excited by this new turn of events that her words came out in one long breath. "I'm flying, Emma! Did you make me fly with magic? Just like Wendie? I'm like Wendie?"

"Uh-huh!" The child's eyes blazed green and she began to float, too. Just a little bit at first, their bare feet only inches from the floor, and then higher and higher they drifted until they could almost touch the ceiling with outreached fingers.

"Emma, you're the coolest ever!" Sofie exclaimed and she grabbed Emma's hands to keep her steady in the air.

"Uh-huh!" the child agreed, and they began to drift around the room, both of them giggling as they did so.

"I can't wait to tell my mommy and daddy that you can do real magic and made me fly!" Sofie's voice was rushed with excitement, but as soon as her words were out, she fell from the air and hard onto the floor.

Emma's feet landed gracefully, but Sofie hit hard, landing on her side, her right hip bone instantly beginning to bruise.

"No! Sofie, you can't tell anyone!" And as she spoke, the child began to grow and twist and jerk and change. The air in the room grew darker as her bright green eyes grew lighter. It was as if the sun was going out and only those otherworldly lanterns were left to bade off the darkness that tried to fill the room.

Emma's eyes grew large, and her bones snapped as they changed form. Her red hair was still in a poofy cloud of curls around her head, but her head grew large and plump, and her mouth became a cavernous hole of teeth and drool and stench. Her arms grew longer, and her legs stretched out tall until her back hit the roof and she was forced forward, bending over Sofie's small frame with twisted arms and claws outstretched above her little body where the poor girl lay spread out beneath her.

"You have to keep my secret, it's what best friends do." The child's voice was gnarled and full of venom and thick with threat. "If you tell your mommy or your daddy I will know and I will come to your house and I will eat them all up. I'll make you watch as I rip their faces from their heads and when I'm done crunching up their bones, I'll crunch up yours, too!" Burning spit flew from the child's jagged teeth as she spoke, and the feeling of the fire-hot drops against her skin broke Sofie from the spell she had been under since hitting the floor. She opened her mouth and screamed a scream like she had never made before. It was high pitched and full of fear and the child sensed that she would never see this girl again, but she knew that she would keep her secret. She could tell by the smell of urine that filled her nose as Sofie's bladder let loose out of pure fright. A dull yellow puddle began creeping out around her as she did so.

The child could hear the sound of the women rushing up the stairs, even through the loudness of Sofie's screams, and just before the door burst open and they both almost poured into the room she changed back to Emma's cute and pint-sized body, a look of confusion and shock across her face.

"What happened in here?" Sarah asked, relieved that there wasn't any blood, but still very much concerned by the sound of whimpering that was coming from Sofie now. A broken sound that had replaced the screams.

"I don't know, Momma. We were just jumping on the bed and pretending we could fly like Wendie and then she went crazy and I think she saw a spider and fell right off the bed. She's super scaredy pants of spiders." Emma's voice was thoughtful as she spoke.

"Did you see a spider?" Jess asked the girl, astonished that such a little thing could make a kid piss herself and scream like the devil was coming at her.

Poor little scared Sofie backed away from Emma but nodded as she did. She didn't stop until she was against Jess' feet and she not once could tear her glance away from Emma's face. "Can I please call my mommy? I wanna go home now," she whispered in a voice they could barely hear, and Jess bent down and picked her up. Grimacing just a little at the feel of her wet leggings against her forearm, but not so the child could notice.

"Why don't we get you in a nice bath first and you can tell me all about the spider. I bet it was huge and scary, huh?" Jess asked as she threw her sister a confused look and headed down the hall with the little girl held safely in her arms.

Sarah waited for the sound of the water running into the tub

113

before she crossed the room to where the child stood, careful not to step in the puddle that Sofie had left behind. She knelt down to bring herself to the same level as her daughter's eyes and looked deeply into them.

"What happened, really?" Sarah asked. Her voice was a little on edge, but she was trying to not sound cold and accusing, even though she felt it creeping through her mind.

"It was a spider," Emma shrugged and picked up the dollies from the floor where they had fallen as the girls began to rise into the air. She dusted them off absentmindedly and then placed them back into their places on her bed.

"Emma, are you sure? Nothing else happened? Just a spider?" Sarah's voice was pleading now, needing to hear the truth in case Sofie told her parents later on. Or Jess as she bathed her down the hall.

"Don't worry," Emma whispered. "Best friends keep secrets." She smiled at Sarah then and that smile told her all the truth she needed to know. She opened up her arms to the child and hugged her in a tight embrace, not so much out of love, but because she didn't want the child to see the look of anger and dismay blooming across her face.

Sarah would have to figure this out as soon as she possibly could. Who knew what poor Sofie had seen, and she had no doubt that whatever it was it would haunt her for years to come though she knew it would be a secret she never told out of fear of retribution. Sarah had felt the evil seeping out of Emma before and knew that if she told you to keep a secret, you would. Until the day you took your last breath on your deathbed would you keep that secret. Because when you felt the evil coming off of the child you knew that it was capable of any number of horrible things and the last thing you wanted was to see it lurking over you as you tried to sleep after spilling her secret to someone.

Jess was her only hope, but she didn't even know how to bring this up and if she did, would Emma know and would Emma get revenge for Sarah telling her secret? She felt trapped and lost and alone again, even though the morning had been a wonderful dream. She should have known that the nightmare was always close by and that she couldn't escape it so easily.

"I love you Momma," Emma's voice drifted up through the mixture of their hair. It was soft and pleading for reciprocation.

"I love you, too, baby," Sarah whispered back, filling it with as much love as she could muster, and squeezing a reassuring squeeze into their hug.

"No matter what?" Emma asked, a hint of fear, but a threat of anger there as well, if the answer she gave was wrong.

"Always, no matter what," Sarah reassured, not yet ready to let go of the hug. Not yet capable of controlling the truth that filled her face.

The child soaked in the embrace from the mommy with a sense that all was right with the world. Who really needed a best friend, anyway, when you had such a great mommy to love you and keep you safe? Certainly not the child. Plus, there was the auntie here now, too. Blood is thicker than water.

Finally, Sarah felt confident that she could keep her emotions in check and she lightly pulled the child back at arm's length. "Do you think you can pick out a change of clothes for Sofie while I clean up this mess?" she asked casually with a warm smile across her face.

"Sure," the child beamed back and immediately headed for her dresser. "She loves unicorns, so I know just what to pick!" Emma's voice sounded happy to Sarah's ears and for just a moment she wondered if all of this really *was* over just a tiny little spider and not something more sinister.

With the puddle wiped up and the area sanitized with the special wipes Sarah kept under the kitchen sink, they headed to the bathroom to show Sofie the outfit the child had chosen for her. A sparkly, shiny affair, with a glittery unicorn running across a cartoon rainbow on the front of the shirt and matching multicolored leggings. Even the underwear had rainbows all over and the child knew from Emma's mind that Sofie would love this outfit.

Sarah swung the door open to Jess kneeling on the floor before the tub. A cloud of soft pink bubbles stretched three feet high and she was busy piling as many as she could onto Sofie's head, which was shaking with laughter and made the job quite difficult, even for an aunt of such high caliber as she.

"More! More!" Sofie squealed with delight. "Make them touch the ceiling!"

"The ceiling, huh?" Jess laughed right back. "I'm not sure we have enough soap for that!"

Sarah began to laugh, too, but then as Emma's tiny body entered the room and she saw what they were doing, a bottle of her favorite soap lying empty on its side on the white tile of the bathroom floor, the child screamed a hateful scream and threw the clothes next to Sofie in the tub.

"Those are my bubbles!" Emma's voice echoed in the small room and the lights above the vanity began to flash and make an odd sizzling sound. "That's my special soap!" she screamed again. This time in an even screechier tone, and one of the oversized circular bulbs actually popped and a sulfur smell began to fill the room, though from where Jess was sitting it seemed like the smell was coming off of her niece and not up from where a spark was busily flashing from the exposed wire of the broken bulb.

That's nonsense, she reassured herself, but there was something off about her favorite and only niece in the whole world. What a weird coincidence for the lights to break at this exact time as if a power surge waited on the whims of a spoiled child who didn't like to share. That, in itself, was odd. Her Emma loved to share. She had always been a generous kid; even as a baby she would pluck her binkie from her mouth and try to stick it into yours.

"Emma!" Sarah bent and plucked up her child, removing her from the room as fast as she could. "It's okay, Auntie Jess didn't know. She's going to rinse off Sofie now and make sure that she gets all the bubbles off, right Auntie Jess?" she called back behind her, her words soothing as well as something more. Something like a warning hidden for Jess to pick up on, but it took a second for Jess to register what had just happened, and a second more for her sister's words to sink in.

"Uh, yeah! We're gonna get you all rinsed off now, aren't we Sofe? And then we'll go downstairs and watch a movie! How does that sound, kiddo?" she asked, turning to the stunned and frightened child in the tub.

Sofie just nodded and stood as Jess pulled the lever that begin sucking away the water and bubbles filling the tub. "I'm sorry," she whispered to Jess and began to cry.

"Aw no, little friend, don't cry. It's okay." Jess stopped and thought for a second, wanting to know the right words to say, but she was just as confused and scared as the kid in the tub. "You know how Emma only has a mommy because her daddy died a couple years ago?" She asked while she grabbed the spray nozzle off the hook that held it to the wall way up high and began to wash the bubbles that were now starting to itch, anyway, as they began to dry to the child's skin and Jess' hands.

"Uh-huh. Emma said he got real sick and had to go away to heaven to be with the baby Jesus and his mommy, Mary," Sofie explained, her voice still soft and scared, but there was sympathy there, now, too. Sofie herself loved her own daddy very much and she couldn't think of a world in which he had to go away to be with Jesus and Mary and the angels in heaven.

"That's right. And it was very, very sad. Sometimes when very sad stuff happens to a person, it makes them have anger inside of their hearts. It hides in there and grows and grows and then one day, for practically no reason at all, it can come out and that has to be what's happening to Emma now. So, we should try to be patient with her and understanding. What do you think?" Jess asked the child as she swept her up in one of the giant fluffy pink towels folded neatly on the shelf above the toilet.

"Yeah. Emma is my best friend, even though the sadness makes her scary," the little girl decided after a few minutes of self-deliberation.

"You're a good kid, Sofe," Jess stated and sat her gently on the puffy pink bathroom rug that matched almost exactly the shade of the towel she had wrapped the girl in. Then she bent over and wrung out the clothes that Emma had thrown in next to Sofie and hung them to dry over the curtain rod that wound around the tub in a circle. "C'mon, let's go find you some comfy clothes, shall we?"

Sofie nodded but waited for Jess to go first. She liked the tall red headed auntie with her funny voices and the occasional bad word sprinkled in. She wished her aunts were like Emma's was.

They were boring and gave her clothes at Christmas and never ever said a swear. Back in Emma's room Sarah was knelt again before the child. Trying to calm her down. Here, too, the lights were flickering, and the air was starting to grow thick and buzzed with a feeling of anticipation of something horrible to come.

"Emma, it's okay. Remember how many bottles of soap we bought? You won't run out, I promise. I'll order more for you tonight, okay?" Sarah stroked the child's cheek and planted a loving kiss on her forehead.

"I don't like it when you babysit. I want Sofie to leave right now or else it might be bad for her to stay," the child stated with such coldness that Sarah was instantly afraid for Sofie.

"I know, honey. I don't want her here right now, either, but sometimes we have to make the best of things, okay? Can you do that for me? Can we choose new clothes and make the best of it until Sofie's mommy comes to pick her up? I promise there will be no more babysitting after this. Deal?"

The child groaned and stomped her feet over to the dresser. "Fine!" she obliged in an angry tone that Sarah had never heard come from Emma's mouth before. Emma who was always so easy going and sweet and kind. She yanked open the drawer and threw items out, this time choosing things she hoped that Sofie would hate. Ugly grey sweatpants and plain white undies. A tee shirt that was just pink with no cartoon animals or pretty designs and had a stain from that time she spilled her pasta in her lap, and it had splattered all over the place.

When she was through choosing the ugliest outfit her angry little hands could find, she stomped away with a defiant look upon her face and the air grew even thicker and more dense.

"Hey, come here." Sarah pulled the child close just before she could make it out of reach and held her tightly in her lap. "Thank you, Emma," she whispered. "I know how hard you're trying right now and I appreciate you for it. I love you. Remember that, always, okay? I love my Emma forever and ever and ever, no matter what."

The child sat stiff in Sarah's grasp for a few minutes and then she seemed to melt into the mother's arms. The soupy air dissipated as the child grew relaxed and Sarah sighed knowing that, at least for now, everything was going to be okay. The mounting crisis had been averted and hopefully they could make it through the next however many hours they needed to make it through before Sofie's mom returned to take this extra burden from Sarah's overburdened shoulders and weary mind.

"Can we come in?" Jess asked from the door. Sofie was peeking in from behind her legs, which she held tightly in her hands as if the woman was her shield and behind her, she would stay safe from whatever dangers they were walking into.

Sarah looked at the child in her lap, who smiled and nodded her bright green eyes which were for now pacified. "Come on in! Emma picked you out some nice comfy clothes, Sofie. Why don't you get dressed and meet us downstairs. I'll make popcorn and hot cocoa. How does that sound?" she asked the unusually timid child who looked ready to run at the slightest sign from Emma that things were about to go sideways again.

Sofie looked up at Jess, silently pleading with the woman to not leave her alone and Jess, bless her wonderful soul, read the words right from those large, scared eyes.

"Throw me that shirt, wouldya, sis?" Jess asked her sister as she walked all the way into the room, scooping up the towel laden child as she did so. She placed her over one shoulder and carried her to the far side of the room, near the dresser where the rest of the clothes had been tossed and sat down in one swift movement that bounced the girl softly up and down. "This is one heavy sack of taters, I got here!" Jess exclaimed and finally the child's wall of dread was broken, and a nervous giggle escaped her.

A few minutes later they had the girls snuggled, each on one end of the couch with individual popcorn bowls in hand. They had given Emma the remote so as not to incite further incident, which Sofie seemed to have no issues with whatsoever. It ended up being a non-issue, anyway, as Emma put it on a cartoon that both girls loved, and within a very short time they were both laughing from their respective ends of the couch, mugs of hot cocoa steaming from the coffee table before them. Huge dollops of whipped cream floating on top and tiny brown chocolate chips resting on the white fluffy clouds of it.

The day passed without further incident between the girls, but each tick of the tall grandfather clock by the front door resonated in both Sarah and Jess' minds. Jess had so many questions to ask, but she sensed not to ask them while Emma was awake. She could tell that something was terribly off about both her sister and her niece, and she wanted answers but found the patience to wait until the child was sleeping to ask. To give Jess credit, that was a very unlike Jess thing to do.

The two women handed out food and drinks whenever they were asked for, which kept the kids both in a state of amiable semi-coherency as the educational TV shows rotted their brains, just a tiny bit at a time. While they all sat on the couch, Sofie, Jess, Sarah and then the child, the women holding the girls off and on whenever they climbed up into their laps, Sarah sent out text after instant message to the mousey child's mother. She fiercely wanted to know when she was coming to pick up her daughter and she was stuck in an uneasy state of panicked worry after hours of getting no replies when finally, the doorbell rang.

"It's my mommy!" Sofie said, so happily and excitedly that Jess' heart melted a little for the kid. She had grown fond of Sofie in that short time she had known her and though she was just as anxious for her to leave as was her sister, she would miss the little rug rat with her easy laughter and always close by smile.

Emma shot Sofie a heated look of warning and Sofie blushed with a fierce red fire. "Don't worry," she whispered when the two women walked out of the room to get the door. "Best friends keep secrets."

The child slid off the couch and stood before her friend who had leaped up at the sound of the doorbell. She held out her arms and wrapped Sofie up in a tight hug and brought her lips to rest just an inch above one ear. "I'll rip off their faces and use them as masks if you tell. Their eyeballs will be delicious." She then held Sofie back and smiled at her warmly as her aunt and mother came into the room with Sofie's mom in tow.

"I really am so sorry to just dump her on you like this, Sarah. You know I'll make it up to you in any way I can. We were in meetings all day, so I wasn't able to check my phone and the battery died and I had to charge it in the car and, ugh, it was just the worst day possible," the new lady was saying as she came into the room behind Sarah and Jess.

"Hi, mommy!" Sofie smiled and ran over to where her mommy knelt down, ready to cover her daughter in a million kisses. Sofie had recovered lightning fast from hearing the threat the child had made because Sofie liked her parents' faces exactly where they were. She didn't want her mommy to ask her if she was okay. If her mommy did that, she might burst into tears of fright. So, she pushed it to the back of her mind and told herself that Jess was right. Emma was just angry and sad at the loss of her daddy, who she had loved so very much. Sofie might go crazy, too, and turn into a monster if her own daddy died. Maybe that's how monsters were born, her child's mind reasoned.

"Hi, baby! Did you have fun? What on earth are you wearing?" the mom gushed all in one breath after covering the little girl's face in kisses that left smudges of lipstick all over Sofie's brow and cheeks and chin.

"Eeew, mom! Your lips are sticky!" Sofie protested delightedly.

"I know! I just put on a new coat after I pulled up! Just for you! I know how much you love my kisses!" She smiled mischievously at her daughter. "Spill it, kiddo! What happened to your clothes?"

Sofie did grow nervous then and looked down at the floor. She could feel Emma's eyes drilling into the back of her skull and she didn't want to answer in a way that would make her mad. "Emma and I were flying super high by jumping on her bed and then a spider came whooshing down from its string and touched my nose. It scared me and I fell backwards off the bed and hurt my side and then…" Sofie did begin to cry now, in shame for having peed her pants. Big girls didn't do that anymore, her daddy told her.

"She had an accident, is all. We gave her a bath and put her in some of Emma's play clothes. Her stuff is in a bag by the door. I didn't know how long you would be, so I didn't wash it. I'm so sorry," Sarah said.

"She has a wicked bruise coming in, too, on her hip bone where she must have hit the floor," Jess added solemnly. "I get it, though,

121

spiders are the worst," she added, trying to break the awkwardness in the room a little.

"It touched your nose?" Sofie's mother asked in horror and then made creepy crawly fingers before the child's eyes. "Did it just reach right out like this?" Her voice was full of empathy and love and playfulness as she snatched her child up and covered her in even more lipstick kisses.

In the end Sofie's mom was grateful that Sofie had had such good care, considering the spider incident. She thanked both Sarah and Jess about a million more times before guiding Sofie out the door, shopping bag of soiled clothes in tow. When they finally drove away, Sarah closed the painted red front door and leaned against it with her body. She had woken up feeling so refreshed, but the overly stressful day had drained her, and she was back to feeling like a dark storm cloud was surrounding her mind.

The child walked into the hall and faced the mother and the aunt who stood just to her right. A look so serious on her face that both of them were afraid of the next words to come from those adorable little lips.

"I'm hungry," the child said. "Let's get pizza!"

Without missing a single beat Jess replied, "But I was going to make a nice big pot of lima beans for dinner!" The child laughed at the joke and ran into Jess's open arms, allowing her to swoop her up high and then place her on a hip. "Can we get a pizza with sardines or anchovies?" Auntie Jess asked and then began to laugh along with the child, who had burst into a fresh gale of laughter.

"I love fish guts!" Emma's voice announced in such a silly way that the laughter intensified as they went back into the living room. Jess sensed that Sarah needed a moment to compose herself, though she wasn't sure she completely understood why.

"You *are* fish guts!" Jess exclaimed. "Big, stinky, slimy fish guts!"

"Nuh-uh! *You* are!" came the child's delighted reply and again they burst into minor hysteria.

In so many ways the child truly was just a little kid, lost in a world with a different set of instructions on how to live. She had to adapt and take what she needed while walking a thin line of self-protection, but she did it all through the mind of a little kid, barely older than a toddler. Like any child this made her lovable in a way you couldn't put your finger on and Sarah was struggling to cope with it all. She only wanted her Emma back, but part of her felt the need to protect this new Emma, too. This imposter who wore her baby as a costume, but there was no zipper she could find to pull to get this child out of her.

I'm starting to have a thing with crying while leaning against doors, Sarah thought and wiped her eyes with angry hands.

"Mommy! Hurry! You have to pick your toppings!' Emma's voice was calling from the living room computer.

"Coming, love!" she called back as she slowly picked herself up off of the floor before the door. Please let this night be short, she thought as she joined the others in the living room. As they laughed over pizza toppings appearing on the pizza builder page of their local pizza place's website, she thought again about how great it would feel to get a shower. Maybe Jess being here was a blessing in disguise. Maybe while they waited for the pizza to come, she could sneak away from it all and lose herself in the steaming hot water for a bit. That would be as close to heaven as she was capable of getting these days and she smiled at the thought of it.

12

The order came up on the screen in the back by where the pizza station was. Stella wrinkled up her nose at the first pizza's toppings and wondered who had ordered such a thing. Probably some old dude. Who else could stand the slimy little things but old dudes. The only person Stella had known who had liked those on their pizza was her grandad Joe and she had tried one once. Nasty was way too lenient of an insult for how they tasted. Stella had almost puked all over him as he chewed in delight at her disgust and she had vowed never again to let one cross the sanctity of her lips.

"Max! I need two cans of sardines for this one! Like, who orders *double* sardines?" she called out to the tall teen who stood behind the register on the other side of the pizza making station.

"Aw, that's rank as fuck!" Max said as he threw down the pen he had been doodling with on his hand and headed into the back where the walk-in cooler was. He grabbed the two cans out of a mostly full box that was stored in the very bottom shelf in the back. He didn't understand these little fishies at all. They tasted like guts and slime and salt. Putrid, if you asked him. He had tried one on a dare not long after he got hired on here and that one time had been enough. He had managed to keep it down, but just barely. The manager had given him mad props and after that people looked at him with respect in a way that they hadn't done before.

As Max came back and handed the tins to Stella from the wall side of the food station where the cashiers stood looking into the dining room, which now sat empty, Drew walked in the front door. He was back from a delivery that had taken him too long to get to and the people had stiffed him on a tip.

"Fuckin' losers always expecting us to be able to fly over traffic or somethin'," Drew complained as he walked through the swinging door which led to the back.

"If you think that's bad, Drew my friend, wait until you get this baby into your car!" Stella said, punctuating her words with the popping sound of the metal tab on the top of one of the cans, breaking the seal of sardines and letting a somewhat rotten fishy smell out into the room.

"Aw, man!" Max exclaimed and fanned his hand before his face as he used the other to pinch his nose shut. "That shit smells like a two-dollar ho in the back of the dollar store parking lot!"

"How would you know?" Stella asked as she pried the lid off and threw it into the giant trash barrel in the corner.

"'Cuz I took your mom there last week!" he replied with a raised eyebrow and a silly shit eating grin spread across his face.

"Oh, ha ha!" Stella reached one of the slimy fishies out and flung it at Max, who had the reflexes of an eighty-nine-year-old dachshund with one leg. It splatted right between his eyes and all three of them paused to consider the incredible shot she had made before bursting into laughter.

"Great, my car is going to smell like Max's sister Lyla when I had her in it last month." Drew sighed as he placed the carryout bag on the hook and washed his hands to help Stella with the order. There were four pizzas in total and this would be his last delivery before heading out to the party tonight. He couldn't wait to end this hell of a day and get down to the finer things in life. Things like good weed and hot babes. There was nothing like a good country party to end a shitty day on a badass note. Besides, today was his Friday!

"Buuuurn!" Stella laughed. She grabbed a pre-doughed pan from the shelf and scooped a giant scoop of the white sauce into the middle of the extra-large circle of dough and spread it out with the underside of the ladle she had scooped it with.

"Huh, that might actually not be too bad, sardines and white sauce," Drew considered as he checked the order on the screen and grabbed another extra-large pan from the same shelf Stella just had.

"Uh. You're nasty," she said and threw a piece of the grated mozzarella that she had just thrown on and pushed around to cover the sauce with. Stella's go to was throwing things and she was pretty good at it. The piece of cheese she had tossed bounced expertly off of Drew's nose and then onto the messy floor at their feet.

"Takes a nasty to know a nasty," Max laughed from the front and then they all joined in at the stupid joke as if it had been the best one they had heard all day.

"At least the three other pizzas are of a more delicious variety," Drew stated, thinking that if the people were a no show at the door, then he could bring these four extra larges along to the party and be a pizza god among mere mortals. He really was curious about how the sardines would pair with that sauce and briefly considered just skipping the delivery entirely before seeing on the screen that it was a prepaid online order. His dreams of calling it a prank order dashed to bits almost as quickly as he had thought of it in the first place.

"Two meat lovers, extra bacon and a Hawaiian with barbeque sauce, chicken *and* bacon. These guys truly are pizza connoisseurs." Stella nodded as she threw the first two finished pizzas in the oven to let them begin their merry journey through the heated depths of hell before being gradually spit out on the other side, nice and toasty and done.

"Hey, make me a personal one of those Hawaiian ones, would you? My shift ends after this delivery and I'm not coming back in until Sunday," Max said as he finished up a meat lover and placed it on the rotary screen behind the other two that were just far enough in to fit the third pizza.

"Sure, man, it does sound good," she said as she sprinkled the final top layer of cheese on the Hawaiian she had been working on and setting it aside to go in after there was room on the grate.

"Yeah, bruh! You get two days off! Fuckin' sweet!" Max shot Drew the double thumbs up and then mimed slicing his throat with one of the extended thumbs as the bell above the door sounded and a grumpy looking couple walked through. "Back to the grind," he sighed. "You two can't be the only ones who earns a paycheck around here." And he turned to watch the couple come storming to the counter.

"Last week we ordered a pizza, and it was doughy when we got it. We called and your manager said you would give us a remake," the lady huffed, clearly agitated beyond what was normal for a simple pizza emergency such as the one she had described.

"Okay, cool, no probs, my lady friend. Just give me the name and I'll check the list!" Max told the lady with much enthusiasm and his best charming smile.

"It's Jeffries, Debbie Jefferies, and we should get drinks, too, because we had to drive all the way down here, which is really quite far out of our way," she told him in her huffy voice.

Max checked the short list that was kept hung on the wall beneath the counter. A Walters, a Smith and a Jefferies. "One large stuffed supreme, hold the 'shrooms," he read off of the list. "Light on the sauce and burn it a little on the edges." Then he turned back to the couple who seemed a little less agitated now that they realized they wouldn't have to argue with anyone about what was coming to them, and Max gave them another one of his high charismatic grins. "Drinks *and* the salad bar, on the house! We here at Luigi's Pizza understand the importance of taking care of our customers."

Debbie smiled and blushed at the grin and grabbed a plate and a frosted red cup from the stacks by the register. Her husband slowly took a plate and a cup, as had his beloved, but he was waiting for the catch. A little less trusting of Max's charming grin as was his wife, and once he had them in his grasp, he scuttled off to join her, already piling the lettuce high up on her plate. He wasn't taking any chances and wanted to vacate Max's area before he dropped the bomb and said they would have to pay for taxes or just get one trip each to the wonderful bar of salad.

Max chuckled to himself as he entered the remake into the system, pushing the comp button and his code when prompted. People made him happy the way they each had their own mannerisms and he had found in his young life that even the most anxious ridden folks could be calmed by nice words and a friendly smile. People, in the end, just wanted to be heard and maybe respected a little. It wasn't a hard thing to do, and Max had gotten out of a ton of trouble at school or in the neighborhood that way. People just liked Max because Max made himself likable with his understanding ways of listening and making sure you felt heard. It was a true gift in one as young as he and he didn't always use it for the betterment of mankind. Sometimes he used it to score with the

127

ladies or get his F's turned into C's in Spanish class. Sometimes both of those things at the same time. Mrs. Gonzales was a hottie, and a cougar and Max had a special place in his heart for that woman. As she seemed to have for him.

The bell above the door went off again as Tommy arrived to start his shift. He was tall and lanky with a sideways cap, though not intentionally so. It just always had a way of sliding sideways, no matter how many times Tommy fixed it during the day. To be fair, his head was a little misshapen. Though not noticeably so unless he gave himself a buzzcut and he had only done that once on a dare. Never again, he had sworn as he walked the halls of his high school and people started calling him Flat Head or Crater Dome Tommy.

"What?" he would yell back at them on occasion, good naturedly, even though he was growing tired of it on the inside. "My mom got a little winded after pushing my huge dick out that I use to fuck your mothers with. So, my head got a little stuck for a while. It's worth it, man. Your moms are good in the sack." Or "My dudes. It's just a little flat from getting bashed when your dad caught me fucking your sister." Everyone would laugh. Tommy didn't know if they were laughing with him, or at him, but he never got jumped in the hall or shoved into a locker. Like Max, people liked him. He was a happy dude, if just a little crude in the mouth.

"Tommy!" Drew exclaimed. "Right on time, as usual! I'm about to clock out, dude. I've got that huge party tonight!"

"Yeah, sorry I'm late, man," Tommy said as he walked through the swinging door that led into the back. "Fuckin' traffic out there is intense as fuck." He grabbed a vest off of the coat rack by the doorway that led into the back area where they washed dishes and held staff meetings and where the manager's office branched off of.

"Tell me about it," Drew sympathized with a sigh in his voice as he pulled the fish laden extra-large out of the oven. Again, he wondered if it would actually be delicious, but he wasn't going to admit that to these clowns. "It's been like this all day. They're doing construction downtown on some building that nobody cares about and roadwork on the freeway. I thought they only did that shit at night." Drew's voice was full of disgust as he used a spatula to slip the pan out from under the pizza and slide the crispy crust onto the wooden cutting board they sliced them on. "Fuckin' city owes me tip money, man. I've been gettin' jipped all day because of being late. Fucking suuuuuucks!"

Tommy turned to head to the sink and wash up for his shift. Washing up was something he always took seriously when handling food. His mom had taught him well in that department, maybe to make up for his serious lack of grammar etiquette. Drew grabbed the giant pizza slicer off its hook on the wall. It was a long stainless-steel beauty, about three feet from end to end, that Drew had always admired. He loved cutting stuff with it. It was like using a sword, only with wooden handles on each end so that you could lean into the flow of the blade as you pressed it down and rocked it through the pizza. The cutting motion calmed him before he went out on his deliveries. He vowed to own one of these someday. He wanted so badly to just cut stuff with it. Hot dogs. Carrots. Those little tubes of biscuits they kept in the section in the grocery store with the orange juice.

Just now though, he had something else in mind. As Tommy began to walk past him Drew, in one graceful swing of his wrist, he brought one of the handle ends down and using Tommy's momentum against him, brought it straight up and into the crotch of Tommy's jeans.

"Dick tap," Drew laughed and brought the blade back up. Tommy instantly fell to the floor, his hands clutched over his genitals that were now screaming with pain inside his boxers and he struggled to catch his breath. Random cooked toppings sticking to his face as it rubbed across the floor while he writhed in pain in the walkway.

"Dude! Every fucking time!" Max shook his head at the cash counter, his words full of sympathy for the hapless Tommy on the floor.

"Glad I don't have a dick," Stella stated as she leaned over the cutting station and watched Tommy try to catch his breath, as if watching an experiment in lab class. She was truly interested in how something so small could cause such a huge reaction in a man and every time she had witnessed this display of crude humor, she had always stopped what she was doing to watch the recovery

129

stage. She couldn't help herself. It was science.

"You can have mine," Tommy wheezed and gave her the best wink and suave smile he could. You know, under the circumstances.

They all laughed then. A good-hearted laugh and a wonderful sound. Even the two in the dining room joined in, though they couldn't see what it was that had been so funny. The vibe in the pizza parlor was always a good one when these guys were on shift. They all genuinely liked each other, even though they each came from a different world than the other. A different layer of the pecking order, you could say. But this place had brought them together, and they were all truly grateful for that.

Above the door, the bell dinged again. Drew helped Tommy up and brushed a withered olive off his cheek. Tommy grabbed his hat and shook it off first, then they both swatted at different parts of his clothes before heading to the sink together to wash their hands.

"Hi, folks! How is your evening? These knuckleheads treatin' you right?" Luigi asked the couple as he walked through the dining area.

"Yes! They're great and this salad is amazing," the husband said through a mouthful of Thousand Island dressing.

"Glad to hear it!" the short, plump and gently balding man said as he reached the swinging door that led into the kitchen. "They're good kids!" And with that he ducked through.

"Luigi!" the gang called out in unison. They all liked their portly boss, who was stern, but fair. Stella had just put the pan-sized barbeque Hawaiian into the oven and Drew and Tommy were drying off their hands.

"Oh, my dear mother in heaven what the actual pizza gods is that?" Luigi asked as he walked past the cutting station and saw the extra-large white sauce with double anchovies sitting there. The mozzarella had browned beautifully in places and the still uncut pizza really did look delicious. In the way that something taboo can be attractive, though you know it should repulse you.

Drew walked past his boss, who came up to his collar bone and had wild tufts of hair sticking out around his head. The top of his shiny scalp haloed in the dark brown puffs of it. He grabbed the slicer again and began to cut as Tommy grabbed a prefolded box from the shelf on the wall behind them so Drew could slide the pizza in. The holding area of the pizza oven's exit was starting to get backed up now and he wanted to help the process run more smoothly if he could.

"It's kind of catching, isn't it boss?" Drew asked as he ran the curved blade over and through the pizza for the last time.

"Wait, don't box it up. Let's put this baby under the warming lights in back. I gotta try this. I can't believe I never thought of this combination before! I could put it on the specials!"

"Aw, but it's a to go with three others. Traffic already sucks, we don't want three cold pizzas and a hot one, do we?" Drew tried. His shift had been full of angry customers, even though the driving time hadn't been his fault at all and he really didn't want to end it that way, too.

"Heck it!" Luigi said, a large smile across his face. "Refire them all and we'll eat these for dinner! You can't say you don't wanna try that ugly broad right there, can you?" He nodded toward the pizza on the board in Drew's hands and Drew knew it was a losing battle. Plus, he really *did* want to try it.

"Refiring, boss!" Stella saluted from her place on the other side of the cutting station and Tommy swiftly grabbed a metal pizza tray to slide the pizza onto instead of the box.

"I'm game for a slice of this bitch," Tommy said, matter-of-factly. "You can't judge a pizza book by the cover."

"He's right, you know," Luigi said and grabbed the dish, now full of pizza, from Tommy's hands and headed toward the back. "Take care of the guys stacking up in the oven and then come on back for a slice or two, you guys. It's dead as balls in here tonight. Fuckin' Thursdays."

One of the reasons they all loved Luigi so much was because he didn't judge them. Plus, he was hilarious. You never quite knew what was going to come out of the guy's mouth. He was short, but sassy. And he always gave a Christmas bonus.

Drew shrugged and he and Tommy finished cutting up the rest of the pizzas as Stella began making more. Max had gotten her two more cans and as she cracked them open, they all made sounds of disgust at the smell.

"Aw, Stella!" Tommy complained, "Take a shower, would ya! It's gettin' a little rank down there."

This time the anchovy Stella threw landed in Tommy's laughing open mouth and he instantly started gagging at the taste of it. Again, the sound of laughter erupted in the kitchen of Luigi's Pizza. In the dining room the couple, who were no longer anxious, smiled. This really was a magical place to be.

13

"Thirty minutes, Auntie Jess!" The child jumped up from where she had been laying on her tummy before the TV. Her legs bent at the knees and her ankles crossed just where the legging style pajama bottoms ended. Her chin had been cradled in her palms as she watched cartoons. The timer had been Jess' idea because the child had taken her bath and then been dressed and still the pizzas had been a no show. Sarah had been trying to calm her down as the child got cranky when she was hungry, and Jess had been a life saver. Perhaps literally.

Jess had picked the unruly child up, cradled her like a baby and pulled up her pink pajama top with her teeth. Exposing her niece's belly button, she then blew raspberries until she heard the beautiful sound of child's laughter fill the room. This was a trick that always seemed to work on Emma before and she was super glad that it still did. When the child had seemed almost out of breath, and so had Jess been, she sat the kid back down and tapped her nose and ran for the kitchen. The child had looked at Sarah. Sarah only shrugged and then ran after her sister after tapping the exact same spot her sister had on Emma's button nose. The child had watched them go, starting to get a little annoyed again at the unanswered need for pizza. Then a weird thing happened. Well, weird for the child, not for children in general. She smiled and ran after the two women of whom she was starting to love.

When they got to the kitchen, first Jess then Sarah and closely behind came the child, Jess plucked the chicken shaped kitchen timer off its spot on the stove and plopped it into Emma's small hands.

"Twist that baby all the way around until the little red arrow touches the thirty-minute mark. Then we'll put on a movie and if the pizza hasn't arrived by then, I'll call, okay?" Jess asked and picked the child up to carry her into the living room.

The child did as she was told and slowly twisted the dial with a look of concentration on her face. Emma had learned time by asking mommy and watching TV. It had been a pretty easy concept for her to grasp, but Sarah was still impressed by the ease in which she saw Emma's little hands twisting the top half and the bottom in opposite directions and stopping at the halfway point. Then the child grabbed the remote and lay down on the floor to watch one of the cartoon movies that came up in her streaming account that was solely a collection deemed safe for kids to watch. The chicken she placed carefully down on a nest of carpeting, and they all began the wait. The two women taking solace in the fact that it should be considerably less time for the pizza to arrive than that. As it turned out, they had been wrong.

Drew finally arrived at the address, annoyed as hell, but at least the pizzas still felt hot through the bottom of the thick red pizza bags he had them stuffed in.

"Please don't be mad," he whispered to himself as he stepped up onto the curb and began walking the pizza up the sidewalk to the front door. What a crazy day this had been in the pizza delivery world and Drew was so grateful he had a two-day mini vacation to look forward to. After the party tonight he was gonna crash over at Dana's place. Find an open couch when the tired took him and just fuckin' pass the fuck out. It was a solid plan. Mostly because he really liked Dana and he hoped that they would have some alone time tomorrow to chat where maybe he could ask her out. To the movies or a club or whatever. Maybe even breakfast if he could get up the nerve in time.

After they had done the refires on this order, he had anxiously waited for the new ones to come out. Grabbing a slice while he did so of that gnarly looking siren of a sardine pizza and actually taking a bite, you know, while nobody looked. Stella was still working on the refires. Tommy was at the exit gate of the oven, waiting to slice and box the pizzas Drew had to deliver and Max actually had some customers by this point at the register. The big boss himself had gone out the back to vape. A thing that Drew thought was very uncool of him to be doing, at his age. What fifty something adult guy wanted to smell like strawberries and cream, he always wondered, though he secretly liked the smell better than when the short dude had been into cigarettes.

He brought the slice slowly up to his lips. He could smell the garlic in the sauce and his mouth began to water in anticipation. The cheese drooled down the sides of the slice a little. White melty ribbons and the fish seemed like they belonged there. A fact that he honestly hadn't ever thought he would ever think in his life. A life he planned on being long and fruitful. With many children and a couple wives. One after the other when the first one got tired of his all-night gaming binges and lackluster performance in the bedroom. He knew who he was and he had made peace with it. It was cool, in his mind, because the second wife would be for love where the first one had been for experience. So, she would stick around where the other one couldn't bring herself to. If only he knew now how this day would end, maybe he could have done something to prevent it.

He took a quick peek around to make sure that he was the only one in the room and then took the plunge. He opened his mouth a little wider and tilted his head back as he brought the pizza up and above his face. Slowly dipping it in so that he could make sure to catch all of the rivulets of cheese that were swaying off the slice's edges. He filled his mouth with cheese and bread and yes, an anchovy. Mixed with that sauce, it was surprisingly delicious. This may be his new favorite pizza combination. It was salty, but not in a fishy way. It had a hint of some meaty flavor he couldn't quite place from memory, and it married itself to the garlicy cream sauce they mixed in house each morning. The cheese and crust and anchovies seemed the perfect mixture with that sauce and as he chewed what was left in his mouth he brought in another bite because it was seriously that good.

"So, it's a hit, then?" Luigi asked from the back doorway as he walked in from the darkening outside. A not unpleasant smelling cloud of strawberries and cream wafting out around him as he walked.

"Oh my god, yes," Drew stated through a mouthful of pale-

135

colored half-chewed food. He no longer cared about anyone catching him eat this delicious delicacy and only frowned on himself for not trying this out sooner. "This is a pizza game changer!" he added as he went in for another slice.

"I gotta try this for myself!" Luigi said as he reached over to grab a toasty wedge. He was just short enough that he didn't have to bend down towards the table at all to get this done and some of his cheese drippings trailed along its surface as he brought it up to his mouth. "Oh, my hecking god this is delicious!" he exclaimed as he took a huge bite and began to chew. "It's going on the specials' board! Get the chalk pen, kid!"

Now as Drew rang the doorbell, he repeated to himself, "Please don't be mad." He could hear commotion inside. Through the small square frosted window which was placed in the middle of the door he saw the blurry outlines of two grownups and a child coming down the hall toward where he stood on the stoop. For some reason his heart began to thumpity-thump quicker in his chest and a voice whispered deep inside his mind to just drop the pizzas, heat bags and all, and get the fuck outta here.

But that was silly, of course, and he would get ragged on at work to no end if they called in to complain. Plus, those bags would probably come out of his check. It was already a shitty day for tips, and he didn't want to add anything else on top of that, monetarily speaking.

Time seemed to slow down then, which was weird. It seemed to take forever for the people inside to make it to the door. Even the sound of the crickets had slowed to long screeeeeeeeeeee screeeeeeeeeeeees. When he had first walked up, he had thought about how annoying that sound was and knew for a fact that they had been screeing much faster a few seconds ago. Again, something inside his mind, and maybe his heart as well, told him to run! Just run! Don't let them answer the door, it said. If they do, you're a dead man! Run now, while you can! And Drew almost *did* run. His grip on the bags began to loosen, but slowly. Far too slowly. One of his feet actually began the act of turning to flee when suddenly time crashed back into pace and the door was jerked open hard enough to crash against the hallway wall. Banging against the doorstop as it did.

He jumped, and the bags fell out of his hands as a little redheaded girl came running out and grabbed his legs in a tight embrace.

"Whoa, little lady!" Drew said with a relieved smile on his face. He was being paranoid of a little kid who just wanted her dinner. "You really love your pizza, huh?" he asked as he patted her back awkwardly and then just stood there with his hands out to his sides as if he didn't know what to do. Drew didn't have any little siblings or cousins, so he really was lost when it came to the munchkins of the world.

"I'm so sorry," a tall strawberry blonde lady said as she bent down to pry the girl off of Drew's baggy jeans. He didn't care how popular the trend, he would be caught dead before you found himself sporting skinny jeans. That was a promise.

"Aw, no worries, ma'am," Drew smiled at the woman, who he pegged as the kiddo's mom, even though the other lady had the same bright red hair as the kid had. There was just something about the way she gently pried at the shorty's fingers and the tired look in her eyes that screamed mom to him. She was pretty, though, he thought, and he would have bet a million bucks that if Tommy had been here to see her, he would have instantly proclaimed her doability.

"You shouldn't have been so late." The little girl looked up at him and as the icy coldness of her voice pulled his gaze down toward hers, he gulped. The child's eyes were almost glowing, even though he knew that was impossible to the max. People's eyes didn't glow. Not even creepy little rug crawlers had glowing eyes. Right? He shivered as he thought about it and then bent to pick up the bag on his right as the mother drug the upset kid inside. The other woman, her sister most likely by the strong resemblance she held for both the child and her mom, came out and joined him on the stoop.

"I'm so sorry about my niece. She's very serious about her pizza." The aunt laughed a nervous laugh and then held out her hands for the first two boxes.

"Was she the one who built that anchovy and white sauce

137

number?" He asked amiably enough, he hoped, after the creepy kid incident just moments before.

The woman laughed and Drew was suddenly aware of how beautiful she was. She was a little taller than he with super curly hair and not too skinny or too fluffy, as his mom would have put it. He wished he was a few years older; he would have asked her for her Insta or cell number. As it was, he was just a delivery kid that had shown up late and so probably put their evening into a bit of a tailspin with the mini human in there.

"Yes! Actually, it was her and I. We dared each other to eat it so I said only if it had white sauce. I couldn't imagine it would be even remotely good with marinara." She blushed, aware of how uninteresting the whole thing was and then held out her arms for the second set of pizzas to be stacked on top of the first two.

"Aw, man, that pizza is why I'm so late. My boss took one look of me cutting the first one and he made us refire your whole order so he could try it." Drew returned her blush, knowing that there was no way to salvage the tip on this one, anyway. "It's actually pretty killer, if you ask me! I had two slices before I left. And then traffic has been a nightmare. I'm so sorry to be so late. I tried to talk him out of the refire, but, well -"

"No worries at all," she interrupted. Her voice was chipper and a little relieved sounding. "I'm glad to hear it's good! To be honest, I've been dreading your arrival!" Then she turned and called back to him from over her shoulder, "Don't go anywhere! I'll be right back!" And she disappeared around a corner. Less than a minute later she reappeared from where she had just gone and was carrying a crisp twenty-dollar bill in her hand, held out toward him.

"Aw, no, man, I can't accept that. I'm super late! And I really pissed off shorty, there. I really don't deserve a tip." He held up his hands, palms facing her in the universal gesture of nah, man, nah, and she smiled. She liked this kid, and she truly was happy to not be so afraid of losing street cred to her niece by chickening out with the anchovy pizza. She already was not a fan of fish. Especially when paired with something as amazing as pizza, which was her favorite meal ever. Like, *ever*.

138

"I insist! Seriously, you fought for us at work and then gave me that amazing review which will help me seem brave when I go to take a bite. That's worth more to a cool aunt like me who doesn't want her niece to know she's been faking this whole cool thing from the start." She winked at Drew and his heart melted. He would have done anything for this red-headed goddess at that moment and he reached out his hand for the money. His forefinger touched her thumb, and he blushed as a hot spark of electricity shot from her pale colored skin to his darker tanned flesh.

"Thank you," he whispered and suddenly found his shoes very interesting. He wasn't used to talking to nice ladies. Especially today, this had been a wonderful treat for him. All day it had seemed like bad stuff had kept happening when it came to customers and he was glad that his last customer of the day had been this incredibly nice, even though her niece had been so pissed that she had given him a rage hug. Ha, a rage hug. That was a new one for the record books. He couldn't wait to tell the guys back at work on Sunday all about it. They would get a kick out of it, he was certain.

As they said their goodbyes and she closed the door gently on him gathering up the bags and stuffing the twenty into his front pants pocket, he smiled. This had turned out to be a great day. He had spent it with good people, minus the grouchy customers earlier in the day. Had gotten to try a surprisingly delicious pizza, plus he still had his personal-sized chicken barbecue Hawaiian with bacon in the car for later. And to top it all off this super nice lady customer had given him a pretty fat tip! His heart was riding high as he pulled his car back out onto the street and headed for Dana's party. Today's my lucky day, he thought as he turned on the headlights to beat out the darkness of the streets around him. I'm gonna go for it! I'm gonna finally ask her out on that date. He smiled, thinking of Dana then. If only he knew he would never get that chance.

14

Drew headed for the gas station to fill up and grab a forty-eight ouncer of Code Red. He loved the stuff and tonight was gonna be long. He needed the extra caffeine if he was gonna make it through! He loved parties at Dana's. Her parents left for long weekends every few months and that meant people would show up on Thursdays and some would crash over until Saturday or sometimes even Sunday. It was awesome. Most of the guests would leave around the time the sun started creeping up and show back up again the next night to start the cycle all over again. That meant that Friday mornings were always quieter, and he could get her alone long enough to make his move.

Drew got his gas and liquid refreshment and headed for Dana's. She lived off a long dirt road about twenty miles down this old highway that wound through the foothills out of town. Her house had an amazing view of the valley and at night the sky was ablaze with stars. It was worth the drive from the city to get to her place and he really couldn't wait for the weekend ahead. He was a little nervous to finally be bearing his soul to Dana, who he had had a crush on for years now, but he felt finally ready and excited for the opportunity.

About halfway to Dana's turnoff, Drew realized that there was a weird green glow coming from the backseat of his tiny white hatchback. It was one of those things that happens when you're driving that you can't really recall when it started, just that it was there and had been for a while. How long that while was you can't quite say. Like when you realize a song you love is almost done playing on the radio. Or suddenly find yourself halfway home on your long commute but you don't quite remember getting there. Suddenly, Drew felt afraid. Not just afraid, either, but terrified.

"You're being an asshat," he told himself, his voice a bit shaky in the quiet car. A quiet that was now thick and tense instead of relaxing. "It's just the Luigi's car topper you threw in there after leaving that last house. It must have turned itself on after you hit a bump or something." The car topper in question was laying on the floor behind his seat. It was shaped like a long, green triangle with Luigi's Pizza in bright red letters and the phone number beneath the logo in matching crimson. He had never had it turn on by itself before and so didn't know what it would look like in his car on a dark, deserted road in the middle of the sticks. Still, it was plausible that it was the current culprit in this situation.

He tried to ignore the eerie glow and keep going. He really just wanted to make it to Dana's as quickly as he could but every second that passed the terror in him grew and grew. It was as if he was running from something, but he didn't know what and he didn't feel alone, either. Even though it was impossible that he wasn't. His car was small, and he would have noticed had someone climbed in at the gas station. He would have seen it before he got back in. He always made a habit to sweep his car before getting in. It was easy to do and only took a second. Besides the fact that he could see everything in his mirror, anyway. As that thought ran through his mind, his eyes darted from the road to his rearview in the upper middle of his windshield.

"See, nothing -" he started to say, but then he saw her. The child from that last house, sitting in the middle of the backseat. A happy smile on her face and her eyes really *were* glowing.

He screamed and jumped and slammed on the brakes all at once. The car swerved and he over corrected and he could feel the back end begin to slide around as his front end skidded and hit the gravel side of the road, which sucked his car in that direction. That motion forced the rear of his car, which was still trying to travel the sixty-three miles per hour he had been going, back in the other direction. Forcing him back on the road and his world began to spin as his car swerved into a giant circle. He could feel the right side of the car begin to lift and tip and so he pulled the wheel in that direction, and it settled back down and finally, after the longest screeching noise he had ever heard in the entirety of his life, his car

141

stopped. He found himself facing in the direction he had been coming but in the opposite lane.

"Holy fuck," he whispered. His body was shaking, and his mind was numb. He checked the mirror again and the child wasn't there. His back seat *was* glowing a bright green, but he laughed as he saw why. A nervous, relieved sound in this dark and quiet place. The Luigi's car topper had bounced up and onto the seat and he could see that the glow had really been coming from it the whole time. He chuckled again and began to slowly put his foot down on the gas. He made a huge u turn and frowned at the bumping his right front tire was doing and he pulled over as much as he could onto the narrow gravel side of the road. His car was still in the lane about a foot, but he thought it would be okay because the road was deserted, and he couldn't see headlights or taillights at all in either direction. Just before he swung his door open and climbed out to inspect the damage, he clicked on the emergency flashers. Better safe than sorry, he thought as he left the hatchback's tiny cab to inspect the damage.

He slowly walked around the front end of his car and could tell immediately that the tires on the right side were shot before he even made it to the front where he could see them. The car was slouched down on the right side at an angle that made it clear something was very wrong. He winced as he made that last corner around the hood and bent down to get a better look at the mangled tire and rim on the front passenger side.

Not that he needed a closer look. His tire was thrashed. The rubber had been ripped open when it had hit the narrow strip of gravel and it was a mangled mess of sharp wire and torn tire. The rims were chipped where the gravel and asphalt had chewed away at them. He couldn't see that well out here, the moon was just a sliver in the sky above him, smiling a Cheshire grin in a sea of brilliant stars. Even through the darkness he could tell, though, that his rear passenger side tire was equally as fucked.

"Goddamnit," he said flatly. His heart was still racing a mile a minute in his chest, and he swiveled around on his heels and sat down with his back against the white fender in between the wheel well and the bumper. There was just over a foot of gravel covering ground between his car and a steep drop off into a ditch that was at least over his head deep if he were standing in it, though it was hard to judge because the bottom of it was so lost in shadow. It was as if a thick soup of darkness lay below his dangling feet.

"I guess I'm lucky," he announced to nobody as he thought about how bad it could have been. How much worse off he would be right now had his car ran off the road instead of just into the other lane. The ditch was about twenty feet wide with sharp, gnarly looking rocks poking out from it here and there. He thought it was probably a drainage ditch of some kind, but he only barely even was aware of the term and had no idea what they were really for, aside from draining. Draining what and to where he couldn't even guess past water, that was. A river? Rain? Toxic waste? Who knew? Surely not Drew.

He sighed as these thoughts raced through his head and he picked up a small stone from among the many from where he sat and threw it into the darkness. He expected to hear a plink as it landed on something hard, or a whisper of grass, perhaps. Instead, there was no sound at all. As if that dark layer prohibited it, and suddenly he was terrified again. Suddenly he realized that he was stuck in the middle of nowhere all on his onesie and even if he had a spare (which he did not) it wouldn't matter because his current predicament would require twice that many.

"My cell!" he almost shouted with excitement as he remembered it sitting in the cupholder, attached to a charging cable plugged into the cigarette lighter like an umbilical cord giving it life. Just as he started to get up, his hands were dug into the gravel, the sharp bits biting into the skin of his open palms, he heard something. Something that made the hair on the back of his neck stand up at the same time that a shiver ran all the way down his spine. A little girl's giggle. A sound that should be sweet, but out here was anything but.

He froze with one foot up and under him, his knee bent, and the other leg still outstretched into the darkness below. The darkness that now felt alive and he knew in his heart of hearts that there was something down there. Something ancient and evil. Something staring at him with predator's eyes and a mouth full of teeth ready to tear his flesh from his bones as the asphalt had done with the rubber from his rim.

He wanted to move but couldn't. Sharp edges of rock were pressing even harder into his palms now as the weight of his upper body seemed to grow even heavier with every passing second. He could feel parts of his skin dimple and were pierced as tiny drops of blood began to spill. He hardly even noticed the pain because down there the darkness was beginning to move. It seemed to swirl around in the same way as the green glow in his car. He hadn't quite noticed when it had started, he just suddenly became aware of the fact that it was happening and had been happening. And still, he was frozen in place. The ankle of his right leg feeling the pressure as his shoe sunk deeper beneath him and the ankle of his left feeling completely exposed as it sat over the edge and halfway down the embankment to where the moving shadows began. They swirled as if a thousand creatures lived just below their surface, churning the darkness as gators churn the swampy waters of haunted southern bogs.

The giggling got louder and louder as the darkness whirled about. And suddenly he saw her. The girl from the house. The one who had hugged him an angry hug full of malice instead of love. Her eyes began to appear from the blackness, slowly fading in. Their bright green going from dim to blazing in seconds and he wished he could squint his eyes against that light.

The giggles grew louder and suddenly he saw her hand slowly reach out from the black shifting veil that even that bright green light couldn't penetrate. It reached up the rocky dirt hill, its small child's hand slowly inching forward past shards of broken glass and tufts of yellow dried grass. Closer and closer to his black and white canvas sneakers with the star on the side it crawled as the giggles grew and grew louder and louder in his ears. He felt like he would go crazy if she touched him. Her hands were dirty. Oh, so dirty. The nails were embedded with mud, or something worse, and the creases in the knuckles were stained with some dark liquid he feared was blood from whatever last victim she had recently fed upon.

Then it happened. The tippy top of one of those reaching

fingers touched the edge of his rubber-soled shoe and his paralysis broke. He screamed as loudly as he ever had before and jerked his foot up and underneath him so that he could stand and run back around and away from that terrible child whose face and arm were the only things poking out of the darkness below him. Her mouth was stretching into an open grin and her teeth! There were so many teeth, too many! And they were sharp and pointy, just right for tearing away his skin and muscle and severing his bones.

I've made it! He thought as he reached his full height, but as he turned to flee his balance shifted as some of the gravel slipped below his sneaker. He could feel himself begin to fall backwards toward that hand and the face that nightmares are made of. Toward that thick blackness that harbored others, he was sure of it. It was full of things that would love to make him a snack and fight for his softer bits like dogs fighting for scraps. His arms began to pinwheel as he desperately fought the battle to regain his footing, and just as both his feet began to slide backward toward that abyss his fingers barely grazed and then caught the thin metal of the white car's antenna and he prayed with all of his might that it would hold.

He felt the child's searching fingers once again touch his shoe and another terror-filled scream erupted from his lungs and he jerked himself forward, just in time. He fell face first onto his hood and scrambled up and over. The child's giggles came again, this time sounding as if she were right behind his head and again he screamed and pulled himself toward the road and away from the death-filled darkness awaiting at the bottom of that spillway. He slid across the white roof, his belt buckle screeching against the metal as it gouged a long line in the paint. He pulled himself over and fell face first into the road on the other side of his car before jumping up on limbs made of jello and pouring himself back into the tiny cab. He locked his doors with the automatic button and took solace in the loud clicking noise as all of the locks slammed down in perfect unison.

He sat there for a minute. Breathless and scared. Suddenly he realized he sat in silence. The giggling had stopped, and he scanned the landscape outside, trying to look in every direction at once. Praying that what he had just seen had been some kind of crazy

145

hallucination. A leftover from the time he had dropped acid with Dustin behind the Shake Stop on Sixth Street and brought on by the scare he had had with the blowout. It could also explain the girl he had seen in the backseat just before it happened.

"Yeah, stupid. That's gotta be it. Dude, you're so fuckin' dumb, takin' that shit," he whispered to himself. His voice full of electric anxiety that seemed to be sparking off of the words like a lightning rod. "The fuckin' bumps in the road turned on the light and it freaked you out, causing you to see that creepy kid and then after you almost flipped your car you saw her again in the ditch. You knew acid could come back atchoo later and you took it, anyway. Fuckin' ass clown," he chastised himself, but he wasn't mad, just relieved.

He laughed that same nervous laugh from earlier and then reached for his cell in the cup holder. He would call his mom and have her use her insurance card to get a tow and then he would have Dana come and pick him up. She would be his hero and that ride back to her place would give him the time to ask her out! It was perfect! His mother had always taught him to look for the silver lining. Mothers are the best.

He tapped the black screen, and nothing happened, so he pressed the button on the side. Again, blackness greeted his efforts and a confused frown spread across his lips. He had this puppy on the charger all day. He knew he did. He had been using it to find his routes and he would have noticed if the wire wasn't plugged in. But that's when he realized it wasn't plugged in and maybe hadn't been even though he could have sworn it was.

"Ugh." He groaned out loud and let the phone fall back toward the cupholder. He didn't really care where it landed. It was basically just an expensive paperweight at this point. This wasn't the first time he had forgotten to plug the tiny cable end into his phone and had it die on him, it was probably just the most important time.

"Where is all the traffic?" he asked the empty passenger seat, the sound of his words out loud making him feel a little better. A little less alone. "There should be bitches headed to Dana's, right? Like, dude, this is the only fuckin' road to her place coming from town. It doesn't make sense that nobody has passed me. And, like,

146

I've been on this road a shit ton of nights like this and there's always people headed down the hill, too." He wondered as the fear started to creep up inside him once again. Drew was a social creature who never had done well alone. He hated making decisions, especially important ones, and right now seemed like a great time to have someone there with him. Someone to comfort him and tell him what to do. Someone to say it was all gonna be okay.

"That fucking light, bro! I can't take that green glow anymore," he complained and reached into the backseat. He flipped the thick green plastic over and pressed the button that turned off the light. The click was loud and satisfying and the darkness was instant and intense. He hadn't been expecting it to be so thick, despite his blinkers steadily flashing on and off outside of the cab, but the stars still shone above him like a beautiful quilt, and he sat back in his seat and looked out the windshield at their brilliant dance above him.

Click.

The green glow filled his car again and he jumped, startled at the loudness of that sound in this quiet tomb.

"It's not a tomb," he whispered, instantly regretting that thought. Tombs were where mummies lived and came alive to murder intruders who came looking for their treasures. Or so he had seen from some movie his mom had been streaming the other day. Some creepy flick from her childhood. It had been a pretty good film, in the end, though Drew was a man with a more refined comedic pallet.

He slowly turned his head to look into the backseat. He was afraid the girl would be there, that teeth-filled grin across her face. That giggle threatening to escape her throat once more. But there was nothing there. Just the light sitting on the cracked leather of his back seat. He checked the floorboard behind him and even crawled through the small opening between the front seats to look over the backseat's backrest and into the rear compartment. Aside from empty chip bags and slushie cups, the place was empty. He scooted back into the front driver's seat, clicking the light off once again as he did so, this time welcoming the darkness that filled the car.

He couldn't take that green glow anymore. He just really couldn't. He didn't understand, either, how that switch could turn itself on without being physically pressed. It defied logic. And he had heard the click, so something had to have pressed it. Things don't just go around pressing themselves, right? Like, that was a major impossibility, right?

His thoughts were growing more and more anxiety-filled inside his mind. Even the hypnotizing beauty of the stars above offered no sanctuary from the terror that was tugging at his mind. Maybe he could walk to Dana's. It would take him a couple of hours but, dude, anything was better than being stuck in this car.

Click.

Again, the light turned on and this time he jerked around so hard to see that the steering wheel was slammed into his hip painfully enough for him to yell in surprised pain. Again, the car was empty, and that green light seemed to be mocking him. It filled the car with an eerie glow, and he hated it. He suddenly hated it with all of his might. He grabbed the Luigi car topper and roughly yanked it through the space between the two front seats leading into the back. He turned it upside down in his lap, a feat not so easy in this small space because of its awkward size and yanked the battery compartment lid off. Drew grabbed out the batteries with one hand and threw them into the back as far as he could. The darkness was again immediate, but this time he took no comfort. This time it seemed like the stars had even dimmed.

He gracelessly pushed the light into the passenger side with a triumphantcy that held no actual feelings of having won a great battle and he ran a nervous hand through his hair. There was absolutely no way possible that the light could turn itself back on now, but still, he stared at it, feeling like it would. At any moment he would hear that click. At any moment he would lose his mind.

"Boo," a voice whispered to him from behind his left ear. Someone in the empty backseat, but that was impossible and with the sound of that voice all he could think to do was escape this place. It really was a tomb, and he knew that now. The voice in the back seat had been that girl's, but girls could be mummies, too, and he reached for the door and pressed it open with the full weight of the left side of his body. As it opened, he just as quickly exited.

Drew had time only to stand before it happened. The semi had been going a little too fast according to the posted speed limit signs, but not crazily so. He had seen the car sitting there, partially in his lane, so he had gotten over to go past the tiny white clown car looking thing. He had laughed at how small it was, imagining trying to squeeze himself into that front seat and still be able to use the wheel.

George was a big guy and he hated little cars. His first car had been a tiny little thing and how the other kids had laughed each time they saw him have to bend down and get in. After that he always bought trucks. Trucks like Lucille here, whom he loved. He patted her burgundy dash and smiled. He didn't notice the door opening and the kid pouring himself out onto the road. But he did hear the crunching of metal when it happened. A sound that he would never forget for as long as he lived. It would haunt him in the early hours of the morning, just before dawn's light would drift through the curtains. That high-pitched screeching sound as metal scraped into metal and twisted and tore. On his deathbed some years later, that would be the sound that carried him into the afterlife as he lay in his hospital bed gasping for breath. It was his life's great regret, that night. That night when that sound changed everything for him and took everything from a kid and his family. That horrible, awful sound.

Drew had just enough time to stand before the front end of the truck pressed his body hard into the door of his car. The force pulled his little white hatchback over against the moving truck and metal sheared into metal and fiberglass and Drew's unfortunate body was grated like cheese against his much-loved hatchback and George's much-loved semi.

His skull was bounced first one way and then the other. His neck snapped with a sound that would have been loud in the quiet Drew had been in just seconds ago but was now lost in that great cacophony of two vehicles crashing against each other. His chest was pinned to the door which had been pushed all the way open against the front driver's side fender and the truck's front passenger side just before the bumper. The force of the truck moving forward,

149

even as George slammed on the brakes, pulled Drew's rib cage to the left as his back was still pinned and it ripped the flesh of his right side wide open and peeled it forward. The skin going with the truck as the bones pressed flat and to the right, shards of ribs ripping into his still beating heart just before the weight of it all flattened it. Not unlike a pancake with strawberry syrup.

Drew's hips were also crushed and the whole front of his body was ripped away, layer by layer, as the truck forced its way across him and the car. It was the world's worst rug burn and as the skin and fat and muscle were ripped from him, so too was his face and nose and an ear. Even his teeth were seized from their place inside his mouth and before the truck could finally stop its deathly run his lower jaw hit the oncoming semi-trailer and was crudely ripped away from his body and flung onto the road ahead.

As George was finally able to get the truck to stop, he sat before the wheel with his head hung down. His whole body shook with the fear of what he knew he would find when he climbed out his door. He had seen the kid stand and he knew there was no way he had missed him. Tears began to fall as the thought of him taking a life began filling his head and suddenly, he was filled with the urge to vomit. He opened his door and jumped down as he had a million times before, only this time all of his grace was gone, and he landed hard and fell on his side with an ooof. He barely made it over and onto his hands and knees before his stomach let loose of everything it held. When it had emptied of his dinner, prime rib at some roadside cafe, still he wretched. He wretched and wretched and finally when his throat was torn and the iron taste of blood coated his tongue, he was able to stand on shaky feet and reach in for his cell. Never in his life had he felt so much guilt and he still couldn't bring himself to look.

As he dialed with shaky fingers and bile still dripping down his chin, he heard something that for a moment stopped his breath. Somewhere on the wind in the silence that now surrounded him it drifted to his ears. A quiet sound that still his frightened mind couldn't quite convince him wasn't there. The sound of a little girl's playful giggle, but from far away.

Back at Sarah's house, Emma was sitting in front of the

television with a happy smile upon her face and the cutest little laughter escaping her at whatever hilarious thing was happening on the movie that played before them. A shiver ran down Jess' spine at the sight of that smile mixed with that sound. There was something about it she couldn't quite put her finger on, though it was a sweet enough combination. Something in her niece's eyes, she thought. Those too bright eyes that hadn't been that bright before. Something inside of Jess told her that things were not right in this house and that her sister needed help. Something deeper whispered that this child was not really her niece, but she pushed that thought away. That was an impossibility she wasn't ready yet to entertain. But she would be. Oh, yes. She would be.

15

Sarah woke up to the sound of sirens growing in the air. The room was already bright from the sunlight that drifted in through the colorful floral curtains and she sat up with a start. They're coming for her, the frantic thought raced through her mind, and she rocked her sister's sleeping body so hard that Jess rolled to the side and started to slip off the bed. She woke from the sensation of falling and was able to lift her head fast enough to avoid hitting it on the white wooden end table on her way down.

"Ouch! Sarah! What the fuck?" Jess asked as she pulled herself up into a sitting position.

She had fallen asleep in her sister's bed last night as they had lay whispering about Emma and how she had changed. Sarah had told her everything. How she feared that something had stolen Emma's body and held her child hostage inside. How the neighborhood cats were missing and how she thought that Emma had something to do with it. How she could do things that no child should be able to do. Move quietly across a room far too quickly for someone her age and size and more.

Sarah told her about all of it. About the temper tantrums that ended with broken windows that nobody was standing near or the room getting so full of this electric feeling that she was afraid to even move in fear of the air itself shocking her with the friction her body would make moving through it. And about the dreams. The dreams where she was stuck in a dark cave or endless hallway and everywhere she looked there were branches like a maze. The whole time she would be lost in this place she would hear Emma, *her* Emma, calling out to her. Her child's voice so full of fear and sadness that she would often wake up with tears streaming down her own cheeks and her heart breaking over again each time.

She even told her about what she would sometimes find when

she awoke from those dreams. Emma's small body standing in the doorway covered from head to toe with grime and dried blood. Her dress would sometimes be torn and always it was stained and caked with filth. And she would smell of death and dank places and always ask for a bath with lots and lots of strawberry bubbles. As she told her sister this her whisper got faster and more urgent. She felt like she needed to get this out of her. She needed to not be the only one who knew. She needed an ally and someone to give her an idea on what to do, because poor Sarah was lost in it.

Jess didn't know what to say, so she did the only thing a big sister could do when she saw the pain and anguish and fear her younger sibling was going through. She pulled her close in a warm and comforting hug and told her it would all be okay. Jess was here now, and Sarah wouldn't be alone any more. She would stay as long as Sarah and Emma needed her to, and together they would figure out a way to make everything alright again. Jess held Sarah and let her cry. She cried and cried and cried for god only knew how long. Eventually they both fell asleep that way. Like they had when they were little, and Sarah had slipped into Jess' bed when the storms brewed heavy in the sky. Neither one of them dreamed that night. Their hearts and minds were too heavy for it. And both of them were grateful because they both knew that had dreams come to them in those wee hours after Sarah had told her dreadful tale, they would have been nightmares.

"Listen," Sarah said, as she jumped out of bed and ran across the room to the window. She peeked through the curtain as if she were a nosy neighbor trying not to get caught, but her whole body was tense with fear. "They're coming for her! I knew that playdate was a bad idea! I don't blame them, I would have called the cops, too. Ugh, what do I do, Jess?" Sarah looked to Jess for help. Her eyes pleaded with her for it.

"It's okay. I don't think it's for Emma. Let's take a second, okay? I'm sure everything is fine, sis." She stood and walked across the room to where her little sister stood. Tired and in desperate need for a shower.

Jess peeked out the window beside Sarah and they both stood there, tense and waiting. The sirens grew louder and louder and both women had a panicked moment where the cars came into view, white and black with flashing red and blue lights on their roofs and loud wailing sounds as they slowed in front of their house. Both women simultaneously let out a sigh as the two cruisers kept going and pulled to a stop in front of the MacGregor residence next door.

"Oh my, god, Emma!" Sarah said and turned to run from the room, but Jess was able to catch her wrist and she stopped, an unnerving look upon her face.

"Sarah, it's okay, they're next door," Jess soothed, a reassuring smile on her face.

"No, you don't understand! It's Emma! She did something, I know it! And if she left evidence, they'll know it, too! Then they'll come for her and lock her away. She's so small, Jess. This isn't her, not really. I'll never get her back if they do that." Sarah slid her wrist free of her sister's loosening grasp and left the room to go find Emma. It only took Jess a second to decide to follow.

"Hi, mommy!" Emma called from her soft perch on the window seat. "The police are next door. I wonder why." But the child's voice sounded as if she really didn't wonder. The child's voice sounded like she already knew.

Sarah rushed across the room and knelt before her daughter. On her knees before the shelf that was also a window seat, Sarah and Emma's heads stopped at the same place so Sarah could look deep into her daughter's dazzling green eyes. Searching for the truth or at least a passing lie that would ease her worries.

"Emma. I need you to be honest with me now, okay?" Sarah asked, almost pleadingly.

"Of course, Momma," the child said, having to tear her gaze away from the neighbor's backyard fence. She could just see the police outside their cars talking to an elderly lady and her husband. They didn't look familiar to Emma, who had spent a fair amount of time watching this house, but the MacGregors had always had a lot of friends from church coming over. At least that's what Sarah had told her when she asked why there had been so many people always coming and going.

"Emma, I need you to tell me if you've gone to the MacGregor's recently? Maybe before you and I took that long nap before Auntie Jess came?" Sarah asked her, placing her hands on her daughter's shoulders gently. Not wanting to hurt the child but wanting to make sure that she couldn't turn away when she answered.

"It was six days, Momma," Emma's voice answered happily, as if she didn't have a care in the world.

At first Sarah couldn't say anything. She was confused all of a sudden and didn't know what the child meant. Then she realized and her mouth fell open in disbelief.

"We slept for six days? But that's impossible. We would have woken up to eat or drink or go potty," Sarah said flatly.

"Nothing is impossible, silly mommy," the child said and tried to turn back to the window once more, but Sarah held her shoulders tight and Emma grimaced. She wasn't used to not getting her way.

"Before we slept, did you go next door? Were you mad at Mrs. MacGregor for coming over and asking about the cats, so you went to pay her a visit?" Sarah asked and with each word her fingers dug a little tighter into Emma's shoulders.

"Ow, Momma, you're hurting me." The child's voice sounded angry and Sarah could feel a small electric current start to build.

"I'm sorry," she said, and loosened her grip, just a bit, on Emma's tiny frame. "But you need to tell me the truth. I'm your mommy, right? It's my job to protect you, but I need to know what you need protecting from."

"Please be honest with us, Emma, you're our family and family is always honest with each other, right?" Jess spoke up from her place by the door where she had stopped as Sarah had knelt down in front of Emma just a few seconds before.

The child sat for a second, looking from mother to auntie and back to mother again. As if she was considering the truth to what Jess had said. Finally, Emma's head nodded, just once, and the child began to speak.

"I did go next door. Mrs. MacGregor was gonna make trouble, so I played a game with them. It was really fun, and they both played super great! But, I didn't hurt them. I didn't have to. It was easy to get them to do all the work for me." The child's voice sounded happy, and Jess and Sarah shivered at the same time. It was as if they were twins instead of born two years apart. Aside from their hair being just a little different in color.

"Are they," Sarah began and then gulped. "Emma, are they dead?"

"Oh, yes." Emma's eyes were big and blazed gloriously at this admission. "Mrs. MacGregor finally stood up to him. Really, she should have done it years ago." The child shrugged and finally turned away. Sarah's hands dropped to her knees, and she sat back onto her bottom. "Will the police come here?" Jess asked as she walked over and sat down next to the child on the comfy window seat.

"Nope." Emma's voice was matter of fact. "But I wonder what will happen to the cat."

Jess and Sarah exchanged looks of relief and alarm all mixed into one. They both knew that something would have to be done, but they didn't know what. They both took comfort in the fact that neither of them was alone in this and Jess was glad that she had come. She hated that Sarah had had to carry this burden alone for who knows how long. Time had seemed to stop counting for Sarah and she couldn't say for sure how long Emma had been like this.

"Sarah, you go jump in the shower. Emma and I are going to get dressed and go shopping," Jess said in her best fun auntie voice as she stood and scooped up the kid. Then she brought her over to her bed and tossed her high in the air. The child laughed as she flew and fell onto the mattress.

"Yay!" the child said in an excited voice. "Mommy never takes me shopping anymore. Can we go to the toy store, too?" she asked. "Only if you're good at the grocery store. We're gonna make breakfast and dinner today," Jess said. "Now you get dressed and I'll meet you in front of the TV when I'm ready, okay?"

"Okay," the child agreed with an exaggerated nod and a happy grin across her face.

"C'mon, Momma! We gotta get you in the shower so I can get this shopping trip started." Jess pulled on Sarah's arms, helping her to stand and ushering her to the door as the child began to dig through her dresser. "Don't forget to brush your teeth," she called back over her shoulder as she maneuvered the shocked Sarah around the corner and down the hall.

"Okey dokey," the child called back.

Both women couldn't help but smile at the simple sound of a happy child excited for the day to come. They were good people, were Sarah and Jess. Beneath the fear and confusion of the nightmare they now found themselves in was love for the child. For Sarah that love was even deeper, because for Sarah it was also the love a mother has for her offspring. But Jess' love for Emma was almost as deep. You can't deny an auntie's devotion to her niece, either.

"Are you sure you can handle this? I don't think you know what you're getting yourself into," Sarah whispered to her sister as they entered her bedroom and closed the door behind them.

"I got this, little sis, don't worry," Jess said, her voice somber and hearing it said so helped calm Sarah's nerves a bit.

"If you make her mad, you won't like what happens. And I'm worried about you. She needs me, but she doesn't need you," Sarah pleaded with Jess. Trying to warn her of the true danger that lay before her.

"Sarah, it's okay. Look, I believe everything you told me last night. I do. And I believe -" Jess stopped, and Sarah could see her throat working as her sister gulped. "I believe she is responsible for the police being next door." Her voice had dropped to a whisper so low that Sarah could hardly hear her. "But whatever else she is, she's still Emma. I believe that, too. And I know you do as well because I saw the worry on your face when you heard those sirens. Even if something is living inside of her, some darkness, some evil, Emma is still there, too. Somewhere. Your dreams prove it. Emma would never let anything bad happen to either one of us. She loves me the most out of everyone in the world after you and her daddy."

Sarah's face jerked back a bit, as if slapped, at the mention of her poor dead husband. She found herself wondering for probably the millionth time how things would be different if he were still here with them. But at least now that Jess was here, she was no longer alone. She felt saner, somehow. Just having someone who believed her was a help.

"I love you, Jess. Just be careful. And take my wallet. Buy whatever you want, it never goes empty. My pin number is nine five two seven, but there's cash as well," Sarah said with a sigh. She was actually starting to look forward to the long shower and she hoped that their shopping trip would go well. She planned on staying in the hot water for as long as she possibly could.

"Wait, what?" Jess asked, suddenly even more confused. "You know how I had a lump sum from the insurance policy and the money that dad had left?" Sarah asked as she got up to walk toward the bathroom. Jess nodded and so she continued. "Well, the amount never goes down. Not since Emma changed. It took me a while to realize it, and I know it sounds crazy, but it never does. Even the cash in my wallet is the same as it was. No matter how much I put in or take out, the next time I open it, it's the same amount as was there before. Seventy-three dollars and sixteen cents. I don't remember the exact date of her change, but I will always remember that number because I've counted it out more times than I could even say."

"Woah." Jess' voice was full of astonishment. "Talk about silver fucking linings!" she exclaimed. "I wonder if this miracle extends to favorite aunties as well?"

Sarah shrugged and turned on the water. Then she turned to her sister, who had stopped at the bathroom door, and met her gaze with a stern and warning look.

"Be careful. I stopped taking her out. I hope you don't have any problems, but please, just be careful. Not just for you, or her, but for others." Sarah stood there, her hand on the pocket door and when her sister slowly nodded she pulled it closed and began to undress. She really couldn't wait to climb in the shower and wash her hair. The smell of her shower gel called to her and she answered the call, gratefully.

16

Jess was proud of herself for her ability to accept all of this with so much grace and only a hint of mind-boggling terror. Their grandmother had come from Ireland when she was a small child and her own mother had brought all of their rich Irish folklore with them. She was afraid of her children losing the most special part, or so she believed it to be, of their heritage when they left for America, so she had placed a visit with her own nana before their departure.

She had loved her Nana dearly and remembered with fondness all of her wonderful tales. Stories of beautiful mermaid sirens and their prized jewel. If a man were to find that jewel, they would win her as a prize. A bride to bear his children and make him rich and keep his home. But, if she ever were to find her precious stone again, she would abandon that life for the sea, leaving behind her husband and children for the call of the ocean's great blue depths.

Tales of the Pooka. Mischievous evil creatures with yellow eyes and the ability to turn into any shape they like. They were beasts of the night who favored to show up as goblins with sharp, pointy teeth or black goats with twisted horns. They demanded portions of the hard-working people's harvests and enjoyed playing tricks on the people they were terrorizing. They were scary to think about as a child when you couldn't sleep in those darkest hours of the night.

Then there were the kingdoms of the fairies. They were a mostly beautiful race of musical beings who loved to sing and dance. Their kingdoms could be found in mounds or caves, and they were quite good at baking and weaving and hunting. But there were evil fairies, too. Ones who would steal away children or curse you with bad luck. The fairy world was rich and diverse and interesting.

Also, there were the trickster leprechauns who hid gold at the end of rainbows and upon capture would grant you three wishes. But you had to be careful with what you wished because they loved to twist your words and turn your wishes into regrets. And there were banshees who appeared to warn of death to come. They would take the form of a beautiful maiden or withered old hag and could be found near rivers washing the blood from the clothes of those who would soon depart their mortal coil.

Another terrifying beast was the Kelpie. Appearing to children as a marvelous looking horse or foal, it would entice them to climb on their back and once there, the child would then become stuck to the
creature's body. Unable to escape, the Kelpie would take them to a bog or other body of water and drown the unlucky lad or lass before devouring their corpse. Leaving only the quieted, unbeating heart and liver behind.

These stories and so many others were important to Jess' grandmother's mother as she had heard them her whole life and when visiting her Nana for that last tear-filled time, she had her retell every single one at least once to ensure they were all stuck in her mind. She meant to raise a generation of children who knew these stories as she did. Who would love them and care for them as if they were family, for, in her mind, they were. They were an important part of who they were and no matter where life took them in the world, she meant to take them, too.

She stayed with her Nana for a week and three days and still felt as if she needed more time. But time had ran out and with a last hug goodbye she left with her husband and small children, with one on the way, to their new beginning. But she had kept her vow to raise her own with the tales of their land. They grew up loving this special part of who they were and never doubted the existence of these creatures or their role to play in the universe of things. In turn they raised their own children with the words of their mother's Nana and their children's children. So, it was no great mystery why Jess and Sarah took what was happening to them and to Emma with such great ease, even though fear was also present. To them the world was full of magic and myths were real. To them this wasn't unbelievable at all.

"What should we make for dinner tonight?" Jess asked as she locked the front door behind her and the child.

"Cake!" the child laughed.

"Cake, huh?" Jess returned the laughter and took the child's hand as they walked down the sidewalk to where her car was parked in the driveway.

"Yes! Chocolate cake with red icing!" said Emma's voice, happy at the idea of it.

"Ooooo! I know! How about we make hamburger cake?" Jess asked, remembering the dish from her childhood. "Your mom used to love it when our momma made it for us."

"Hamburger cake?" The child's voice was confused but interested. "What's hamburger cake?"

Jess opened the back door and folded down the center console which turned into a booster seat. She had bought this car just for that feature a few years ago with her niece in mind. "It sounds gross and icky, I know!" Jess said, scrunching up her face as she moved aside for the child to climb in and buckle up. "But, it's actually super good! You make a kind of meatloaf and put it in a cake pan. After it's cooked you slice it in half and fill it with mashed potatoes mixed with cheddar cheese. Then you put the top back on and cover the whole thing with ketchup and bake it a little bit more. When it's done, it's a delicious cake you can eat for dinner."

The child took a second to consider what her aunt had just said. "Can we put candles on it?" she finally asked.

"Yes!" Jess exclaimed happily. "Emma, you're a genius. I'll even let you pick out the candles!"

Emma clapped as Jess closed the door and a few minutes later they were off to the store. Jess put on a station with silly kids' songs, and they sang along to the ones they knew. It was a pretty great start to their morning, and both were looking forward to the day ahead. Neither of them could predict how this trip would end.

They pulled up to the grocery store. It was one of the fancy kinds which prided itself on a wide selection of non-GMO products, a huge variety of gluten-free choices and eggs from chickens who lived cage free, on top of the normal items found in every other grocery store chain. The child loved this store because there were always ladies wearing hair nets and plastic gloves handing out tiny portions of all kinds of delicious delectables. It had been a while since Sarah brought her shopping, though, choosing instead to have their groceries and household items delivered. Which was quite boring to the child. Sarah couldn't be held in any negative regard for this, however, because each time she had ventured out into the world with the child in tow, bad things had happened around them.

"Yay! It's the free sample store!" Emma's voice was excited as they slowed to a stop in a parking space up front. "I love this place! Mommy doesn't take me anymore."

"Why not?" Jess asked as she turned off the engine and unbuckled her seatbelt.

"Because of the worker guy who told me to stop running. He slipped off his ladder and hit his head on a shelf. I think he died," the little girl said matter-of-factly, and Jess paused in the act of opening her door.

"He died?" Jess asked, to which the child just shrugged and unbuckled her own seat.

"And this other time a mean old lady glared at me 'cause I was crying because Momma wouldn't let me get a ball 'cause I was making bad-asking choices so a shelf fell on her," Emma's voice added as if she were talking about nothing more important than the weather.

Jess sat for a second, thinking, and then turned around in her seat so that she could face her niece. "Emma." Her voice was stern, an odd thing for Jess when speaking to her most favorite kid in the whole world. "You're gonna be on your best behavior today, right?" The child nodded gravely. "And you're not going to throw any temper tantrums, right?" Jess continued and Emma's head shook side-to-side, her eyes never leaving Jess'. "Okay. If you're good and nobody gets hurt, I'll take you to the toy store and you can pick anything you want that costs less than fifty dollars, okay?" Jess finished, using every aunties' favorite method of behavior control in children, bribery.

Emma's bright green eyes grew large, and a happy grin spread across her face. "You're the bestest, most awesomest auntie in the whole wide world!" the child gushed.

"You have to promise to be good first, okay?" Jess prompted.

"I double super-duper promise!" The child hopped up and down in her seat as she assured her aunt that everything was going to be okay.

Jess nodded and smiled warmly. "What are we waiting for then?" she asked, and they both got out of the car and headed into the store, hand in hand.

The bakery was just past the carts as you walked into the building and the child ran to the window displaying all of the beautiful cakes. Sarah had told her she could get one for her birthday next year and she already knew the one she wanted. It was tall and covered in real hardened chocolate and it had chocolate dipped strawberries on top laying in fluffy white clouds of whipped cream. They had one like that now and the child smiled happily. But the reason that she really loved the bakery section was because they would give you a cookie if you asked nicely. Her favorite thing in the world was food; she loved the textures and flavors as she chewed and then swallowed with her human mouth and teeth and tongue.

"Excuse me, miss, but may I please have a cookie?" the child asked in her sweetest little kid voice as Jess walked up behind her, pushing a dark brown cart. They both stared as the bakery lady continued unloading a box of what looked like cake toppers into a bin on a counter where cakes were made.

"I don't think she heard you, toots," Jess said.

"Uhm. Excuse me, please." Emma's voice was louder and a little less sweet this time around. "Can I please have a cookie?" Still the lady unloading the box did not turn around and Jess and the child both stood, staring with matching frowns. Jess because she really wanted this shopping trip to be a good one, and the child because she really, really wanted that free cookie.

"Excuse me!" Jess tried, a lot louder than what was maybe socially acceptable, but at this point not caring. She just wanted to keep the kid in the cool zone and now she kinda wanted a cookie, too. The woman behind the counter jumped and turned. She used one hand to take out the wireless earbud she had been listening to and Jess laughed. "Emma, that's why she couldn't hear us, she was listening to music while she worked."

"That's not very nice." Emma's voice held a hint of disdain, but also, relief.

The woman flushed and looked embarrassed as she walked up to the counter. "I'm so sorry," she said happily enough. "This isn't my department. Our baker called in with a family emergency this morning. Her son was in a horrible car accident last night. It was super sad. So, I'm just unpacking some stuff for her while she's gone."

"Oh, my god," Jess said, suddenly not wanting a cookie anymore.

"May I please have a cookie?" the child asked, undeterred.

The woman behind the counter frowned down at the child, "I'm sorry, kiddo, but we don't have any cookies behind the counter today." The woman knew that she could simply walk over to the ones for sale from yesterday's batch. They were in bunches of twelve in thin plastic containers not too far behind where the red headed demon child (the woman hated kids and this one seemed particularly annoying to her) stood, but the uncaring way she had asked for the cookie, almost a demand, really ruffled the woman's feathers. The woman made it a habit to not give in to pint-sized terrorists like this one.

The child looked up at the woman, an angry line forming in her forehead and Jess could feel a small bit of electricity starting to jump out from her. Warning bells began to ring in Jess' ears, and she knelt down next to her niece and swiveled Emma's small frame so that she was looking eye to eye at Jess instead of the lady behind the counter.

"It's okay, you can pick out a package of cookies and we'll have even more than one that way! We can dunk them in milk when we get home! They can be scuba cookies and the milk can be shark-infested waters," Jess said. It only took a second for the anger to drain from Emma's eyes and the air to neutralize back to its more normal self.

"Have a nice day," the woman behind the counter almost sneered as she watched this pitiful display. It was parenting like this that created spoiled brats. Shameful, really, the woman thought as she watched the red headed woman usher the kid over to the packaged cookies. I hope they're all stale, she added to herself as she put back in her earbud and turned back to her work.

"These ones!" the child said with excitement as she found the pack she wanted. It was the kind that had brightly colored candies instead of chocolate chips. Jess smiled down at the happy look on Emma's face as she carefully placed the cookies into the cart. Kids were lucky that such simple things could make them so happy. "Can we get chocolate milk for the dunking part?" the child asked, and Jess smiled wide and nodded.

"That just may be the best idea I've ever heard in my whole life," she said and ruffled her niece's unruly hair. "My whole entire life!" she added, and they walked to the dairy section, which was in front of them at the back of the store.

When they got there a man in his early thirties was just standing back up from where he had leaned over to grab the last jug of delicious- looking chocolate milk. The child watched longingly as he placed it in his cart. Drips of condensation were welling up on the outside and the rich, dark brown liquid looked even more tantalizing through them.

"Sir," the child spoke up, again trying to sound as sweet as possible. "You took the very last one." She did her best to give him the most adorable puppy dog eyes she could muster, outside of having them look like actual eyes from a furry baby dog.

"Oh, yeah! Sorry, kid! I love the stuff." The man shrugged and began to walk away. The child looked up at Jess, her eyes beginning to well up with tears. It was hard to be good when you weren't used to having to, but the child, for some reason she couldn't quite put her finger on, really wanted to make Auntie Jess proud and earn that toy. A fifty-dollar shopping spree sounded like a million bucks to her kid ears, and she wanted to prove to her auntie and herself that she could do it. Change was hard.

"Aw, kid, I'm proud of you, you're doing great," Jess said and smiled. "We can get regular milk and chocolate sauce and make our own!"

"Yeah!" the child agreed, appeased by the solution, but looked longingly after the man as he turned a corner into an aisle. How much she wanted a wheel to fall off his cart in a way that would cause him to fall over, toppling the cart and spilling the milk all over him. She smiled as she thought about it. The air began to grow heavy with electricity once more as she envisioned a gush of thick, chocolate deliciousness flooding into his nose and mouth and she could almost see him choking on it. She could almost hear him gasping for air and only sucking in more of the dark brown liquid. A trickle of blood from his busted upper lip he got from the fall mixing in with the milk and adding a hint of color to her already vivid imagining.

Out of their sight, the man's cart began to wobble a bit as the front right wheel began to shake. Jess turned when she realized the air was once again electric and she tapped Emma's shoulder, releasing the child's concentration and dissipating the thickness that had been gathering around Emma in an invisible cloud. The man's cart leveled back out, leaving him unaware of the disaster that almost befell him.

"Which kind does your mommy buy?" Jess asked, knowing it was the light blue fat free one on the lowest shelf, but needing a way to get her niece's attention off of that bit of space where the man had disappeared down the aisle.

"I'll get it." Emma's voice was happy again. Just thinking about what she had wanted to happen and seeing it in her mind's eye had been enough to quell her anger at the man for now.

They continued shopping for breakfast and dinner pretty uneventfully until they made it to the meat department. There, a friendly looking little old lady wearing a bright red apron stood behind a small cloth covered table with tiny squares of pizza in little white cupcake wrappers. As Jess got what she needed for the hamburger cake, the child rushed over to the lady behind her booth and began to reach out for one of the samples. She had her eyes on the biggest piece she could see. It was in the back row and had the most cheese floating atop a bright red layer of marinara sauce. On top, as if a cherry on a sundae, sat a slice of pepperoni that had slightly burnt edges and was cupped up around a round ball of scrumptious looking sausage like it were holding its very own little meat baby.

The child loved burnt pepperoni on her pizzas and her mouth watered at the sight of it. Just as her fingers were about to close around the white cupcake liner, her tongue pursed in her lips as she anticipated the bite to come, a sudden loud smacking sound followed by a small burst of pain erupted from her hand. The elderly lady looked down at the child with an angry look on her face and pointed at the child with the same hand that she had used to slap Emma's smaller one.

"That is very rude to take something without asking," the woman said. Her voice a little high pitched and exasperated sounding. "Where is your mother?" she demanded, shaking her head as if she had just witnessed some hysterical and uncalled for behavior when in reality the child was actually being very good by her normal standards.

Tears welled up in Emma's bright green eyes and anger began to course through her body. She was so exasperated at this morning's trip. It was supposed to be fun, and she had been so excited to come here. Now she just wanted to go home, and she didn't care about the toy store at all. The child then did something that she had never done before in the real genuine sense where she wasn't just trying to manipulate those around her. The child began to cry.

It was a real emotion of sadness and confusion and fear. She was confused at why the woman would hit her for just taking a sample, something she had done before with encouragement. She was confused at why the man had taken the last chocolate milk even though she had wanted it and he was a grown up and she was just a little kid. She was sad at the pain and confused at why she felt so adamantly that she should not be getting back at all of them right now. She wanted nothing more but to make her mommy and Auntie Jess happy. She didn't want to let them down and that was the most confusing thing of all.

The child had liked other parents she had had before Sarah; it was rare, but it had happened. The silly couple in Baton Rouge who tried very hard to figure out why their daughter had suddenly changed and had tried to fix her by feeding her ice cream and going to the theme park. That had ended badly with a roller coaster car derailing after the attendant said that she couldn't ride because she wasn't tall enough. The guy had been super nice about it, and he had pointed out the funny looking cartoon woodpecker that was holding the tall sign that said you had to be this tall to ride and it had been so tall that she could barely reach it with her outstretched hand reached as high up as she could reach, even on tippy toes. She had liked the rollercoaster guy well enough and had seen that he really did mean it when he said it was the park's rule and not his, so she had spared him the lesson and taken out her frustrations, instead, on the car full of smiling people who got to leave as she stood there staring longingly after them, being forced to remain behind. Her then-daddy had been one of the people in that coaster car and his death had made her then mommy very sad and angry at her.

That's when the child had stopped liking her and had had to move on. After the then mommy had tried to hurt her with a knife and had instead fallen on it hard after swiping it at the child, unsuccessfully. The knife had lodged through her sternum as she fell and barely missed her beating heart. The child stood over her and watched as the woman had bled to death. Her mouth had opened and closed and opened and closed like a fish lying on the sandy beach, trying to breathe the air that was foreign to it. The then mommy had died like that, and the child had abandoned her host.

Sally had been aware of everything and when suddenly she had been thrown back into control of herself, she laid down next to her mommy, who she loved very much, and cried until she fell asleep. Eventually she had woken up, covered in her mother's sticky semi-dried blood and walked out the front door. She had only been just shy of five years old and still didn't know how to work a cell phone to call for help. To her, it was just a portal to games and hilarious picture filters. She and her mommy had often taken funny pics of themselves, and the phone had turned them into puppies or bunnies

168

or even scary monsters at Halloween time. That was before the real-life monster had come to live inside of Sally. That was when they had all still been a happy family.

It had been very early in the morning when Sally went walking down the sidewalk for help. The sun had just crept up and a nice jogger lady had come across the girl as she walked in a shock-filled daze. Her blonde hair was matted with the blood of her mother and the whole right side of her face had been covered in it. That was the side she had fallen asleep on as she cried. It was a sight that the jogger lady would never forget. *Could* never forget.

There had also been the nice gay couple in Vermont. They hadn't had their daughter for very long and so they assumed the child was acting up because of past trauma. Laci, their adopted little girl, had really never experienced any trauma before her body had been suddenly hijacked and she had been forced to watch uncontrollably as the child took over her limbs and invaded her mind. Laci had lost her parents in a fire. It had been scary and very traumatic, but it hadn't been abuse that caused her nightmares before the child came to call.

At first it had just been little things; the cat had gone missing, and they assumed that Laci had accidentally let Mr. Wigglemunster out when she went into the back yard to play. Houseplants began to wither up and die and the fish in the downstairs playroom all went belly up in the same afternoon. Andy and Greg whispered to each other, wondering if maybe Laci had poured something toxic into the planters and the tank, but they couldn't see how because they had carefully locked away all of the poisonous chemicals, as well as the knives and medications.

Next, they noticed that the neighbors who played their music too loud on Friday nights suddenly stopped making any noise at all and after the parents of one of them had an officer make a well check on their house next door, they were found totally decapitated in pools of their own blood. The police had eventually made a statement that the couple had decapitated each other, using their last dying breaths to get the jobs done. Something that seemed like an impossibility to both Andy and Greg. They added the thoughts that the child might be responsible for murder into their late-night

169

whispers. The first time that Laci had shown up in the living room as they watched some romcom that Andy loved but Greg only tolerated, assuming that she had been asleep for a few hours now, completely covered in blood, their paranoid whispers seemed to be less paranoia and more fact.

They didn't know how to deal with having a monster for a child, but they had grown to love her in the short time that they had had Laci. Mostly because of the bright and wonderful kid she had been before the child had come into the picture. The second time the child had come home drenched in filth and blood, Greg had had enough. He put his foot down even though Andy thought it was a bad idea.

Andy was terrified of the child by this point. He never left drinks setting around where they could be easily poisoned by their mousy little daughter with the wavy brown hair and bright brown eyes that seemed so much more alive than they had when they had first picked her up. But Greg was out of nice ideas, and he thought that maybe discipline would do the trick. It was more desperation than anything.

They had wanted so desperately to have a family and all of their visits with Laci prior to the adoption going through had been extremely happy affairs. She had seemed to be working through the guilt and anger and fear and sadness that the loss of her parents had caused her, and she seemed willing to accept them as family. So, the fact that it all had suddenly changed was confusing to the two loving men who only wanted to create a home full of happy memories.

"Laci, enough is enough," Greg had told her that second time that she had turned up bloody and covered in mud and something far more foul, by the smell. They had all been watching cartoons together in the den. It had been a relatively nice morning without any tantrums or outbursts and they were hoping that perhaps this would be the turning point as the day before had been easy going as well.

Greg and Andy had gotten super tired and had both leaned against one another, as they had since they met seven years ago during the Love Vermont volunteer clean up event, and they had

170

fallen peacefully to sleep. It was rare for them as of late to not have nightmares terrorizing their slumber and so they slept within a veil of comfort. They awoke sometime later. The light had changed drastically against the wall and Laci had been standing before them grimy and holding a worn brown teddy bear of which neither of them had ever seen before.

"You can't leave like this by yourself, it isn't safe and we just want to keep you safe," Andy almost pleaded, kneeling beside the child with a worried look upon his face.

"And you can't keep hurting things." Greg's voice was drenched in anger more than the fear that his partner's voice held, and he was sad and upset that the child they finally had been able to add to their home, the child that was supposed to on some grander level complete them, had turned out to be so, well, bad. Nevertheless, Greg was in it for the long haul, as he held his commitments in high regard, and he and Andy both felt that you should never give up on a child. Especially your own, and they both loved Laci like their own. To them she *was* their own.

"Is it animals?" Andy asked gently, though the teddy bear she held made him terrified to hear her answer. "Are you angry about your parents and so you take it out on animals?" He hoped, even though it was a grisly thing to hope for, it felt like the best option, all things considered.

The child had just smiled a bright and happy smile and turned and actually skipped toward the bathroom. Each hop she made left a tiny red smear on the dark and shiny hardwood floor and something snapped inside of Greg.

"You will not walk away from us like that!" he had called after her, almost a scream. "We are your parents now. You need to respect us so that we can help you."

"We're not trying to take the place of your real parents, sweetie," Andy added, trying to soften his husband's harsher tone.

"Bubble bath, please," was the child's response. That same happy smile across her lips, only now it also seemed smug as well as cheerful. Her brown eyes blazed out at them, and they knew that they were close to some invisible tipping point. They could feel it in the air. An electric current starting to emanate out of her toward

171

them. Andy's heart began to race, and Greg was even more determined to win this battle of wills. If he did not, he was worried about what it would mean for the girl's future. He was terrified that she would grow to kill humans and not just animals like their poor Mr. Wigglemunster, if she hadn't already, that was. There was just something about that teddy bear that cried out that it was far too late for them to stop her from crossing that threshold already.

"No. No more bubble baths. You can take a shower, but you're grounded for a week. Starting from right now until next Saturday night. No bubble baths, no cartoons, no special desserts or breakfasts with sprinkles and whipped cream. You can listen to music instead of the TV and no devices." Greg's voice had the edge of finality that he hadn't yet used on his new daughter, and he hated how it sounded as it came out across his lips, but he knew they had been spoiling her. Children needed boundaries, too, and they would just have to find a balance between both of those things.

The child stared at them for a moment that seemed to drag on and on but in reality, had only lasted a few seconds and then she began to laugh. A chilling sound in the thickening air and as the sound tinkled out of her, the TV on the wall behind them made a popping sound and the screen turned black. Andy and Greg both jumped at the noise and looked behind them, both of their mouths round o's of shock and their eyes large with fear.

"I want a bubble bath, please," the child spoke again. Her words no longer happy and instead oozed with warning and demand.

"Okay, honey, come on, I'll get you a bubble bath," Andy said and started toward the bathroom doorway.

"No." Greg's voice was soft but firm and Andy stopped and turned to look at him.

"It's just a bath, Greg. How can you ground a child from a bath?" he asked.

"No bubble baths for one week. She can take a shower," Greg repeated.

Suddenly the child screamed. A high-pitched scream of anger, and the floor actually shook. She had thought she liked it here with these two men. They had been kind and giving and not too bossy. But now Daddy Greg was being mean, and she didn't like it anymore. She didn't like *him* anymore. She began to stomp her feet as the scream went on. Andy smashed his palms into his ears to protect them from that sound that seemed to be shaking his skull with the mere vibration of it. But Greg stood firm and planted his hands on his hips with his legs spread wide. His posture telling her that he would not be moved by her display of defiance. That was when the ground really began to shake.

It jerked hard to the left, and then the right, knocking Andy off balance, and he almost fell onto the floor. He would have, in fact, had it not been for the staircase banister next to him. Greg was able to keep his balance, though he did have to take two large steps backward to do so. And still he stood firm, his eyes blazing with an inner light of their own. The two locked gazes, the child and Greg. Both of their wills fighting against each other's and both determined to win this battle.

"I don't like you, anymore. I only like Daddy Andy," the child said and when the last word of that sentence left her lips there was a loud splitting sound as if a tree had fallen right here in the entryway between the den, the hallway and the stairwell. But it wasn't a tree at all. A huge beam came crashing through the ceiling just above Greg's head and Andy inhaled a breath to call the warning, but it was too late. The heavy chunk of wood fell hard onto the top of Greg's head, caving in his skull with so much force that Andy watched as both of his eyes bulged out of their sockets, swinging a little as he was pushed forcefully to the ground. A puddle of blood began to form around his dead corpse almost immediately as it trickled out from his mouth and nose and eyes and broken skull.

Andy stood there in shock at what he had just witnessed. His heart shrank up into a ball so tiny and dried out that his chest burned with grief and fear. The child walked across the small distance between where she had been standing and where Andy leaned against the highly polished wood of the banister and took his trembling hand in hers.

"Bubble bath, please," she said, again cheerful as if she didn't have a care in the world. She tugged on Andy's hand, and he had followed in a daze. He made her bath warm and full of bubbles,

173

just how she liked. He hadn't even bothered to rinse her off first like he would have normally before getting the water dirty with all that covered her. He just plopped her in when it was done, and she had undressed.

After she was in her bath, Andy silently left the room, closing the door behind him. She continued to bathe and didn't even startle a few minutes later when the sound of the gunshot crashed through the house upstairs. She calmly finished her bath and then climbed out when the water finally started to cool. She wrapped herself up in a giant white towel and crept slowly up the stairs to her room. Once she was dressed in her most comfiest jammies, the ones with the little pink puppies chasing tiny red bouncing balls, she climbed into her bed, tired from the day's many twists and turns.

It was about four days later when the little girl awoke, scared and alone. The child had slipped away in the dark and Laci was left in the house with the corpses of her dead adopted daddies. She was terrified to go downstairs and stayed locked in her room for two more days before someone finally came to check on why they hadn't been answering their phones. Thankfully there was a small half bathroom attached to her room where she had been able to drink from her tiny pink plastic cup with the purple elephant smiling happily on the front. Otherwise, she may have had to risk going downstairs, and she didn't think her heart could take seeing another dead parent, lying there on the floor.

There had been many others she had liked more over the years, and many she had hated from the very beginning. Parents who rejected her from the moment they saw her too bright eyes and those who waited a while before deciding to give up. Sarah had lasted the longest and the child had never had feelings like this before toward anyone. She didn't know exactly what love was, but part of her whispered that maybe how she felt toward Sarah, and even Auntie Jess, could be it. So, she cried before the old woman who had slapped her hand because she was confused at the turmoil that was going on inside of her. She wanted so badly to make Auntie Jess proud, and for Auntie Jess to go home and brag to Sarah about how good she had been at the store. She wanted Sarah to smile and hold out her arms for her to run into and to hear Sarah to tell her how much she loved her and how happy she was that she had been so good. Restraint was not the child's strong suit, though, and so she cried, too, with frustration.

"Aw, now, what kind of monster makes a little girl cry like that?" a man's voice spoke up to the child's left and the woman in the red apron frowned.

"She was grabbing at the sample without even asking and it was very rude and unsanitary, too. Instead of taking one in the front she reached over all of them to get one in the back. She could have gotten germs over all of them that way," the woman huffed.

"So, you slapped her?" the man's voice asked incredulously. "I don't even think that's legal! You can't just lay your hand on someone else's kid like that."

The child looked up at the man who had come to her rescue and smiled a grateful smile. He was tall and handsome with hair almost the same color as her own and thick black rimmed glasses over soft hazel eyes. She suddenly liked this man very much and as quickly as they had come, her tears dried up in her eyes.

"Fine, here," the older woman huffed and grabbed a square of pizza that was closest to the child's face, which popped up just above the top of the tablecloth.

"Oh, come now, surely you can do better than that." The man laughed, a good-natured laugh and pointed at the sad little slice the woman held in her gloved hand. "There's hardly any cheese on that piece. Kids don't like pizza for the sauce." The man reached to the back row and grabbed the piece that the child had had her eye on when she first came up to the table. "She'll take this one, and this one aaaaand this one, too," he said and plucked two more choice pieces off the cloth and handed them all to the little redheaded girl who he had helped to turn her frown upside down. Finding that her smile was contagious, a grin spread across his handsome face which revealed two dimples at either end of it.

"Well, I guess I can see where she gets her spoiled, entitled behavior from," the woman remarked snarkily and sneered at the man, anger flushing her cheeks as well as embarrassment from having had someone catch her slap the child's hand. Something she had not done on purpose, but out of instinct. When her children were small there was absolutely no way she would have let them get away with that type of unruly behavior. Parents these days were ruining an entire generation, as far as she could tell.

"Oh, I wish I was lucky enough to have such a cute kid," the man said and as Jess walked up, he winked at her in a way that should have come off as unnerving but was instead quite appealing. "I think that she must belong to this beautiful lady right here, if I'm not mistaken. The resemblance is uncanny."

Jess stared at him, unimpressed with his charms, as to her he was just some strange creepazoid who was talking to her niece in the store. "Can I help you?" she asked, her voice cold and on edge. He could tell that it contained a warning, and he knew that the whole situation could suddenly get away from him if he weren't careful.

"I'm sorry, miss, but this lady here made your daughter cry. She reminds me a bit of my little sister and so I couldn't help but come over and make sure she was okay. She slapped her hand for trying to get a sample, and in my book, that's pretty much wicked witch material." He dropped his gaze and kicked softly at the bright white tile he was standing on in a nonchalant way.

"You slapped my niece?" Jess turned to the woman behind the sample booth with raised eyebrows and cheeks that were starting to burn. "How dare you slap my niece! She's just a little kid and you have absolutely no right at all!" Jess stepped away from the cart and pulled Emma's small body behind her own. Then she walked up to the woman who was cringing back away from the angry redhead who was pushing her way into the table to get closer to her. The angry aunt pointed a single finger at the woman's chest and pressed it hard into her upper right breast with each word as she continued to speak. "If you want to take this out back, I'll show you what happens to someone who likes to slap little kids."

Now it was the older woman's turn to start to cry and frightened, angry tears burst forth from her tired-looking eyes and poured down her cheeks. She stood there for a moment, behind the table covered in tiny squares of pizza each in their own individual cupcake liner. Her face red and wet now with the streaks that were running down from her eyes.

She looked at the redheaded man and then the little girl peeking out from behind the curvy ginger woman with the mad face and then around where they stood. Searching the area for anyone who could back her up and tell her she was right. That the little girl should have known her place and not assumed that she could just take whatever she wanted.

That little kids these days should not be so loud and demanding. But all she saw in the eyes of the other patrons who had stopped to watch the spectacle go down was harsh judgement directed at her and her final straw of righteousness broke. She grabbed her apron with both of her hands and pulled it up to dry her eyes and hide the crumpled look of her face as she burst into even heavier crying. She turned from all of them who stood before her and around her, staring angrily at the woman who had laid her hand on such an adorable small child, and ran to the back and through the large brown swinging double doors.

"I'm so sorry," the man told Jess a few seconds after the woman had disappeared into the back. "I didn't mean to intrude. I saw that you were over there, and I knew that you hadn't seen what had happened. I just hated to let that woman get away with that. Nobody should hit a little kid just for taking a treat."

"He's a nice man, Auntie Jess. He got me the pizza." Emma's voice only held a hint of sadness. Mostly she felt proud at her auntie for sticking up for her to the mean old lady and her heart warmed to her fierce aunt a little more than it already had.

"Yeah, I'm a nice man. Cross my heart and hope to die," the man swore as he made a gesture of crossing his heart with his index finger and then held up two fingers in the time-honored traditions of scouts who were swearing true.

"And hope to die!" the child repeated excitedly through a mouthful of one of the slices of pizza. The man laughed, not noticing that Jess didn't seem to think it was funny, but a second later she joined in. His laughter was contagious, and she couldn't help herself. It felt good to laugh with someone. There had been so little of that in her life these past couple of days.

The man's name ended up being Ben. He and Jess spoke for a bit in the meat department as the child stood before the vacated sample table and ate to her heart's content. They talked about where they were from and why they were in town. Jess explained that she was staying with her sister, who was a widow, and Ben told her how he was visiting with his parents while his dad recuperated from surgery. Jess and Ben ended up having a lot in common and as the child started to get restless, she exchanged numbers with him before heading to the checkout. They had pretty much everything they needed, and Jess felt like they had avoided too many catastrophes already and that they were running on borrowed time.

When finally they made it out to the car, the child had even helped to unload, and both were buckled in Jess turned to her niece and smiled.

"Proud of you, kid," she said. "You handled all of those sticky situations like a champ."

The child giggled at the thought of the mean people she had encountered in the store being all sticky with ooey goo and everything they touched became a part of them until they grew bigger and bigger and -

"What's so funny?" Jess asked, her eyebrows raised.

"I was thinking about sticky situations." The child laughed and then her face got very serious. "Did I do it? Did I be good enough while I was in the store? Do I get a shopping prize now?"

"Yes! You were very, very good. Even though there were people in the store who were naughty. You definitely get a prize! Fifty whole dollars for anything you want. But what do you say we go home to check on your mommy and then after we unload the groceries you can show me how to order toys on the computer?" Jess used her best super excited voice, hoping that it would rub off on her niece so that she wouldn't have to repeat the exhausting walking on eggshells dance she had just performed in the grocery store.

"Yeah! I'm really good at it! Mommy lets me pick out stuff for shopping all the time," the child bragged and smiled. In truth, she didn't want to risk anymore shopping trips, either. She was relieved to have gotten through this one without making Auntie Jess angry. Thinking about the mean lady at the cookie counter and the man who had stolen the very last milk and the wicked old witch who guarded all the pizzas and slapped her hand made the child a little angry again. They had almost made it where she didn't get a prize, and even worse, they had almost made it to where Auntie Jess wasn't proud of her.

The child's gaze looked straight ahead at the store, and she could see them in her mind inside. The man with the chocolate milk was standing at the ice cream display looking at all of the flavors without a care in the world. The mean cookie lady was now in the canned food section, unloading cans of sweet peas onto a shelf, her head beating along to the music playing in her ears. Then there was the pizza witch who was now back at her booth, throwing away all of the empty wrappers and leftover squares so that she could disassemble the table and take it back into the storeroom.

"I won, right? I for realsies get my prize money on anything I want?" the child asked.

"Of course. I wouldn't lie to you about something as important as shopping," Jess said as she slid the key into the car's ignition.

What happened next happened so fast that in retrospect there really had been no way for Jess to stop it. The car filled with a thick electric feel that made the hair on Jess' arms stand on end and her teeth seemed to vibrate a little in her head. Then the ground beneath her car's tires jerked one way and then the other and then back again. The whole store wobbled with the shake. The roof jerked to the right then the left and then back to the right. But though the car stopped jerking, the roof of the store kept on sliding during that final sway. A great noise of metal ripping loose from metal filled the air around them and then the roof came crashing down, bringing the walls with it. A great cloud of dust and debris came rushing outward, crashing into cars and causing alarms to blare out into the morning air, but Jess' car remained untouched. Even of the dirt that seemed to cover all that was around them.

Inside the store they could see the shocked look of people standing up from where they had fallen or hid during the quake, or so the people thought it. Faces of shoppers covered in dirt with small cuts and bruises, all lucky to be alive. Through the cloud of filth still drifting down from above Jess could see Ben, standing where a checkout line had been. A piece of ceiling had fallen and wedged atop a tall shelf that had blocked him from the falling chunks of ceiling and wall and glass. His bright red hair and pale skin was even clean of the dust, though his face wore the same look of surprise as did everyone else's.

Later on, they would find out that only three people had perished among the thirty-two folks who had been inside the store during the surprise earthquake. A quake that had only affected that particular store out of all of the businesses downtown, and it was being considered as quite the miracle. The news would do reports on the three people who had died, and Jess recognized all of them.

Jarod Miles, a single man who enjoyed the nightlife and who loved chocolate milk. Chocolate milk had been the reason he had been in the store that day. He normally ordered his groceries online but had woken up with a craving for the stuff and had told his roommate he would just get all the things on their list while he was there. He left behind a dog but no other relatives. The roommate would keep the dog around for a few weeks and then tire of the incessant barking and take it to the pound. Luckily Banjo ended up finding a loving home with a man who loved to fish and had a hearing problem that made the barking a non-issue. He was just happy to have a friend around since losing his wife from cancer last winter.

Marjory Thomason had been working that day, though it had been her scheduled day off. Marge had gotten a phone call that they were shorthanded, and could she come in to stock shelves and prep the bakery for the emergency baker who would be coming in later on that afternoon. She was cool with it because she really could use the money. She was saving up to get her own place and get out of her sister's spare bedroom. Her sister's kids had been driving her crazy and she swore if she never seen another little kid again, it would be too soon.

Then there was Grace Elliot. Grace was scheduled to work that day and had shown up promptly on time, as she did every workday. She was a stickler for the rules and was the kind of woman that Ralph would have appreciated had he gotten to know her. She probably would have appreciated him, too. She had had seven kids, all of whom had grown up to be successful. She attributed their

180

success to her stern raising of them and the fact that not one of them had made her a grandmother hadn't bothered her at all in the least. None of them had had fond memories of their childhood and when their mother passed, they had felt a little sad about it, but weren't too taken aback in the scheme of things.

"I'm gonna get a doll house," Emma's voice drifted up to Jess' ears from the backseat. She sounded content and relieved. Jess just sat there as the dust settled. A look of disbelief on her own face. A few minutes later she slowly put the car into reverse, backed out, and headed for home. She absolutely did not want to be there when the police arrived. She didn't even know how to begin to explain the situation if she were asked.

17

The doll house ended up costing way more than fifty dollars, but Jess didn't care at that point. She wanted something extra fun so that she could have some time to talk to her sister without little ears nearby. Her only care was that it was something that could be delivered that day from the fulfillment center. They found one that came with one hundred and twenty-five accessories and Sarah insisted they use her card that was already attached to the account. Jess and Sarah had been left a decent-sized chunk of money, as was their mother, when their father died, but it didn't seem to matter anymore to Sarah since Emma's change, and Sarah didn't want her sister to spend so much money unnecessarily. Jess even insisted that they should get as many extras as they could because she was so proud of how well behaved her little Emma Bug had been in the store, when, really, she just wanted as much time as possible alone with Sarah.

While they waited for the packages with all of the child's new toys, as well as some household items Sarah threw into the cart before they were finished because she thought she might as well while they were at it, Jess nervously paced around the living room, chewing on her nails and checking her phone for the time. While she waited, Sarah fixed a big breakfast of rainbow pancakes and sausages and bacon.

The packages had still not arrived by the time the food was ready, so the two women sat across from the child as she ate. Jess pretended to be excited for the hearty meal, but Sarah could tell she was feigning interest and as they sat there Jess just took a few nibbles and then pushed around the food with her fork. Sarah could feel the tension rising off of Jess in waves and was reminded of how it was to be near Emma now when she was upset, and the air changed into something charged and ready to bite.

"Emma, take smaller bites, would ya?" Jess asked, a worried tone filling her voice.

"I won't choke," Emma's voice responded, muffled through a mouthful of syrup-covered purple and blue and pink bites of pancake.

"She won't, I promise," Sarah said, trying to keep her voice as casual as possible, but the anxiety that was seeping off of Jess was greatly troubling her and she was dying to know what had happened at the store. Sarah wasn't dumb by any means, and she knew that her sister had purchased such an elaborate gift to keep Emma busy while she filled her in.

Jess stared at her niece as she chewed the biggest mouthful of food she had ever seen and then watched as she swallowed. She gripped the edge of the table, ready to run to the other side of it when the obvious happened and her niece began to choke. She couldn't believe that Sarah was so relaxed about this new eating habit. Every other time Jess had witnessed her sister and her niece eating, Sarah was very careful to make sure Emma took tiny bites or she would cut everything up into small pieces. Now it was as if she didn't care if the kid breathed in a lung full of whipped cream and sprinkles. When the kid finally began to swallow, Jess understood Sarah's lax attitude about the whole thing.

Emma's mouth couldn't even close around the bite she had, and she was forcing more into her mouth with her fork. It was as if the child was starving and hadn't just eaten a whole pizza to herself last night on top of a few slices of the other two AND the entire free sample table at the store. Jess' nails bit into the shiny polished wood of the table and she watched Emma's throat work as she swallowed. It bulged out and Jess actually began to stand as she watched the lump of food travel down from below her chin to where her neck was attached to her torso. And still the kid shoved more and more food into her mouth. It was as if she didn't need to breath at all. It was as if her body was changing its natural shape to fit the food inside of it and get it to where it needed to be. Jess sat back down hard and for a while lost herself in the act of just watching her niece eat. It was mesmerizing and defied the laws of nature and for the rest of the meal she forgot about checking the time.

Jess had texted Ben earlier to make sure he was okay, and he had texted back almost immediately that he was fine. He couldn't believe what had happened and that nobody that he saw was hurt. It wasn't until later that he would find out that the pizza lady had been one of the three victims, and he would feel an odd mixture of guilt for having helped make her cry just before her death and relief that it wasn't someone nicer. Someone that didn't make it a habit of going around slapping the hands of innocent little kids. Ben thought it was odd that not a hair on his head had been harmed when everyone else seemed to get scratches or bumps and that not a single fleck of dust had even landed on him at all. Not even his shoes had gotten dirty in the collapse.

Jess told him how lucky they were as well and how their car hadn't gotten scratched even a little. When Ben asked her why they had left so quickly, Jess made up an excuse about not wanting her niece to see anything horrifying in case there were people who were hurt, and it seemed to make sense to Ben. She felt bad about lying, but how could she tell the truth? Even if she didn't like the guy and want him to like her, too, she couldn't have ever told the truth in fear for Emma's safety. She loved her niece and that was the most important thing to her right now, Emma's safety.

Just as Emma's tiny hand was forcing three whole sausage links into her child-sized mouth the doorbell rang. Jess checked her phone and smiled over at her sister with relief.

"Two hours almost on the dot!" she said and scooted back her chair to head for the door.

"Oh, no. You stay there until you're done eating and then you go straight to the bathroom and wash up and brush your teeth. All that syrup is going to rot them right out of your head if you don't," Sarah said to her daughter as she had started to get up from the table to follow after her aunt. The child frowned through her sausage chewing but stayed where she was. She swallowed the sausages in her mouth almost whole and Sarah had to look away as the chunk made it down her throat. Then the child jumped up from her chair and ran up the stairs as Jess closed the front door and began scooting a large box down the hall with her feet because her arms were full with two smaller ones.

"A little help," she called through the two boxes in her arms and Sarah grabbed them both and the two women headed to the living room to start unpacking. The child joined them a few minutes later, the smell of minty freshness heavy in the air around her head.

"Did you rinse?" Sarah asked and Emma's cheeks flushed red with the lie she couldn't quite muster up the courage to tell because she knew that Sarah would see right through it. "Go rinse," the mother told the child, though kindly so. The child sighed and ran into the kitchen, excited to be done with this part of her morning so that she could play with this amazing new thing. The best part of which was that she had *earned* this toy. She had never earned anything before, and it felt amazing to her little kid's heart and mind. The child didn't think of the collapsed building as a bad thing. She had waited until the trip was over and she had spared everyone except the three mean people. That was an unusual kindness for her. She had even kept the super nice man that she knew Auntie Jess liked in that adult way of liking from getting hurt or dirty at all. She was a hero, really.

A few minutes later, after the giant box was unpacked, the three redheaded girls made quick work of putting the house together. It was as tall as Emma when they were done. The chimney poking just above the child's spiral curls as she stood with her back up against it so that her mommy could measure the difference between the two. She almost grabbed her phone to snap a pic, but then she remembered what had happened when she had taken pics of Emma in the recent past. Every single one would emphasize her too bright eyes and they all looked eerie instead of cute.

"Ope. It's just a hair taller than you," Sarah said, and the child smiled wide and jumped up and down clapping with pure happiness. Both of the women smiled at the sight of their Emma so excited, even though they both were dying to talk to the other alone and both were frightened of the little girl before them. They still loved her and took joy from seeing her so elated.

Emma traced a finger over the detailed roof of the house. The small black plastic shingles were bumpy beneath her fingers and the chimney poked out smooth with stone colored plastic bricks. She then peeked into the attic, which had one window on the other side that was round with bright blue shutters on the outside and light pink curtains on the inside. The floor was dark brown plastic with a wood grain feel and she couldn't wait to fill this space with tiny cardboard boxes and holiday decorations like the real one they had upstairs. She wondered if they made those things for doll houses, and she hoped she would find some in the giant dollhouse box.

Then she got down on her knees and looked into the second floor. There was a master bedroom with its own bathroom and walk-in closet on one side. A hallway that had stairs going down to the main floor and stairs going up to the attic. Then there were two other bedrooms and one giant bathroom where the children dollies could sleep and take bubble baths. All of the rooms were void of furniture, but they all had different colored curtains on their windows.

Finally, the child sat all the way down and bent her head over to see the gloriousness that was the first floor. There was a kitchen and a bathroom and a giant living room. A laundry room branched off of the kitchen and led to a real swinging door to the outside. The hallway had doorways to all of these rooms and the first flight of stairs. A lump of pride filled Emma's chest and the child was so happy and excited. She had EARNED this fantastic house and she couldn't wait to fill its walls with a family full of love.

"Okay, Emma," Jess began, her voice as casual as she could make it. "Mommy and I are going to go do stupid boring chores, okay?" She opened the second box and found that it had the stuff that Sarah had added. Less exciting things like shampoo and dish soap and she moved it to the side to open the third box which was full of accessories for the dollhouse. Each individually wrapped. "Here's the box full of furniture and stuff and there's more still in that big box the house came in, so you can put everything in the house where it goes and make sure you throw all of the garbage back in that giant box when you're done, okay? But get out all the good stuff first."

"Okay," the child agreed and dove into the big box with the picture of the dollhouse on it that had come in an even bigger box.

She pulled out a mommy doll and a baby doll and moved the mommy's arms in a way so that it could cradle the baby. She didn't even notice when the two women disappeared up the stairs. She hated boring chores, and she had hours of entertainment before her.

Jess pulled Sarah up the stairs and into her bedroom. Looking around for a good place for them to talk, Sarah took the lead and pulled Jess across the room and into her shower. They left the bathroom door open but closed the bedroom one so that they could tell if Emma came looking for them. Once she was satisfied that they could talk without being overheard Jess let loose a frantic whisper, telling Sarah everything that had happened.

"But Ben said that nobody that he could tell was hurt. He didn't really know for sure," Jess said. "Maybe she couldn't help it. Maybe it had been an accident, but she spared all the people? Or maybe it had actually been an act of God, or whatever. An actual earthquake?" she added, her voice dripping with hope.

"No," Sarah said. "I'm sure that it wasn't. I'm sure it was her. I'm impressed, though, that there were so many survivors. I wonder about that man and those two ladies. If they were mean to her at all, I bet they weren't as lucky as your friend, Ben." At the mention of his name, the sisters smiled. Jess because it had been a long time since she had had a crush on a guy and Sarah because she knew that about her older sister.

"Okay, but what do we do?" Jess went on. "How do we stop her? How do we make sure that nothing like this ever happens again? And the neighbors next door?"

"I don't know, Jess. I've been trying and trying to figure that out since I realized what was happening. I didn't enroll her in kindergarten this year because I was afraid for all of the other little kids, and I don't take her out ever. We play in the backyard instead of going to the park and I order everything online or over the phone. I try not to let her even answer the door when stuff arrives. I'm so scared all of the time. I'm going out of my mind with it all." Sarah leaned back against the fiberglass wall of the shower and slid slowly down until she was sitting with her knees up to her chin in the tub. Jess sat down next to her in the same position. It was as if they were both scared little kids again, hiding in the shower together as their parents had a very rare fight downstairs. Jess put her arm around her sister and pulled her close for a hug. Sarah leaned against her, and they both sat silently staring at the closed bedroom door through the bathroom doorway. Lost in thought.

"Emma's still in there, though. I can feel her," Sarah finally added. "And she comes to me in my dreams. Begging me for help. Calling out to me." A lonely tear fell from Sarah's right eye.

"We'll figure it out, Sarah. Together. I promise," Jess told her and they both just sat in the quiet comfort of the other's company. They sat until they fell asleep, younger sister's head on the other sister's chest. Older sister's arm around her. Their knees resting on the other's. They slept for hours like that and when the child finally came looking for them, she smiled down at her mommy and her auntie and then climbed into the tub. They scooted over without even thinking, creating a place for Emma in between them and fell back asleep. Their bodies should have been aching with stiffness, but they weren't. They felt comfortable in that small space and when all three of them were together, they dreamt of happy things instead of terrifying ones as was their recent norm.

18

Sarah woke up sometime later to the sound of the doorbell downstairs. At first, she didn't know where she was, someplace hard and dim. Then she remembered that she and Jess had fallen asleep together and she smiled down at Emma, who was laying with her head on Sarah's knees and Sarah had wrapped her own arms around her daughter's waist, holding her tight against her in their sleep. She wasn't sure when Emma had joined them, but it made her feel a simple joy that she had sought out her company. It gave her hope.

The doorbell rang again, and Jess sat up suddenly, being torn from her peaceful sleep all at once. Her movement woke up Emma and they all stared at the darkening hall as the doorbell rang once more.

"I'll get it!" Emma chimed and jumped up and out of the tub with the grace and speed that only children seem capable.

"Wait for me," Sarah said and pulled herself up and out of the shower tub combo.

"Me too, kid. Stranger danger, remember?" Jess yawned and followed them out to the hall.

When again the doorbell rang Sarah called down, "We're coming!" She didn't know why, but she was starting to get a sinking feeling in her stomach. Something deep inside told her not to answer the door at all. She reached out and picked up Emma and sat her on her hip when they reached the bottom of the stairs and stepped aside so that Jess could go ahead of them and answer the door. Jess did so with her own reservations about who might be calling, and she turned the bolt slowly as if twisting it through thick molasses. When finally Jess swung the door open, just enough to get a peek at first and then all the way when she saw who was there, both women laughed at how silly they were being.

Standing on the stoop of Sarah and Emma's home was a tall and slender woman with dark brown hair cut into an A-line, short in the back and longer on both sides. She was wearing tan khaki pants, a plain red button up shirt and a powder blue cardigan sweater. She wore no makeup and had kind eyes and a warm smile. In her hands she held a giant platter of chocolate chip cookies and the crow's feet around her eyes and the laugh lines aside her mouth seemed to indicate that she was in her mid to late fifties.

"Hi," she said, her voice friendly and upbeat. "I'm so sorry to bother you all. I'm new to the neighborhood and when I was taking a walk this morning to see what all the commotion was about, I saw that you had a small child about my grandson's age. I was thinking that maybe when he comes to visit, we could come by sometime and have a play date. He's so shy and doesn't easily make friends on his own." The woman walked through the door and pushed past Jess and slid by Sarah and Emma and disappeared into the kitchen as the two women watched her go, dumbfounded by having the strange lady enter so unexpectedly. "I'll just put these cookies on your table and please, help yourself. I just baked them before coming over so they're super fresh," the stranger continued, though now her voice was muffled from being in a different room as they were. Sarah and Jess exchanged a worried look and Emma's mouth widened into a yawn as she lay her head on her mother's shoulder and laced her hands together around Sarah's neck, perfectly content to be held so close. Sarah and Jess followed her into the kitchen just in time to see her disappearing through the doorway into the living room.

"My name is Karen, by the way." The woman laughed. "I know, I know. My daughter tells me, mom, she says, you really need to change your haircut. You're a walking meme with that thing on your head. But I tell her every time, I've had this haircut since two thousand and five and I'm not changing it now. Especially not for no internet trolls. Oh, what an adorable doll house," Karen continued and again when Jess and Sarah entered the living room the woman was already disappearing down the hall back toward the front door.

"Now where did you all disappear to?" she called and when the three of them finally caught up to her she was standing at the foot of the stairs with her hand on the banister, craning her neck up as far as she could to get a look upstairs. "Oh, there you are." She smiled, a smile that seemed genuine enough, though it didn't seem to go all the way up to her eyes. "Shall we have some coffee or tea to go with those cookies? Maybe a glass of milk for the little one there?" she asked and turned back into the kitchen.

"Oh, dear baby Jesus," Jess said, already exhausted even though she had just woken up from a pretty solid nap.

"Ma'am?" Sarah called and walked back through the living room to get to the kitchen from the doorway there with Jess fast on her heels. "Really, we would love to chat a bit more, and welcome you to our neighborhood, but it's getting kind of late and we really need to start our evening ritual if we're gonna get this one to bed on time. Perhaps you can stop by again next week?"

"Oh, I completely understand and that sounds like an amazing idea. Next week it is," Karen said chirpily and started opening cabinets until she found the one with the coffee mugs. "Do you want tea or coffee?" she asked as she sat out three mugs on the counter. "Oh, good. You have one of those instant jobs where you just put in the pod. My late husband would never let me get one. He said they were too wasteful, but a busy woman in today's world should have more things at her fingertips, wouldn't you agree?" Karen asked without even waiting for an answer before continuing. "Oooo, I love your flavor choices. Chocolate raspberry, vanilla and caramel, extra strong." She swung the silver rack filled with K-cups around as she read off all of the titles and then plucked one from its metal ring. "Dark chocolate mint, yes please."

"Ma'am, I'm so sorry, perhaps another time? Really, we have to get dinner started and I still have to clean up from breakfast. As you can see, it's a mess in here."

"Oh, I don't mind messes. I remember what it was like to have children. Mine are all grown now, you see, but it wasn't too long ago that I don't remember." Karen laughed and popped the small plastic cup into the top of the coffee maker, then shut the arm and pushed the button. Hot brown water began to pour from the nozzle

191

and into one of the mugs. "Be a dear, would you? And hand me the creamer? I absolutely insist that we set down together over a cup of coffee and share some of these delicious cookies. Then I'll let you all have your evening. I'm bored sick at my place and I don't know a single soul, can you believe it? Having to move to a place and start over at my late age in life? It's a horrible thing. A lonely and horrible thing." Her voice was suddenly filled with great sadness and Sarah had empathy for her, being a fellow widow herself.

Karen set aside the mug that was now almost full of rich smelling coffee and then plucked another pod from the stand. "You both look like chocolate raspberry ladies to me," she said as she replaced the empty coffee pod with a new one and began the brewing process all over again. "Here, you all set right down, and I'll handle the drinks," Karen insisted, and she gently guided each of them to a chair and pushed them softly into it. Jess and Sarah exchanged looks, both resigning themselves to the coffee and cookies, and besides, the coffee did smell delicious.

As the second cup finished brewing, Karen opened the fridge and rummaged around, bringing out the gallon of milk and the bottle of sweet cream she found inside. "There is nothing like bonding over sweets and caffeine when meeting someone new, my late husband always said, and he was most often right, was Harold." She rummaged in the same cupboard where she found the mugs and brought out a bright pink plastic cup. "This will do nicely," she said and turned her back to the women once more. Her hands a blur of pouring and making the drinks. When finally everything was stirred to her liking, Karen presented Sarah and Jess each with a steaming mug of delicious smelling coffee and in front of the child she placed the pink cup of milk. Then she grabbed the last mug and sat it down before the single empty chair and joined them, passing out a napkin to each from the holder in the middle of the round table.

"Now, young lady, would you like a cookie?" Karen asked the child, who smiled and nodded at the same time.

"Yes, please," the child said and reached to remove the clear plastic wrap from the plate and grab one of the giant chocolate chip filled cookies. They were still kind of warm and when she broke it apart to dunk it in her milk, she saw that it was going to be gooey, and her mouth began to water.

"You two, now. Don't make me feel self-conscious about my baking. I'm an amazing baker. My late Harold would tell everyone that, he would." Karen smiled and held the plate out to Sarah and Jess, in turn. Letting them each take a cookie before she would remove it from before them.

The cookies turned out to be delicious and the child ate three and drank her entire cup of milk before stopping. Sarah and Jess each had two and their coffee cups were both all but empty. Karen hadn't actually eaten a cookie, she had one on the napkin before her, but had been too busy talking to get a bite in. She did drain the coffee from her mug, though. Talking was thirsty work, her late husband Harold often said.

Sarah was sitting there, watching the woman talk, on and on she went, but suddenly Sarah realized she couldn't really follow along with what the strange woman was saying, and she started to giggle. The woman's mouth yapped and yapped and yapped and Sarah thought it was the funniest thing in the world and her giggles turned more and more hysterical. Jess looked over at Sarah and she, too, started to laugh. She didn't know why Sarah was laughing so hard, but it was the funniest thing Jess had ever seen and she laughed so hard that she thought she might pass out. Seeing her mom and her auntie become hysterical, in turn, made the child start to laugh and Karen finally stopped talking.

She sat there, watching the three of them before her with their hands on their sides or gripping the table as their faces turned bright red with the effort it took to cackle as they now were surely doing. A smile spread across the woman's thin lips, one that actually reached her eyes, and she scooted back from her chair. Slowly and quietly so as not to alert the three gingers before her of her actions.

"I feel weird," Sarah said as she gasped for air. Her chest burned and her head felt as light as a feather.

"I feel fucked up," Jess snorted, and the child gasped and pointed at her auntie.

"You said a swear." Emma's voice was high pitched with the effort it took to talk, and they all stopped and stared at each other

193

for a few seconds before they burst into another round of hysterical laughter.

Alarm bells were starting to go off in Sarah's mind, but in a faraway part that she didn't quite have access to at the moment as everything continued to just seem so silly and her head was swimming with it. The room began to tilt and sway, and she tried to stand, but fell sideways, missing the chair and landing hard on the floor. Her teeth bit into her tongue as she hit, and pain and the taste of iron filled her mouth. Which only made her laugh harder than ever and the spectacle of it caused her sister and the child to burst into a new round of chuckles as their worlds began to spin and yank and turn as well.

"I think she drugged us," Jess added and each word that came out of her mouth became more and more slurred and inaudible. Her tongue felt heavy like lead, and she slipped from her own chair, landing softer than her sister had. She found herself laying on her back and looking up at the light fixture on the ceiling above them. A tiny spider was making its way across its fluorescent surface, and she wondered how it didn't burn its tiny little legs. Which seemed like a very silly thing, and as she pondered that her eyes closed, and she drifted off to sleep. Next to her, tiny snoring sounds escaped Sarah's lips as she, too, became lost in slumber.

Only Emma's small body was left sitting in the chair at the table. She had stopped laughing because suddenly she didn't find it funny anymore. Suddenly she was terrified, and the child wasn't used to being terrified. The child was the one who inspired terror and never had it been the other way around. So, she sat still in the chair and willed with all of her might not to fall asleep as had her mommy and Auntie Jess. She could feel sleep calling to her and dragging her away. Its iron-strong fist was around her ankle and pulling her into the crashing waves of lethargy and she fought against it. She willed herself to grow and change, but nothing happened. She was caught in a stupor and even her eyes seemed to dull as finally she let her lids close over them. A second later she, too, was lost in dreams. Terrible ones where she had no control over her body or her senses and was at the mercy of a monster. Finally, she was fully aware of what it was like to be her victims.

And anger coursed through her veins, though there was no outlet for the fury that heated her blood. She was lost in it and lost to it. For the first time ever, she was helpless.

19

It was Sarah who awoke first. She was sore and felt groggy and her tongue ached and felt swollen in her mouth. She tried to reach a hand up to where the pain was but found she couldn't move and then felt the rope that was digging into her arms and legs and waist and ankles. She blinked her eyes a few times and the room cleared before her. She found herself tied to a metal chair in some dark place she had never been before. It looked like an old factory long abandoned, but what kind she could not say. It was dirty and the windows let in only darkness so she couldn't even tell what was out there to help place where she had been brought. Next to her, tied up in a similar chair with the same kind of rough rope sat Jess. Her head was lying forward, her chin resting on her collarbone and a small line of drool reflected shiny pinpricks of light from the ones that had been set up on stands around them.

Sarah was scared, but when she saw what was in the center of the room, she became completely terrified. It was her child, her Emma, bound not to a chair, but a large wooden beam that looked like it had been painstakingly carved and crude symbols had been etched and burned into the rough surface. The beam was laying sideways, the middle over open air, and two large metal boxes lay under each end. Emma's body was on her back on the beam, which was about two feet wide and the same thickness as width. Her face was bent over to the side facing Sarah and Sarah took relief in only that her little girl's eyes were still closed and her chest rose and fell as if she were still lost in slumber.

Emma's body seemed to be attached to the large beam with dark metal chains that wrapped around her tightly from her feet all the way up to her neck. Her hands were bound to her sides and even from this distance Sarah could see where Emma's flesh was white where the chains bit tightly into her skin. The most horrifying part, though, was what was underneath the open space beneath her daughter's sleeping body. A large pile of wood was neatly stacked in a circular shape. It looked like a deliberate pattern, though Sarah couldn't figure out of what or why it would be placed so. All she knew was what it must be put there for and that was to burn.

Sarah pulled her hands as hard as she could, which were bound tightly behind her, and she felt only the tiniest bit of give. The rope was fibrous, and the fibers tore at her skin when she wiggled her wrists and fingers and forearms. She could feel an angry rash forming, but she didn't care. All she could think about was getting free and saving her daughter and her sister. She knew that something was living inside of Emma. Some dark and sinister thing that was capable of the most unspeakable evil acts. But she didn't care. She was her mother, and it was her job to love and accept and protect. She knew that Emma was still in there and she had seen the evil herself diminish, if even just slightly, it was a start. Her daughter needed her, no matter what lived inside of Emma's small body, and she was going to do whatever it took to save her.

"I wouldn't bother," a voice from behind her spoke up. A woman's voice that she recognized, though now it was not as cheerful as it had been back in her kitchen. "I tied those knots well and there's absolutely no way that you can escape. And, even if you could, you can't help her now. Unless you can rip through iron with your bare hands, there's nothing you can do." The woman's voice sounded almost sad as she walked around the chair and came into Sarah's view. "At midnight she's going to burn and nothing you can do or say will stop that. When it's over, I'll call nine one one and they'll come and rescue you and sleeping beauty over there, but the girl must die."

"Why?" Sarah asked, her voice was shaky and cracked. Her throat was dry and raw, and her tongue still throbbed. "She's just a little girl."

The woman laughed. A hearty and heartfelt laugh but it was tinged with grief as well. "Oh, come now, Sarah. You know as well as I do that that little girl is not just anything. Just can't even begin to describe her." The woman pulled up a third chair, similar to the

197

ones in which Sarah and Jess were now bound and sat down facing her so that Sarah could see into her cool blue eyes. "That little girl is a monster and no longer your daughter. You have to have seen the signs by now. The missing pets in your neighborhood. The times she's had to have shown up drenched in blood and gore. The murdered people in the cities and towns surrounding your home. Heck, just last night a pizza delivery guy that your address was the last stop for stepped out in front of a diesel truck for no apparent reason that anyone could figure out. He exploded on impact. Brain and blood raining down on the poor truck driver's windshield. How long do you think that's gonna haunt the man? Probably forever."

"What?" Sarah asked, her voice was honestly confused, and the woman looked surprised.

"You mean you have that kid living in your home and you don't scan the morning papers looking for any tragedy you can find to link to her death toll?" Karen asked. Sarah blinked as if the woman had slapped her. She quite honestly hadn't even thought to do that, but now that the idea had been brought to her attention, she realized that it was something she should have been doing all along.

"That's a horrible accident, but you can't blame that on my daughter," Sarah urged. "We were at home watching cartoons all night before putting her to bed. She didn't leave the house at all."

Karen rolled her eyes and looked at Sarah as if she were the stupidest human on the face of the earth. "Come now, Sarah, are you dumb? You must have witnessed her powers by now. I mean, it wasn't hard at all to figure out where she was, just by using a simple search engine. Tons of missing cats posted to local social media groups. Weird deaths popping up all around. Dismemberments and bodies drained completely of their blood. Internal organs ripped from torsos and half eaten or strewn about. Heck, your house was practically at the center of a gruesome map with a bright red neon light pointing at it," the woman scoffed. "I'm surprised the FBI hasn't broken down your door by now as careless as the little brat has been about it. I was already in town and had finished setting this place up when the pizza delivery guy ate it and was casing your place when the cops were called because of your neighbors' bodies being found. And I tailed your sister and the brat to the grocery store. I saw what happened there. I saw the look on Jess' face. That look said she knew what happened when that building fell. I repeat, there is absolutely no way in hell that you two didn't know at least somewhat of what you were dealing with. Especially since your family has been the longest family that she's ever stayed with, as far as I can tell. Every time I get a place pinpointed, by the time I'm there there's nothing left but ruin and death. You're super lucky or super smart to have lasted this long, to be quite frank."

Next to them Jess began to wake. Her head moved from side to side, and she blinked her eyes as she lifted her chin. "Where am I?" her groggy voice asked, though she had no idea who she was talking to yet. She could barely see through the blurriness of her vision let alone tell who was in the room with her.

"Good morning, Princess," Karen spoke, looking from Sarah to Jess. "How did you sleep? Like a rock it felt like as I moved you over here. You're heavier than you look, you know."

Jess' head swiveled to where the voice was coming from and she blinked a few times, clearing away the blurriness and then glaring at the woman in the chair before them. "Karen, I'm going to beat the ever-loving shit out of you when I get out of whatever the hell kind of fuckery you've wrapped me in you cunt-loving bitch of a whore."

Karen chuckled and sat back in her seat, placing her hands behind her head as she did so. "My my, you are the firecracker, aren't you? Such naughty language, and in front of a child, too." Karen shook her head in disdain, though mockingly so. Jess' eyes moved from the woman to her niece chained up before them and she began to pull and buck in her chair. Trying hard to loosen the bonds and break herself free so that she could do whatever it took to bring harm to the woman who had drugged them with cookies and coffee.

"Who drugs people with baked goods, anyway?" Jess demanded. "Cookies should be a sacred thing that you can always count on. Not some petty weapon to sneak attack a motherfucker

199

with." When Jess got angry, she tended to curse a lot. It was a gift her dad had bestowed upon her. She and Sarah had always laughed when he would hit his knuckles on a wrench while fixing their car or when he would stub his toe on the coffee table. The lines of foul language that would string from his lips would be delightfully bad and so, to the girls, also very hilarious. Their mother always tsk tsk'd their dad during those moments, but she would always do it through a smile she couldn't stop from popping up on her own lips. Those had been good times and both girls regarded their father highly, for his faults as much as for his strengths.

"A smart woman uses any tools at her advantage, my late husband used to say. He was a wise man, he was." Karen sighed and stood, checking the watch she wore on her right wrist as she did so. "It's only a quarter past nine and we have a lot of chatting to do before the main event. I'm sure that you wouldn't take anything I offered since the unfortunate cookie and coffee incident, but I'm quite parched and a bit hungry from the effort it took to get you all here and set up, so if you will excuse me, I'm going to go and grab my dinner now. Can I offer you ladies anything? Some lemon lime sports drink, perhaps? It's full of electrolytes, you know?"

"Let us go. You have the wrong kid. Emma's just a normal little girl and you're making a horrible mistake," Sarah pleaded, and Jess just glared at the woman before them, still wearing the same powder blue cardigan as she had been before.

"Oh, Sarah. This would all go so much easier if you would just accept the truth as fact and move on. I promise I'm helping you, even if you don't see it right now." With those words, Karen walked away, disappearing through a tall metal door which closed behind her with a loud clang.

"Jess, can you see my hands?" Sarah asked, trying to crane her head as far as she could to see how Jess' hands were bound behind her back. The chair was turned just enough that it was impossible for her.

"No, are you okay? You sound funny, like you're hurt." Jess' voice was strained from the effort of trying to scoot her chair closer to her sister's. It moved, but just barely. Her feet were tied tightly at the ankles, and it made it difficult to get any momentum going.

"It doesn't matter, we have to get Emma out of here, she's going to burn her." Sarah was wiggling in her chair as much as her ties would allow her to. Like Jess', her chair was moving, but too slowly to really make a difference, and she was beginning to fear that no matter what she did it wouldn't be enough.

"I swear to all the gods in the universe, when I get free, I'm going to kill that bitch," Jess said with so much anger and hate and revulsion in her voice that Sarah was grateful to have her there with her. Her sister was fierce when she needed to be and right now Sarah figured that they could use all of the fierceness they could get. Just then the large metal door swung back open, and Karen came back in, carrying a brown paper lunch bag and a tall reusable blue plastic thermos.

"Less than three hours to go, ladies, and then the show begins. I hope you brought marshmallows and graham crackers." Karen chuckled as she sat back down on the metal seat across from them.

"You're sick," Sarah sad softly. "You're going to kill my daughter over some crazy fantasy you have in your mind. Just let us go before it's too late."

Karen stopped laughing and sat forward, her eyes blazing with a fiery anger. "That's enough, Sarah. Your lies are not impressing me. I know the monster that's living in your child's body. I know her all too well. She's responsible for the loss of everything I held dear in this world and later on you'll come to understand that I'm saving you from the pain that I've had to live through."

Karen reached her hand into the brown bag and pulled out a sandwich with the crusts cut off and neatly packaged in a large square of wax paper with a small, yellow smiley sticker holding the folds together. She spread the wax paper out on her lap with the sandwich in its center. It was cut in two and had a thin layer of cheddar cheese and ham with mustard. She picked up a half and considered it before setting it back down again.

"Let me tell you my story, before you judge too harshly, shall I?" Karen's voice was reminiscent as she talked.

"I don't want to hear it," Jess said angrily and began tugging at the knot of the rope that was tying her wrists together with her fingers, trying to find a way to loosen it somehow.

201

"If we listen, will you consider what we have to say?" Sarah asked as she was busy doing the same thing with the ropes binding her own hands behind the back of the hard-cold metal chair that Jess was.

"That's fair." Karen gave after a short pause for consideration. "But time is growing short so please don't interrupt me if you want your chance to tell your side."

Sarah sighed. She needed the woman to get lost in her words so that she and Jess could try to test their bondages and figure out any soft places that they could try and wiggle free from. They just needed one tiny give to wriggle their hands free and then the rope would loosen everywhere else for them. She wouldn't stop trying and she knew that Jess was the same way. They were fierce women from a line of fierce women, and they would never ever give up even if it meant their lives in the process. You didn't abandon those you loved to danger or death. It was the way of their lineage.

20

Karen picked up the sandwich again and took a small and dainty bite. She was a simple woman with simple taste and enjoyed the simple pleasures in life. This ordeal was far outside of what she considered simple, but she knew that it was something that had to be done. For her children. For her husband. For her sister and her sister's children. Even for the man her sister had married that Karen hadn't been too fond of, though he was a nice enough fella. He didn't deserve the end he got. None of them had.

"I had to go away on a training retreat for work," Karen began after she swallowed that first bite. Her voice was of a woman who was remembering something hard. A story she did not want to tell but knew she must. She had to make these women understand why she was doing something that seemed so horrible, for she was not a horrible person by nature. "They called them retreats, but they were silly and boring things. We had to go to meeting halls and listen to people drone on and on about things that most of us knew by common sense. How to run the new programming that we'd already figured out on our own. The proper way to speak to those of the opposite sex, though we all had to watch those videos when we were hired. And then there was the retreat part. A bunch of phooey nonsense where we had to sit in circles and talk about trust and then play these silly games that were meant to build our team spirit, but none of us wanted to be there, that was plain enough for all of us to see."

Karen sighed and wrapped the sandwich back up, haphazardly, shoving it back into the bag with far less care than it had originally been placed. "But the worst part was that it was mandatory and went through Friday to Sunday at this camping place with cabins up state. A nice enough place if it was where you wanted to be, but the

Wi-Fi was horrible and I hated to be away from my Harold and the little ones for that long." Karen looked away, but Sarah saw the tear that streaked down her cheek. It glinted in one of the lights she had set up around the room.

"My sister's youngest child was celebrating a birthday that weekend," Karen continued solemnly. "The cutest little niece an aunt could ever ask for. Three years old and all blonde curls and bright blue eyes." She sighed. "Her older sister was five. She had been an amazing kid, too. Same blonde curls and blue eyes as her little sister. Her mom had been worried about her lately, but she wouldn't tell me why. She wanted to cancel the party, but I talked her into it. I told her that sibling rivalry was normal and that it was important for each child to feel special on their birthday. Especially when you had four kids and planned on adding more. Individual celebrations are even more important with so many children in a home."

Karen laughed a sad and tired laugh. "If only I would have known the truth behind why she wanted to cancel. The words she couldn't find to tell me because she didn't even understand what was happening." She looked up and met Sarah's gaze then. Her eyes were sad, and Sarah felt a tug of empathy for the woman. She understood the pain and grief and guilt she must be feeling, but her empathy didn't change the hate she had for her. The overwhelming need to escape her ties and fling herself at the lady who was planning on murdering her child.

"It was partially my fault," Karen continued. "Had I let her cancel maybe none of this would have happened at all. My husband and children would still be here and perhaps my sister and her family as well. But I doubt they would have made it through much longer. The cracks were already forming before the party." Karen looked back over her shoulder at where the sleeping child lay restrained to the heavy wooden beam. "I had insisted to my husband that he film as much as he could since I couldn't make it. I hated missing any part of my children's joy because of work. It was my biggest regret as a mother up until that point. That I had to work and be parted from them. That I had to miss so much to give them the life I thought they needed."

The woman in the chair sat back and stared at her hands. They were trembling with the emotion that coursed through her body with the retelling of her tragic tale. Another sigh escaped her thin lips, and she began to talk once more.

"There was a bounce house and a clown and candy and cake. Everything seemed fine enough until it was time for presents. The birthday girl, Eliza, sat front and center on an oversized chair they had placed in the middle of the back yard and a beautiful tiara sat atop her tiny little head. It sparkled in the sun, and she looked so happy. Her little three-year-old face was lit up at being the center of attention. When you have three older siblings it was a rare thing, to be the sole recipient of so much happiness and the mountain of presents before her caught her toddler mind full of anticipation and glee." Karen twisted the lid off her plastic jug and took a long drink. Jess expected her to say that talking was thirsty work again, but she didn't. Instead, she picked back up the thread of her story and went on. Her voice tired and full of ache.

"At one point her older sister, Jemma, tried to grab the tiara from her head and my Harold told her in a kind voice to leave her sister be. That right now it was Eliza's turn to be the princess. And in the video this is the part that got my attention. I've watched it so many times over and over and had this not happened I would have never known." Her voice grew sharp, and her words became quicker. "Jemma looked at my husband, and so the camera as well, and her eyes shone so bright and so blue that I thought at first it was a trick of the light. There was so much hate in that look and the video glitched. Grey lines shot across the screen then, but those eyes shone bright even through those horizontal, snowy lines. That's when my sister came and swooped her up and planted a giant kiss upon her cheek. She told her that her birthday was coming soon and that she could wear the tiara then and wouldn't she look amazing?" Karen laughed a tiny laugh.

"My Harold was a kind man, especially to children. He thought that they all deserved the best and safest childhood they could. He had been an orphan and had bounced around in the system and it had left him with this need to give back and nourish the smaller minds of this world. Correcting children came natural to him and he did it in a way that normally didn't upset them. He tried to teach them right from wrong but not take away their dignity in the doing. He was a good man. A kind man. This world is a greyer place without him in it." Tears now began to flow from Karen's eyes more freely. Silently she cried as she continued to speak.

"As soon as her mind had been redirected the lines cleared up in the video. You could see as plain as day that Jemma wasn't happy with her mother's words, and she spared another glare at her uncle, a man who she had always loved beyond measure before. And those eyes were still so bright. Too bright to be those of Jemma. Too bright to be human. Just like those of your little girl." She looked at Sarah and Sarah licked her lips but said nothing. She was working on the knot behind her and making slow progress. Painstakingly her fingertips were pushing and pulling and loosening. She was getting closer to being free.

"My sister sat down with the other children, holding Jemma tightly in her lap. Whispering nice things in her ear as her husband began handing gifts to Eliza to open. He looked nervous himself in the video and you could tell that both he and my sister just wanted to get this part over and done. He rushed Eliza through the gifts and in the lower corner of the screen you could see Jemma getting more and more impatient. She seemed to hate it when the crowd oooed and ahhhhed as the presents were opened. And whenever Eliza would squeal with delight, Jemma would make a fist and a few more times static shot across the screen."

In her chair, her face as blank as she could make it, Sarah pulled an end free of its knot and began working it back through itself. She could feel sweat began to pool in the hair at the nape of her neck and something inside of her was telling her to hurry. Her time was running out. She looked sideways at Jess and could see a similar look upon her face. It gave Sarah strength to continue even faster. Ignoring the harsh cries of pain from her skin as it was rubbed away by the coarse rope when she worked her fingers and wrists. Before them, Karen's lips began to move again as her words once more flowed forth.

"Then Eliza pulled out a bright and flowy pink princess dress from a bag. It was beautiful and had to be expensive. Everyone

206

whispered about how pretty it was, and someone even said what a gorgeous little princess Eliza would make with that dress and that tiara. And that's when Jemma's patience broke. She stood and snatched the dress from Eliza's hands and Eliza began to cry. Several people in the small crowd of parents and children expressed their dismay and the father grabbed up Eliza, a look of panic on his face. I want this! It's mine! Jemma screamed and a mother I didn't recognize tried to take it from her hands. Jemma wouldn't let it go and you could hear a loud rip as the arm tore away from the bodice. Everyone hushed and Jemma's face turned red and her eyes blazed out at that random mother who had seemed to have her fill of my niece's spoiled attitude for the day. That's when the ground began to shake, and the picture grew fuzzy. It was hard to see what happened next, but you could hear the dismay and panic from the party guests easily enough. The ground ripped open, and people began to fall. Sinkholes, they called it. Gas pipes were broken and ignited. Screams of pain joined the screams of panic and not only did the ground open up, but it crashed back closed as well. People were buried and crushed and burned. My husband dropped the camera and later they would tell me that he died with our children scooped up in his arms. He had tried to save them, but they all had been knocked over and the earth had torn apart beneath them. They had fallen into a crater that shouldn't have ever been able to exist and the dirt then slammed back around them before opening again. It was as if the ground was trying to eat them up. My children were crushed. Their skulls pushed in and unrecognizable. Their brains were flattened and mushed out of cracks in their head, and I puked when the coroner showed me their bodies for identification."

A grimace spread across Karen's face, and it seemed for a minute that she was done talking. The tears were pouring now from her eyes and down her cheeks. They were dropping onto her bosom and disappearing into the powder blue fabric of her cardigan. Finally, she went on.

"My family was erased in one supernatural temper tantrum from a monster that wore the skin of my niece as camouflage. My husband's face had been twisted into a terror from a dream, a nightmare, and I see it often when I sleep. My sister and her husband and their other three children burned. You can hear them screaming as the crackle of the flames ate away at their clothing and their flesh in the video. And then, the very last frame is of Jemma picking up the camera and looking in. She smiles and her eyes flash and then it's just my niece standing there. A panic builds inside of her and her eyes are back to their normal blue and then the ground tears apart beneath her and she falls in. She lay there at the bottom of the ditch. Clutching the camera and crying in pain and fear. It took the emergency crew almost an hour to be able to get to her through all of the chaos and fire and the ground giving away in places as they worked. She had broken bones in her chest and legs and wrist when she fell. Causing internal bleeding as the new sharp ends cut through veins and tore through muscle. They tried to save her in the hospital, but she only lasted a few short days before a blood clot tore through her body and stopped her heart. They hadn't let me see her because her condition was too severe, and they had been working tirelessly around the clock to stop the bleeding. I never got a chance to talk to her or perhaps she could have told me what took me years to find out on my own. Perhaps I could have gotten to the monster sooner and you never would be living this nightmare that my sister lived at all."

"What do you mean?" Sarah asked. Genuinely curious now. If this woman knew anything at all about what was wrong with Emma, she wanted to know also. Behind her back the knot was almost out. She continued to work the slowly lengthening ends as the woman spoke.

"I researched, of course. That video in the camera that the police gave me after they concluded their investigation made me wonder and I watched it again and again and again. A hundred times I watched it. A thousand, even. Over and over. For days and weeks, it consumed me. Those too bright eyes and how they flashed and made the film go weird. The way the very earth opened up and swallowed people whole at the very moment the dress was ripped, and Jemma's anger hit its peak. The way it ended, and my niece seemed herself again, just long enough to be swallowed up as well. It all added up to something I couldn't wrap my head around

208

and so I went to libraries and bookstores. I searched the internet and visited people who had similar stories to tell. Stories of wrecked lives and wrecked homes. Of children left orphaned and locked up in asylums for murdering their families or for spouting crazy tales of having their bodies taken over and seeing it all through eyes they couldn't control. Of watching their fingers grow and change and tasting the flesh of humans and animals alike. Crazy stories their doctors thought. And those were just the children lucky enough to have survived." Karen stood and walked over to where Emma's sleeping body lay. She let her hand trace the carvings and burnt etchings on the wood and lightly feathered her fingers against the chains.

"It took me most of a decade to put all of the pieces together. To figure out what it was that stole the lives of so many, leaving a trail of chaos and carnage for centuries, if you knew where to look. And almost half a decade more to figure out how to finally stop it. To stop her. She always seems to inhabit the bodies of girls, never a boy that I could find. She prefers to be the only child but has been known to take on a host with siblings, though I'm not sure why. Boredom or desperation? Who knows?" She walked up the beam toward Emma's peaceful face and smiled a loving smile down at her and then looked up at Sarah. "She's beautiful, your Emma. It's a shame that she had to be the one here now. From everything I've learned about you, your family seems nice enough, it's true. And the tragedy you've already had to overcome, losing your husband like that. It can't be easy, what you're going through now. And it's very admirable, how hard you're fighting to keep her safe. Even though you know what lurks inside her. I could see it in your face when I first showed up at your door. I could tell the terror that lived inside your home was real and even still you try to deny it. You are a wonderful mother and still young enough to start over. Meet someone new, fall in love, have more babies. Your life is still ahead of you."Karen turned her back to Sarah and checked the chains around the child's neck to make sure they weren't too tight or too loose. She needed her body to stay alive until the time was right but wanted to be sure that she couldn't escape if she awoke too soon.

"But why kill Emma, then? It makes no sense. Why not just force it out of her?" Jess asked. "An innocent child doesn't have to die."

"Of course, she does. It's the only way," Karen answered. "It took me a long time of searching through ancient lore and superstitions. I traveled to South America and spoke to women and men whose bloodlines went back centuries and whose lineage passed along their knowledge of such things that creep through the darkness all around us. I can't even be sure that this will work, but I have to try. It's the only thing I can do. The iron in the chains will bind the creature to Emma's body. She won't be able to grow or change and she won't be able to flee. The runes I've carved and burned into the wood should keep her from being able to access the magic that courses through her being and the beam itself is doused with holy water, just in case. I've taken all the precautions I could think of since there are only whispers of creatures like her. Perhaps all of the creatures have just been her throughout time. I cannot find any trace of there being more than one of her at once, but so many different cultures reference a monster that can change its shape and feasts on man and beast alike. A malevolent thing that steals the bodies of their children and makes them do unspeakable acts before leaving the child and all around it in complete devastation."

Finally, Sarah's right wrist was free, and she worked now on getting the left wrist unbound. She couldn't tell what progress Jess was making but she hoped she would play it cool and wait for the perfect moment if she was able to get free at all. Sarah herself was almost there and trying to formulate a plan.

"The only way to take the monster out is to bind it to its host and burn the flesh to ash in the hour of the witch. That hour between midnight and one AM. I will douse her body good just before and when the clock strikes 12, I will light the match and together we will witness the creature's demise. I'm hoping your Emma will not suffer. I gave her the biggest dose of sedative that the curandera in this little village in Latin America gave me. She had the most extensive knowledge of the old gods and monsters of the world before time of anyone I had ever found. That's what they were called, it seems, the creatures from the world before time. It is said that they once walked the earth and stars and cultivated all that grew and breathed and bore." Karen turned away from Emma's body and looked at the two sisters before her. "Now tell me what it was you wanted me to hear?"

Sarah couldn't get her other wrist free. It was tied so tight, and the knot just wouldn't give. "Let me whisper it to you, please." She looked shyly at her sister then, as if she were ashamed of something horrible that she couldn't readily admit to her. "Please. Jess wouldn't understand. I can't take her judging me for this." And at that, Sarah began to cry.

Karen stood still for a moment. Trying to gauge whether or not this was a trick. Karen was confident in herself, perhaps too much so. She had always believed that her ideas were best and that her suggestions should be taken as gospel. When she did something, she did it with care to never mess up and even when a mistake was made, she searched for reasons why it couldn't have been solely her fault. That party she had insisted her sister throw haunted her because, deep down, she blamed herself. Though, even then, she felt that her advice was solid for the information she had been given. She wanted to blame her sister for not trusting her enough to help. Had she just reached out, all of this could have been avoided. They could have figured it out together. Karen had come so far since the disaster. They could have thought out a different way much sooner had they worked together. It was a shame. A true and horrible shame.

"Alright," Karen agreed, and began to walk across the space between where Emma lay chained to the beam and where Sarah was tied to the chair with rope. "But I can't promise I won't tell Jess if I deem it something that she should know."

"That's fine. I can't say it myself to her, but it might be good to hear the words spoken by someone else."

Jess just watched the woman move, closer and closer to where Sarah sat, her face full of confusion and anger, but really, she knew that Sarah was about to do something, and Jess was ready.

Karen reached Sarah's chair and bent down close so that her ear was by Sarah's mouth. "What is it, dear?" Karen asked. She felt a sort of kinship with Sarah, thinking of how hard all of this must be. As she felt the intake of Sarah's breath to say whatever it was she was about to say everything went sideways in the most unexpected of ways. Karen had expected something bad could happen if the child were to wake, but this was completely not even in the wheelhouse of things she had prepared for going wrong.

Suddenly Sarah's right arm reached up and grabbed the back of Karen's head. Her fingers digging in an entire handful of that A-line cut and pulling her face even closer to Sarah's mouth. A mouth that opened and screamed a long and guttural sound as Sarah's teeth closed down sharply and with all of her might onto Karen's entire ear. Sarah's teeth had been well kept and they slid down through the gristle and bone that held it to Karen's head, severing it from her scalp and leaving a red and bloody hole that instantly began to gush hot blood down her face and neck and Sarah was doused in it.

Karen tried to pull back, but there was nothing to push against aside from Sarah's body that was now sticky with Karen's own blood, and she couldn't find a purchase that was firm enough to give her any force of which to push away on. Sarah's right arm held firm to the hair on the top back of Karen's skull and even as Sarah spit out the entirety of Karen's severed ear, Sarah pulled her back in for a second bite. This time her teeth sunk into Karen's cheek and Sarah bit just as hard as she had before and ripped away a chunk of fat and skin, revealing muscle that gleamed in the lights and moved as Karen opened her mouth to scream.

The hot and salty blood sprayed out, coating Sarah's vision red and again she pulled her in for a third bite. This time Karen was able to get a hand on Sarah's head and she pushed back, hard. Sarah yanked her own head to the right and Karen's thumb slipped into Sarah's gnashing mouth and again Karen screamed as her thumb was nearly sliced off with the force of Sarah's chomping bite. Finally, Karen was able to break free. There was so much blood leaking from places on her head and shooting out from her hand that even the back of Karen's head was drenched with it and Sarah's grasp slipped. Karen was able at last to relieve herself of her captor who was supposed to be her victim.

"I tied those knots so perfectly, there's no way that you could escape!" Karen screamed into Sarah's face, though not close enough where she could be grabbed again. Her head ached and ran with pain and she held her left fist tightly against her chest as it bled and screamed and stung. She raised her right hand high up in the air, her nails affixed as if they were the sharpest talons, ready to carve sweet Sarah's face to ribbons. Just before Karen was able to strike, a crack filled the room and Karen hit the floor from the force of Jess' heavy metal chair striking down upon her head and shoulder. She sat there, on her knees, blood now dripping down from her hairline to join that which already ran from her cheek and ear. She looked up at Sarah with a look of surprise and disappointment.

"You will regret it if you allow her to live," Karen said and opened her mouth to speak once more, but Sarah couldn't take another word and reached forward with her free hand and grabbed a handful of hair on the side of her head and slammed her face against the corner of the chair in which she was ensnared.

Again and again, she slammed the woman's face into the metal edge. It made a dull smashing sound and that gave way to a wet cracking sound. Her face went from recognizably human to something from a nightmare. Her eyes were punctured and bled white ooze mixed with blood. Her nose was broken and shattered and splintered and torn. It looked like a purple squash that had burst into pieces and instead of white fruit inside it was red and raw and lined with yellow tissues of fat. Her muscles visible from the bite she had sustained just moments before were severed in two from the force of her head being slammed into the edge of the place she had thought she had secured Sarah to. The bone beneath shone out white before it, too, became broken and fractured. Her teeth were thrust through her lips and broken away from her jaw. Some were forced back into her throat and others flew around them like hard little bones of confetti. Her jaw was seeping blood mixed with spit and still Sarah didn't stop slamming and slamming her face into her chair.

She kept going and screamed with the effort of each thrust. She screamed away all of her anger and sadness and confusion.

213

She screamed until her throat was raw with it and still, she screamed and screamed. Jess just stood and watched, shocked at the display of violence at her younger sister's hands. Jess had assumed that when she was able to undo the knots that held her wrists, she would be the one to get her hands dirty with the woman's blood. But she was proud of her sister, who had always been the gentle one. Jess had always protected her from the darker parts of life and now she saw that perhaps there had been no need. Perhaps Sarah could have protected herself all along.

Jess waited until Sarah's hands slowed their gruesome work and then finally stopped, dropping the fist-full of hair and letting Karen's head fall with a quiet sloomp noise when her now gone face hit the concrete of the factory floor. The screams from Sarah's mouth fell silent, too, and she just stared at her fingers which were tarred and feathered with the woman's blood and broken bits of hair. Her eyes welled with tears, but they did not fall, and she looked up at Jess, a terrible smile across her face, and her eyes shone almost as bright as Emma's had of late. Not with supernatural force, but with the fierceness of a mother protecting her young and her family.

"She was the only monster here," Sarah said. "I would have regretted it had I let her live."

Sarah's words snapped Jess from her stupor, and she rushed behind her sister and began working at the knot that held the other wrist. Once that was free, she moved to the front and worked on the bindings that held her ankles to the front legs of the heavy throne on which her sister sat triumphant.

"I'm proud of you, sis," Jess said as finally the ropes binding Sarah were free and she helped her sister to stand. Sarah shook with the effort of it. All of her strength had gone into beating Karen's face into an unrecognizable human pulp. The woman had tried to stop Sarah's strengthy thrusts, but she had still been dazed by Jess' attack and had not the strength to stop her.

"Can you check her body for keys?" Sarah asked as she walked toward her daughter on the beam. Jess knew immediately what keys she was referencing, and she began to check the pockets of the body lying in the expanding pool of blood, though no new blood was added to the puddle as Karen's heart no longer beat. It just continued to spread until it reached the limits of its reach as it thinned out away from the source.

21

When Sarah reached her daughter's sleeping body, she sighed gratefully at the tiny snore that escaped her child's mouth and her cute little button nose. She would recognize the sound of Emma sleeping anywhere and it had been such a soft sound that she had not been able to hear it from where she had been held prisoner across the room.

"I love you, baby," Sarah whispered in her ear and stroked back the curly hair that was stuck to her sweaty brow.

"Found it!" Jess exclaimed from where she had been digging through the blood-soaked pockets of Karen and Sarah smiled at the lovely sound those words made to her ears. Jess rushed across the space to where her sister stood by her sleeping daughter's body and began to unlock the locks which bound the chain using the full keychain she had taken from Karen's dead carcass. As she worked on finding the right key on the ring of many for each lock, the child's eyes sprang open all of a sudden and a horrible scream erupted from her tiny throat.

"It burns!" Emma's voice was loud and piercing. Much too loud for her small frame and both Sarah and Jess bent down, covering their ears with the palms of their hands. They couldn't help it, the sound coming from the little girl's grimacing face was so loud and so sharp they acted on pure instinct.

The room seemed to fill with electricity all at once, it didn't build a little bit at a time like it had before, but in a sudden rush of thick and painful air. The temperature changed just as quickly and Sarah sprang up to her daughter's frightened form atop the beam.

"It's okay." Sarah's voice was calming but lost in the sound of the child's scream and the very walls around them began to shake. "It's okay," she tried again and placed her hands on Emma's face, forcing her to turn and look at Sarah. "It's okay." She tried a third time when those bright green eyes met hers. "You're okay." Sarah's hands could feel the heat rushing through her daughter and it was all she could do to not pull them away. She could feel them start to blister and burn, though Emma's skin stayed perfect and pale and freckle filled.

"It burns," Emma said again, but blissfully stopped screaming and Jess began to work at the locks that were holding her niece in such agony against the grainy wood once more.

"Auntie Jess is unlocking the chains that the mean lady wrapped around you," Sarah soothed, and Emma's eyes blazed with a fierceness that Sarah had never seen in them before. The child looked around the room, searching for the woman who had done this and when she saw her crumpled body and broken face, she smiled at the wreckage that had been left behind.

"You killed her for me?" the child asked, incredulous curiosity filling her voice.

"I would do anything for you," Sarah said and laid a kiss atop the child's burning forehead. As her lips met the skin, she could feel the heat draining from the child's being and the room lost its electric feel. Even the building stopped its groaning as the child slowly calmed and quieted her inner beast.

"We both would," Jess stated as the last lock was finally opened, and she was able to start unwrapping the chains which wound around the child and the wood.

"I love you both," the child said and began to cry. A little girl's cry full of relief and happiness. A feeling of safety and security of which the child had never known crept through her mind and heart, and she felt as if she was finally home with these two women.

"We love you, too," Sarah said as she pulled the child free from the chains and held her in her tight and loving embrace. She then sat down hard upon the floor and cried warm, fat tears of relief and held Emma's body tighter than she had ever held her before. "I'm so happy you're safe," she whispered into Emma's ear and the child held her back and cried her own happy tears into the lighter red of her mother's hair.

Jess joined them and held them both in her arms and together they unleashed their fear and celebrated their victory in wave after wave of tears and happy laughter. Finally, Sarah held her daughter's face at elbow length and again wiped away the strands of curly, red hair that dipped into her eyes so she could search deep inside them.

"I know that you're not Emma, but I know that she's in there, too," Sarah said with a great calmness to her voice that held the child in rapture to her words. "I know that you've done great evil, but I think that you could stop, if you really tried," she continued. "And I need to know, is there any way at all that we could have you *and* Emma? As sisters, perhaps? And we could guide you and teach you what's right and what's wrong? We could help you understand that killing is a horrible thing, even to those who have made you angry. We can show you how to be happy and how to let things go that make you sad or mad. We could be your forever family and we could all be happy together. Would you like that?" Sarah asked, searching the child's eyes for understanding.

The child forced her gaze away and upon the woman across the room. "But you have killed," she said.

Sarah gently turned her head back so that she had to see her mother's eyes as she spoke. "Yes. I killed out of necessity to save your life. I killed because there was no other way for you to live. But you cannot kill out of anger or hate or sadness. You have to bear the harder parts of life with grace and understanding and acceptance."

"You would want to keep me, if you could? Forever and always as your own?" the child asked with so much want in her voice that it made Sarah's heart sad for her. She was just a little girl who needed love and had never found it until now. After who knows how many years or centuries she had walked the earth, searching for a family to accept her and guide her and teach her, they were the first to ever make her feel like true love was a possibility and her heart broke with it.

"Yes. We want you. We really do. But we want Emma, too. We need you both to be truly happy, can't you see that? You are my daughter just as much as she is now. Haven't I proven that today?" Sarah asked, and the child nodded.

"I love you, Mommy," the child said.

"I love you, too," the mother replied.

"I love you, three," Auntie Jess added, and then suddenly they all felt tired beyond control. They yawned and held each other tight. Jess' arms were wrapped around Sarah and the child in her lap, and Sarah's arms were under Emma's head and knees, holding her as if she were a baby needing rocked to sleep. The room around them grew dark and peaceful as they drifted off and they felt as if they were not merely falling asleep but being taken away to some other place some other where and some timeless when.

It was a peaceful place and as Sarah and Jess slept in the factory, both of them creating a loving circle of protection around the sleeping child's body, they two awoke in the place of their nightmares, holding hands. They didn't feel frightened or in danger. They felt as if they were brought here and had some last duty to perform to end this once and for all.

"I recognize this place," Sarah said. "I've been here in my dreams. This is where Emma is. Inside the mind of the child."

"I've been here, too. Just once. The other night," Jess added, and they held each other's hands tighter as they began to walk forward down the dusty trail that wound through a rocky cave with many branches. Lichen clung to the roof and walls and offered a calming glow of which to see by. And somewhere in the depths before them they could hear Emma calling to them.

"We're coming!" Sarah yelled and her voice echoed forward as if paving the way of their journey to find Emma. Finally, they would be reunited. Sarah wanted to run, but knew it would be dangerous to do so, even though it felt like safety here. The walls were covered in sharp edges of rock and stone, and she thought if she were to die here, she would also die back on that factory floor and she was too close to the end for that to happen. She could feel it in every fiber of her being.

"Let's go." Jess said and squeezed her sister's hand reassuringly. "Whatever this place is, it's the beginning of the end. I know it, but I don't know how I do."

Sarah nodded and together they began to walk forward, stopping at every new turn and listening for Emma's calls among the sounds of water dripping and creatures rustling. They slowly picked a path through the winding labyrinth of caves. Passing quiet pools of water and small mossy oases with fungi and pale flowers. Turning this way and that and the closer they got to Emma's voice the brighter the lichen glowed above them and below. They walked together silently, listening to Emma's call somewhere far off in the distance. She didn't sound scared now as she had in their dreams, but relieved and happy that they were now so close.

Finally, they rounded a corner and there before them stood a great pool of water with a black mirror for a surface. Reflecting in its still waters was a gorgeous canopy of lichen glowing in pinks and yellows and greens and blues. It was a great cavern above the pool that seemed to drift on forever as if it were a nighttime sky ablaze with stars. A thick carpeting of soft moss covered every stony surface that surrounded the pool and there was a shelf of green covered stone with a stair of sorts leading down and to the water's beautiful edge.

Both women gasped at the beauty they found here. Growing near the water and next to the shelf there was a great tree of golden leaves and bark and bright red apples. Even though there was no sun here to kiss its fruit or leaves. It was the biggest and healthiest looking tree either of them had ever seen and its branches hung low and full of fresh, ripe, sweet-smelling fruit. Upon the shelf sat Emma, her eyes her own normal shade of green, and as she saw her mother and aunt enter into the cavern her face lit up and she climbed swiftly down the stairs and ran, barefoot, to where they stood, dumbfounded and excited to see her.

Sarah grabbed her up and swung her around, planting a million kisses on her forehead and cheeks and nose. Tears of happiness sprang from everyone's eyes and laughter filled the cavern.

"Oh, how I missed you my sweet Emma," Sarah said in between the kisses she rained upon her daughter's face.

"I missed you, too, mommy, and I was so scared. I got to watch it all in the lake as if it were a movie and it was so scary and so sad. I called out for you and sometimes I heard you calling back, but it was always far away and you never got closer until right now," Emma said, her voice happy and sad all at once.

"Oh, kid! You're a sight for sore eyes!" Jess exclaimed and pinched her niece's cheeks, playfully, but softly, when her mother's reign of kisses finally ended.

"I missed you, too, Auntie Jess!" Emma said with the biggest grin across her face.

"Are you okay? Have you been hurt?" Sarah asked, setting Emma down to examine her more fully.

"Yes! Other Mommy has been taking care of me. She said it's safe here as long as I don't go too deep into the water. It's warm and feels nice for baths, but I only go as deep as my waist," Emma gushed and grabbed her mommy and her auntie by the hand to lead them across the thick carpet of moss to sit underneath the tree near the edge of the water. "And it's very good to drink, too. It tastes sweeter than regular water, which is kinda icky."

Sarah and Jess laughed at Emma and they both were happy, oh, so happy to be reunited with her. Emma reached up and plucked an apple from a branch that rustled away once the burden of the fruit was gone. It did so in a slow and carefree way, as if it had all the time in the world.

"Here, Momma! Taste this! They're so delicious!" Emma held the bright red apple out to her mother, who took it gingerly from her daughter's hands and started to take a bite. But then she stopped, remembering the blood and hair that was covering her and she examined her hand that held the apple. It was perfectly clean, not even her fingernails stained and there was no hair to be found. She smiled and took a huge bite from the fruit. It was the sweetest tasting thing she had ever tasted. Though, not in an overbearing way. Clear juice dripped down her lips and onto her chin and she laughed a childish laugh as she wiped it away with her other arm's sleeve.

"Oh my god, Jess, you have got to try this," Sarah said and passed it on to her sister, who bit and had the same reaction of bliss from how absolutely scrumptious it tasted.

"This is without a doubt the most yummiest apple I have ever had," Jess said through a mouthful of juicy fruit and they all laughed again, together. The sound was magical in this place and the lichen seemed to glow in time with it.

"Who is Other Mommy?" Sarah asked, suddenly concerned bywhat her daughter had said.

"Her," Emma said and pointed happily behind her mother and her aunt who both turned toward where the little girl was pointing.

The being that stood behind them was otherworldly and beautiful. Her hair was long and as silver as the stars. Her face was pale and shone with a soft brightness and her lips were as red as the skin of the apple that Jess now held. Her eyes shone out as blue as the oceans that made up the seas and her frame was tall and slender and curvy. She was the very definition of beauty and grace. Her hands were clasped lightly before her below her waist, and she wore robes of soft ivory that were clenched with a rope as gold and shining as the sun in medieval paintings and the leaves on the tree they stood under now.

"Hello," the woman spoke. Her voice as if a million angels singing drifted across and to their ears. A sound so beautiful that tears of joy sprang to their eyes, and they were humbled before her grace and repose.

"Who. . ." Sarah began but lost her words.

"Who are you?" Jess finished, but with some difficulty making the sentence.

"I have been known by many names throughout the ages by your kind. Leto and Lillith. Arianrhod and Bast. Frigg and Inanna. Juno and Venus. The list goes on. But it doesn't matter what you call me, for deep down I am a mother, like you, Sarah, and that is what defines me." The woman came and sat with them, creating a circle of four.

"Are you -" Sarah began but didn't know how to finish. Which didn't seem to matter because Other Mother already knew.

"Yes. She is my child. I never got the chance to name her, as a name would have bound her to me in a way that would have been dangerous to her. I had to let her go, nameless, into your world for her own protection." Other Mother lifted up her hand which was now full of glittery dust and gently she blew. A cloud of what she held drifted on her breath and formed a shimmery globe in the middle of the circle they had made. In it they could see the sea of stars and then a story began to unfold before them as she spoke.

222

"I was the daughter of a great and ancient god and the sister to many brothers. It was my job to birth the stars, though on my own I could not create true life. Just burning balls of gas, though they held such beauty that with each one my pride in what I did grew and grew. I loved them each with a mother's love and I was happy in my work, though it was as painful as it was a beautiful blessing. Giving birth to suns is not an easy task and it took up all of my time." Other Mother's words carried them away into the scene as if they were witnessing it firsthand and not through a magical globe of shining dust.

"One day I decided to take a break and soak my feet in a milky pool of dust created by the stars and worlds around me. I sat there, in the ever-ongoing expanse of space, admiring my children as they glittered and shone in the universe around me and beyond. Then I saw him. He was the eater of worlds and much hated by my father and brothers who were the architects of these planets. But his dark beauty was beyond any I had ever seen, and he looked upon me as if he had felt the same." Other Mother sighed and paused in the remembering. Finally, she continued.

"There was something to the excitement of his attraction to me. Something forbidden that made me want him more. It was as if we were made for each other, and our love was instantaneous and great. But it had to stay secret. I met with him as often as I could and for a while our love was all that mattered in the worlds and all the space above them. That was until we were seen by my eldest brother, who ran and told my father at once at what he had spied. They found us sleeping here, in this very cavern. A place we had built together. He was used to destroying, as was his way, but he took to the wonder of creating with ease and this place was filled with our love and longing for one another in its very fibers. The tree was a symbol of the beauty we could create together, and we often lay in this very spot, wound in each other's embrace and sleeping peacefully in the comfort of our company and the thick softness of the moss beneath our skin."

Her voice grew sad now as she recounted what happened next. "I awoke to them ripping him from my embrace. His screams of surprise and pain as they bound him tight with iron binds and etched leather straps across his lips to muffle his cries. His long dark hair was grabbed and cut and left behind to be a sign of his shame and loss wherever they took him. My father had the witches in the farthest reaches of space curse him by having his darkness consume him. It ate away at his flesh, and they flung him as far as they could into the vast expansion of space itself. He was left an empty shell who only could feel hunger and they labeled him Leviathan, The Eater Of Worlds, and his hunger was all that they allowed to remain. He was drawn mad by the overwhelming need to eat, but he was frozen in place and only allowed the ability to draw in his next meal so slowly that the hunger consumed him." Beautiful shining tears welled in her eyes and fell as soft as dew onto the lush green of the moss on which she sat. And still, she continued.

"My father was so hurt by my indiscretions that he had the Priest of the Moons cast a spell of death upon my soul. But still, my father loved me, as did my brothers, and they could not bear to watch me die. They took their leave and escaped across the galaxies, to the edge itself, to continue their creations. Only there are no stars, for I am no longer with them. Instead, they call the very stars I have already created to drift that way, ever so slowly, as they push the darkness ever onward, leaving planets as they go. Creating something where once there had been nothing. And it is a magnificent work." In the moving circle before them they saw the beauty that came from their efforts and each one gasped in unison at the true splendidness of what they saw. Other Mother's words were drenched in sadness now and it brought tears of empathy to each eye circled around the story cloud.

"The Priest of the Moons was kind but bound to the service of my father and could not disobey. Though as soon as his withered old hands lay upon my own in a gesture of comfort while I was in my saddened state, he knew. He knew even before I did myself. Something other grew inside of me. Something made of love and not necessity. Like my own mother before me, I grew a child of the gods within my womb. He placed his hands then upon my belly. His old grey eyes turned milky white, and he saw into the future. He frowned then, a frown so horrified and filled with the purest form of repulsion and sadness." Other Mother's words continued to weave the story cloud into action, and they saw the old man's face and each of them understood what it was that he must have seen to cause such a look. His white hair the color of drifting moons was long and full and lay straight down his back and over his shoulders. A long beard the same bright color disappearing into it at the sides.

"Finally, when his eyes returned, swimming up from the cloud of whiteness in a way I had never seen done before, though I had heard the whispers of his great powers to see beyond the threads of time, he ran an old and gnarled palm against my cheek and led me back inside this place. He ran his hand against the bark of our gorgeous golden tree and these red apples began to form and grow and the limbs grew ever heavy with their burden, but they seemed happy to do so. He dipped a finger into the shimmering pool and a great white cleansing spread out from its tip and all the way to every edge of the water before flashing bright and disappearing. He explained that though he had to place the curse and could not stop its end, he could prolong my undoing for just a little while. He sat me down upon the ledge over there and joined me, hanging his feet over the side and dangling them, like a child would. His old toes sticking out from the sandals he wore, and he smiled at me with so much kindness that it brought tears to my own eyes. I was so grateful for his good will even when I had brought shame upon my family and caused my one true love to be locked away, forever surrounded by a great blackness and doomed to only consume for the rest of eternity."

The cloud grew hazy and dark when she mentioned her love and she bowed her head to hide the shame she felt. They all sat silently as she wept openly before them. Sarah and Jess both placed a comforting hand on her shoulders and she in turn placed her hands over theirs. Her touch was cool and full of love, as was theirs to her. Finally, she went on.

"He gestured out to this wonderful place and explained that here I would be safe. He would bind me here and here he would tuck away in some other when and where in a pocket of time and so I would be allowed to live until the day I could find my child a mother to care for her and love her as a mother should. He whispered words and moved his great long fingers in a weaving pattern before us both and the labyrinth of caves you both wove through to get here was laid out around my cavern. The caves were sharp and dreadful to all of those who entered with foul intentions. Hideous creatures lurk there and eat all that come to harm but let pass those who seek me out, though they do not know it at the time." In the story cloud the women saw a little girl walking through the tunnels, lost and scared and sad, but the creatures pushed their way back into the darkness and let the child pass. A lovely sound of singing filled the caves, leading the child down the correct twists and turns to eventually find their way to Other Mother and her loving embrace.

"He told me then that I would have until the child was four years old to love her and guide her and bestow all I could, but at the end of that time she would be ripped away from me to a place called Earth. A place where people had the same beauty and grace as I have, but also the same basic need to destroy as had her father. He said that he could not let me have any more time than that because he had seen my father hear the cries of the child if she stayed even a second past her fourth year and he would come for her. To rip her limb from limb and throw her into the burning heart of one of my stars. I wept so hard then at his words. My hands covering my eyes." In the circle they could see the great pity in the eyes of the Priest, and they all felt love for the man as he gently reached up and pulled away her hands.

"Do not fret so, my dear, is what he said and then he explained. This place called Earth would be a great challenge for my child. She would not remember me or her time here. She would be forced to move from host to host to find the right family for her. He told me that humans had the greatest power of love as well as hate. That they were the closest to our own kind in that way, and that it would be a long journey but that my child would one day find a mother as fierce in her love as I am myself." Other Mother looked at Sarah then and smiled. A smile full of gratefulness and appreciation.

"His ancient voice grew tired as he spoke. He was not used to the effort it took to communicate for so long, but he was determined to go on until he was finished. He said that while my child inhabited the bodies of these other babes, they would come to me here to love and keep safe. He told me that the apples would nourish their bodies and the water would satiate their thirst, but I must keep away their sadness as best I could. Then his words grew dark, and a chill filled my very soul and the air around us grew ever so cold." The edges of the story cloud seemed to frost and turn icy with her words, and she continued talking even though they all dreaded what she was about to say.

"He gave me one last gift, the ability to watch what was happening through my child's eyes as she wandered. The pool would show what she saw, always, only growing dark when she slept. He warned me that without my love and guidance the child would draw from both of its parental contributions, and she would feel the need to consume and destroy as much as her father had. Not because he was evil, but because it was in his nature to do so. He had no choice as the child would have none without a true mother there to guide her. She would abandon a host if the time there had ended and there was no hope left for a mother's love. She would then be pulled across the world and into another body to start all over again. I sensed in his words the great tragedy this would be, the great effort and slim chance of success." The cloud grew dark and dissipated. The shiny dust floated away on some wind they hadn't felt before this moment and it smelled as sweet as honeysuckle in the spring.

"Take heart, he told me, take heart in the knowledge that one day she will find a mother full of love and kindness. When that day comes your child will become hers and she will guide her true and strong. Her will will be as yours is. She will take her father's looks, but leave behind his destructive ways, as long as the mother's guidance is true and good." Other Mother paused then and took Sarah's hands.

"I believe you are that mother," she spoke. "I believe it with all of my might, and it relieves me so."

Sarah squeezed her hands back and smiled. A happy laugh escaped her lips as she nodded. "I can't explain the love I've felt for your child even through the fear and agony of not knowing what was happening to Emma," Sarah said. "I came to know that Emma wasn't herself and I still felt the need to protect your child. And I do love her. I do. But I can't sacrifice my baby for yours. I'm so sorry. I just can't." Sarah put her palm against the woman's cheek to comfort her, but instead of frowning as Sarah expected, Other Mother smiled a great smile.

"You misunderstand me, dear one. You do not have to choose one over the other. My child needed Emma's body for a time, but that time is through. I took great care of your little one while she was here, and she brought me great comfort with her company." Other Mother smiled down at Emma happily, and Emma smiled back. "I would never expect you to make such an awful choice as that. But I do put a choice before you. Will you take my child into you as your own? Will you grow her in your womb as I once did? Will you welcome her into your family and guide her through life as if she were yours, as indeed she will be? Will you teach her right from wrong and love her even when she makes mistakes, for everyone does from time to time? And will you, dear Emma, be the best big sister you can be? And Jess, will you love my child as your niece, for your family's blood will surely course through her veins?"

Sarah, Jess and Emma each exchanged a glance. Many silent words were passed between them as they did so and when they all looked back into the gorgeous blue eyes of Other Mother, they were all smiling.

"Of course, we will," Sarah said and at the same time Jess spoke as well.

"It would be my absolute pleasure!" Jess' words were overlapped by Emma's.

"I will be the best big sister in the whole world!" Emma explained and then reddened and looked at her Auntie Jess. "Well, second bestest ever," she added.

Everyone laughed and that sweet-smelling wind rustled the leaves of the great golden tree as if it were laughing, too.

"My child already has gifts, some of which you already know. As long as you care for her you will never have the need to work, for your balances will always stay the same and your pocketbooks will never empty. She ages slowly compared to that of humans and your aging has matched hers, though it has not been long enough to truly notice. Once she is born into your family she will age normally for some time and then her aging will slow, as will all of yours and those you love and bring into your family. For you three are a family now in the closest sense of the word. More than just sisters and daughter and niece. You will be the inner circle of support and love for my child, and through that love she will truly be yours." Other Mother looked at them, trying to convey how serious this was to her, and they looked back in a way that eased her fears.

"I cannot say what of her father will remain but it's up to all of you to help her see right from wrong. When she was here, she was kind, always, but apples were all there were to tempt her with, and she ate of the tree with a mighty hunger. I do not know what other powers she has that will follow her into your world as her own being, but I have faith that through your guidance she will prosper and make you proud." Other Mother stood then and reached down to help Sarah to her feet. Sarah took her hands and allowed her to help pull her up and then Other Mother embraced her and held her tightly in a friendly hug.

"Thank you," she whispered into Sarah's ear and then stepped back to take her in.

"No. Thank you. I couldn't bear to lose Emma, but also, I have come to love your child as much as my own. Thank you for trusting me with her. I know it can't be easy. I do," Sarah said.

Other Mother smiled and placed her palms upon Sarah's lower abdomen. "Are you ready?" she asked. Sarah thought it over for a moment and then smiled.

"I am," she said, with a nod.

Other Mother began to sing. A beautiful sound that left all who heard in awe of its delicate elegance. For a while nothing happened, and then Other Mother stepped back and looked toward the entrance to the labyrinth of caves and continued her magnificent song. Eventually, after time unknown, a light began to grow in the softly glowing cave. A brighter light than the lichen steadily produced, and it grew in its radiance and finally a dazzling ball of great white brightness entered the cavern. It looked like a tiny star, and it gently glided across the room in a lazy and slow drift that seemed to bounce along to the rhythm of Other Mother's song.

"It's magnificent," Jess whispered, and Sarah was lost for words at its miraculous form.

It drifted ever closer to Sarah and finally it reached her and as if a dandelion caught on a breeze it swirled before her and down to where Other Mother had placed her hands. Once there it seemed to disappear into Sarah's abdomen and Sarah felt a warmth enter into her belly and plant itself deep inside. She placed her hand above where it settled and grinned. She felt that the child was safe inside her now and that it really would be hers to love and nurture and grow and guide.

Sarah looked up at Other Mother and a great and happy smile bloomed across her face. "Thank you," she repeated, and tears of joy began to course down her cheeks.

Other Mother smiled and then knelt and held her arms open wide for Emma, and she ran into her embrace. "Goodbye, dear one," Other Mother said, and Emma began to cry.

"I'll miss you," Emma said, and Other Mother wiped away her tears.

"I'll miss you, too," she told the adorable little redheaded girl with the not too bright green eyes. "Thank you for keeping me company."

"You're welcome," Emma said and ran to Sarah when Other Mother stood once more. Sarah plucked Emma up in a tight squeeze and sat her on her hip. She never wanted to let her down again, she thought as she was comforted by the fact that they were once again reunited.

"Goodbye," Jess said as Other Mother hugged her, too.

"Goodbye," Other Mother said and then ran a loving palm down Jess' face before turning away and walking into the pool of water. When she got to where her waist was covered, she turned back to the women and the little girl. "Go back the way you came and on your way, you will find yourself awake as if this were all a dream. And please always love each other and be kind to one another for my child will be yours and that will be the example she follows." She turned then. Her long silver hair floating on the water's surface and then she dove beneath. A ring of water drifted out and away from where she slipped under. The ring in the water grew bigger and bigger until it reached every edge of the pool and then there was stillness.

They waited for a few minutes but nothing more was seen and the lichen above them began to darken, and so they left. They picked their way back through the cave and the farther away they got from the cavern the darker it grew. They were silent on their journey back, each one growing more and more tired and eventually they slept, even on their feet.

22

They awoke all at once, still held in each other's arms. Sarah stood and picked up Emma before the girl could see the bloody corpse of Karen, faceless on the floor. The girl had not seen her mother kill the woman, as the child had been sleeping at the time, but she knew she had seen the mangled face of Karen already, through the reflection in the pool, though Other Mother urged her not to look. Emma couldn't help but watch all that she could, fascinated and terrified by what the child would do with her body next.

Other Mother had told her stories of kindness and understanding. She had explained why the child acted so and told Emma about how the child had been before she was thrust away from her bosom. How she had laughed and played like any other tiny babe and how she had found excitement and joy in everything she saw. Other Mother had woven stories from the shiny dust she blew, and Emma had watched it in fascination. The child had had a cherub like face and raven black hair and naturally red-colored lips. And the child's eyes had been so bright. Bright like the stars and moons and oh so shiny. Emma had fallen in love with the child through those stories and forgiven her fully for borrowing Emma's self. She had felt great empathy for the child then. Walking alone in the world. Searching for love and understanding time after time. Not able to understand the wrong in which she did and only ever wanting a mother's true embrace. It was terribly romantic and romantically terrible.

Emma held on to her mother's neck, letting herself lay against her chest and feel at home in her true mother's arms once again. Other Mother had been very kind and had often rocked her to sleep, but there was nothing like being home, and to Emma, Sarah's embrace *was* home.

"I'm going to go look for our phones. Mine was in my pocket when this happened. I'm assuming yours was, too?" Jess asked Sarah as she stood to join them.

"No, I mean, I don't remember. I think it was on the coffee table or the kitchen counter, but I honestly couldn't say one way or another," Sarah said and walked away from the wooden beam and toward a door marked exit. It was a dusty sign that no longer shone with light, but she could read the red letters through the buildup of dirt and webs and flecks of dead bugs.

"Mine has to be around here somewhere. Or even hers would do." Jess nodded toward where Karen lay and then turned and walked toward the room in which the woman had disappeared earlier to get her food. Food that still sat on the cracked concrete floor next to where the third heavy metal chair had been placed.

Sarah opened the door and carried her daughter out. The sun was just peeking above the empty buildings around her, and she knew where they were immediately. The old vegetable factory where they had made dehydrated things like powders and salts and soup mixes. They had moved their operation to Mexico a decade ago and the factory and all its buildings still sat here empty for sale. There had been talk of the land being sold to a house manufacturer last Spring, but Sarah hadn't cared enough to listen to Mrs. MacGregor drone on and on about it at that point. She had been worried about Emma and why she wouldn't leave the window in her room for the past few days. Still, she had done her best to be polite and listen as much as she could and now, for the first time, she was grateful for the older woman and a lump of sadness moved up her chest and into her throat. If it hadn't been for her, she wouldn't have known where they were now. She was going to miss the woman, with her plain dresses and stern face and gossiping mouth.

She had been a hard woman to like, at times, but Sarah had no doubt that Mrs. MacGregor could have said the exact same thing about her. She had been so impatient to listen to the stories she wanted to share, especially since the child came, and now she felt so guilty. She would miss her neighbor greatly over the years and she vowed to teach her child that grew in her womb the importance of life and how to respect it. She held Emma even tighter and together they stood and watched the sun rise.

A short while later Jess joined them, holding a phone that Sarah didn't recognize. "She must have left mine at the house, but I found this. I had to charge it for a bit because it was almost at zero, but I have thirteen percent now. It should be enough." She paused and looked around, smiling at the sun against her skin. "Why does it smell like garlic powder? Where are we?" Jess asked.

"At the old vegetable plant, out by the river," Sarah said, thanking the spirit of Mrs. MacGregor as she did.

Jess nodded and dialed the police and brought Karen's phone up to her ear. A few minutes later she was asking for help and explained to the person on the other end where they were and that they had been kidnapped by some mad woman. She told the operator how the woman had gone on and on about burning her niece at midnight and Jess said she thought she had been a part of some cult or something. That she was convinced that Emma was some otherworldly monster that had killed her family over a decade ago, which was impossible, of course.

When Jess got to that part of the story, she and Sarah had exchanged a grim look. Jess then went on and told about how they had had to escape. That they had had to kill the woman to keep themselves safe as well as Emma, who was still bound to the beam at that time. Jess waited on the line and the three of them stood there, sun on their cheeks, listening as sirens began to sing far off in the distance. Closer and closer they came and finally help arrived. EMT's and officers ran toward them. They saw the dried blood on Sarah's hands and face and arms and chest, and she explained that it wasn't hers. That she had gotten a hand free and used it to stop their captor. A female officer took her and Emma and Jess to the back of the ambulance to be checked out as the rest of the officers carefully swept the building.

About nine months later Sarah lay in a hospital bed. Her arms were wrapped around a brand-new little girl who was latched on and eating happily. Small sounds escaped the child as she fed, and Sarah smiled down at her. With the hand that wasn't holding the baby close she gently stroked the infant's coal black hair, thick for a newborn and beautiful. The baby's perfectly bright eyes shone up at Sarah with love in them and Sarah looked back upon the new life she held with a love even greater in her own pale green eyes.

"Momma!" Emma rushed into the room, followed by Jess, who's belly was full of its own growing new life, and just behind her walked in Ben.

Ben saw Sarah breastfeeding and stopped in his tracks, covering his face with both of his hands. "Uh. I'm so sorry. I can wait outside, if you'd like."

Sarah laughed. "Don't be silly. It's a completely natural thing to feed a child. Besides, you better get used to it because yours will be here in another few months," she said.

"Ben, it's okay. In college, Sarah was always…" Jess stopped at the inquisitive look her niece now gave her.

"Mommy was always what?" Emma asked, suddenly more curious than she had ever been. She loved hearing tales about Mommy and Daddy before she was born and thought them the most magical things in the world.

"Yeah, I was what?" Sarah laughed and waited for her sister to find a way out of this mess. She had no doubt that Jess would. Jess was used to digging herself out of holes her mouth made for her.

"Why, feeding babies, of course." Jess smiled and everyone laughed, including Ben, who turned his back and walked sideways to the chair by the window.

"I have no doubt at all that breastfeeding is the most beautiful thing in the world. I just don't want to make you uncomfortable so I will stare out this window and watch, oh, cool! A squirrel!" Ben said and Emma ran to join him. Together they watched the fuzzy little creature run around the grassy lawn outside the window. They laughed and pointed, and the women smiled warmly at their backs.

"You've got a keeper there," Sarah said to her sister with so much pride that Jess blushed.

"I really do," She said simply and eased herself into the chair. "I never ever believed in love at first sight until I met that man."

"That's exactly how I felt about -" Sarah's breath caught in her throat, and she looked down at the hungry child she held. A tear fell and splashed against the baby's blanket that Sarah had gently swaddled her in earlier that morning.

"Aw, you guys were the best couple ever," Jess said. Then, to change the subject she asked, "What are you going to name her? She's gorgeous."

"She should be. Her mother was the Mother of Stars." Sarah smiled.

"No," Jess said, and her voice was so stern that Sarah looked up to meet her gaze. "You are her mother. Your blood runs through her veins."

"Sarah nodded and gently squeezed the child a little tighter in her grasp. "Her name is Levi," she said.

"Levi," Jess repeated. "You know, that's perfect."

Ben soon forgot about the feeding baby and that he was supposed to be embarrassed according to the code of men of which his father had once taught. He and Emma joined them around the bed, and they all gushed over the baby and its ten fingers and ten toes. They marveled at her dimples and her gorgeous head of hair. Ben knew the story of how she had come to be by now and doubted it not even a little. For he, too, had Irish roots and his mother, and aunts and grandmother had regaled him with the tales of his heritage every bit as much as Jess and Sarah's mother and aunts and grandmother had.

Ben and Jess had dated for less than a month before deciding that they were soulmates. They had married and bought the house next door. The house that had been robbed of a happy family when the MacGregors had moved in was finally full of laughter and love. They even kept the cat, Georgie, and he was a happy cat, indeed. The house vowed to stand strong and protect its new inhabitants and it was full of purpose, finally. Ben and Jess breathed a new life into its frame and wood and glass, and it was happy. Happier than any other house had ever been, perhaps.

In less than a month of being married, Ben had sparked life within his love, and they had rejoiced. The room that had been meant for sewing was turned into a nursery and Jess and Sarah had spent the coming months dreaming of their children growing up together as sister cousins when they found out that they both carried girls. Cousins that were as close as sisters they would be, and Sarah was finally truly happy again after losing her own true love the way she had.

Life was a beautiful thing for them. A happy and beautiful thing. Full of hope for the future of their families and they spent long hours wondering what it would be like for their children. Especially because they had no idea what to expect would happen as Levi grew. They all vowed, even Ben, to guide the child. All of the children, for surely Emma and Jess's baby would need true guidance as they grew as well. They would teach them right from wrong and the meaning of love and safety. The Priest of the Moon had been correct about humanity being full of love as well as hate and they all understood the burden of raising children who would spread one and not the other. And together, they knew they could accomplish this. For together, anything was possible.

T hank you, Dear Reader, for taking this journey with me. I hope you enjoyed this book as much as I enjoyed writing it. And thank you to all my family and friends who not only inspired me, but who were there with constant support. This includes Heather Ann Larson, who edited this version, which is the best version because of her efforts. She took my story and made it better, and for that I will always be grateful. Also, I must thank Shannon Ettaro for her beautiful synopsis. Without her, this book may have never found its way into your hands. I love you all.

Until we meet again,

-A Housewife With A Pen.

Printed in Great Britain
by Amazon

24733980R00138